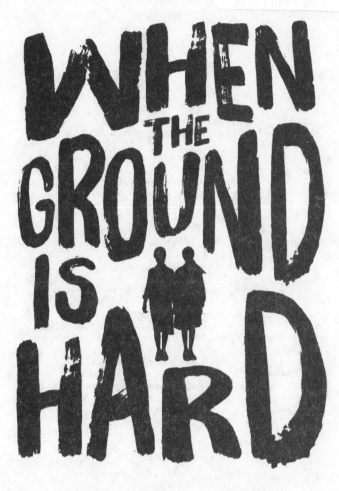

WHEN THE GROUND IS HARD

MALLA NUNN

putnam

G. P. PUTNAM'S SONS

G. P. PUTNAM'S SONS
An imprint of Penguin Random House LLC, New York

First published in the United States of America by G. P. Putnam's Sons,
an imprint of Penguin Random House LLC, 2019
First paperback edition published 2021

Visit us online at penguinrandomhouse.com

THE LIBRARY OF CONGRESS HAS CATALOGED THE HARDCOVER EDITION AS FOLLOWS:
Names: Nunn, Malla.
Title: When the ground is hard / Malla Nunn.
Description: New York, NY: G. P. Putnam's Sons Books for Young Readers, 2019.
Summary: At Swaziland's Keziah Christian Academy, where the wealth and color
of one's father determines one's station, once-popular Adele bonds with
poor Lottie over a book and a series of disasters.
Identifiers: LCCN 2018040602 | ISBN 9780525515579 (hardback) | ISBN 9780525515586 (ebook)
Subjects: | CYAC: Racially-mixed people—Fiction. | Social classes—Fiction. |
Boarding schools—Fiction. | Schools—Fiction. | Popularity—Fiction. | Swaziland—Fiction.
Classification: LCC PZ7.1.N86 Whe 2019 | DDC [Fic]—dc23
LC record available at https://lccn.loc.gov/2018040602

Manufactured in the U.S.A.
ISBN 9780525515593

3rd Printing

Design by Marikka Tamura
Text set in LTC Kennerley Pro

Praise for

WHEN GROUND THE IS HARD

WINNER OF THE 2019 *LOS ANGELES TIMES* BOOK PRIZE FOR
YOUNG ADULT LITERATURE
2020 JOSETTE FRANK AWARD WINNER
A *KIRKUS REVIEWS* BEST YOUNG ADULT BOOK OF 2019
A YALSA BEST FICTION PICK, 2020
A WESTCHESTER FICTION AWARD WINNER, 2020

★ "Excellent writing and an evocative setting make this novel a standout."
—*Booklist*, starred review

"Absorbing . . . A cautionary tale as well as a coming-of-age one . . . *When the Ground Is Hard* may be historical fiction, but its themes are as modern as ever."
—*Book & Film Globe*

★ "The richly evoked setting may be strange to American readers, and the vivid racism may be shocking, but teens will be drawn into the girls' growing friendship and search for self."   —*Booklist*, starred review of the audiobook

"Accidents, lies, thefts . . . secrets . . . dead bodies, and illicit rendezvous make for riveting reading in this taut novel."   —*School Library Journal*

"*When the Ground Is Hard* heralds a truly unique literary voice. In prose poetic and fierce, Malla Nunn gives us profound insight into the racial and class pecking order in 1960s Swaziland and the violence that shapes women's and girls' lives—and their futures. Taut, ambitious—a stunning debut."
—Marina Budhos, author of
the award-winning *Watched* and *The Long Ride*

"The gorgeous imagery sets the scene wonderfully . . . An engrossing narrative that gently but directly explores complex relationships."
—*Kirkus Reviews*

"Racial prejudice has never been exclusive to the United States, and this title provides American readers with a sensitive exploration of how it affected a very different place."   —*School Library Connection*

"Swaziland-born Nunn writes with keen perception of an intricate caste system and the layers within it . . . Readers will find plenty to discuss here as they explore the parallels in our own culture."
—*The Bulletin of the Center for Children's Books*

ALSO BY MALLA NUNN
Sugar Town Queens

For my mother, Patricia Gladys Nunn

When the ground is hard, the women dance.

—African proverb

1

Dying Days

It's Thursday night, so we walk down Live Long Street to the public telephone booth at the intersection of three footpaths called Left Path, Right Path, and Center Path. My flashlight beam bounces the length of the dirt road and picks out uneven ground and potholes, of which there are many. Mrs. Button, who lives in the pink house behind the mechanic's workshop, says that all streets should be paved like they are in England, but we're not in England—we are in the British protectorate of Swaziland, fenced in on all sides by Mozambique and the Republic of South Africa—so what does she know?

"Pick up the pace," Mother says in a fierce whisper. "We can't be late."

We hurry past cement-brick houses with cracks of light spilling from under locked front doors. Dogs bark in fenced yards. A curtain twitches, and a face peers at us through a space the width of a hand. The face belongs to Miriam Dube, the church minister's wife, who makes it her duty to spy on our weekly pilgrimage to the public phone box. It's dark, but I imagine that Mrs. Dube's expression is smug disapproval.

Mother holds her head high, like she is balancing the weight of an iron crown or suffering a garland of thorns. The neighbors are jealous, she says. Jealous gossips who frown on her high heels and her dresses straight from Johannesburg that show too much leg. They know we have carpet in the living room, she says. We also have Christmas bicycles with flashing chrome, in the backyard, and new Bata school shoes that still smell of the factory, under our beds.

They have concrete floors, and if they do have rugs, they are sure to be ugly when compared to the tufted field of purple flowers that blossom under our feet when we walk from the settee to the kitchen. That's why they hate us. That's why they don't stop to give us a lift when they see us walking at the side of the road, weighed down with shopping bags. The Manzini market is three miles from our house, Mother says. Three miles across dry fields pocked with snake and scorpion holes. A dangerous walk. A Christian would see our suffering and pick us up. But our neighbors—who call themselves Christians and stuff the church pews every Sunday—they drive by and leave us in their dust.

The phone booth appears in my flashlight beam: a rectangle of silver metal cemented into the red earth. Right Path, Left Path, and Center Path split off and disappear into vacant land covered in weeds. Bored children and drunks have left their

2

initials and their boot prints on the glass walls, but, by some miracle, the interior light still gives off a dim glow, which attracts a circling cloud of white moths.

Mother feeds four silver coins into the change slot and dials a number. Her hands shake, and her breath comes short from walking the uneven road in high heels. As a rule, she never leaves our house in flat sandals or, Lord save us, the loose cotton slippers worn by women who value comfort over fashion sense. The coins drop, and she shapes her mouth into a smile.

"It's me," she says in a throaty voice that she reserves for the telephone.

The voice on the other end says something that makes her laugh, and she flashes me a triumphant glare. *You see?* her look says. *I call every Thursday night to talk about what's happening with you, me, and your brother, Rian, and he answers just like that . . .*

Mother wants me to know that, no matter what names the church ladies call her, her relationship with him is special. She has a good man she can rely on, and how many "loose women" and "tramps" can say the same thing? Zero. *That's* how many. Mother, I think, wants me to be proud of our weekly walk to the phone box.

I pick a twitching moth from my hair and blow it into the air. Its wings leave a fine white powder on my fingertips, and I brush it off onto the front of my skirt while Mother talks low and soft into the receiver.

"Of course. Adele is right here." She snaps her fingers to get my attention. "She's dying to talk to you."

I take the receiver from her and say, "Hello. . . . I'm fine. How are you?"

The voice tells me that he's tired but it's good to hear my voice and Mother's. Did the rest of the Christmas holidays go well? Am I ready for my second-to-last year of high school, and, good heavens, where does the time go? He pays the fees, so I tell him, "Yes, yes, I can't wait to go back to Keziah Christian Academy." It's January 21, three days before the term starts, but my bags are already packed. "It will be good to see my friends again." Phone time is precious. I can't waste a second of it by mentioning the bad food or the sharp edge of Mr. Newman's ruler that raps against my knuckles when I get a wrong answer or look at the mountains through the classroom window for too long. Mother says: *Have some pride, girl. Nobody wants to hear your problems. Nurse your sorrows in private like the rest of us.* She double-snaps her fingers to let me know that my time is up.

"See you soon, I hope." I surrender the receiver and step away to give her privacy. A cloud of moths beats a white circle around the phone box while others lie on the ground with broken wings.

I pull a strand of wild grass from the side of the road and chew the sweet end while Mother whispers promises into the telephone. Her right hip and shoulder press against the glass, and in that moment, surrounded by fields of rustling weeds and the low night sky, she seems small and completely alone. Just her and the moths dancing together in the pale light while darkness swallows everything around them.

4

Minutes pass. She hangs up and strides across the pock-marked road with her high heels clicking and her hips swinging to a tune that only she can hear. A loose curl bounces against her flushed right cheek, the way it always does after she's talked to him on the telephone. I can't tell if winding a strand of hair around her index finger is a nervous habit or a soothing motion. She throws her arms wide and hugs me tight. Air escapes my lungs with a hard whoosh.

"He's coming," she whispers into my ear.

"When?" I want dates and times. In one way or another, he is always on his way. He tells us he'll be in Mkuze, only five hours' drive from us. Or he has a meeting coming up in Golela, and it's a quick hop across the border from South Africa to us. Next, he's visiting Kruger Park with the other children and he might drop by for a few hours. Maybe he'll show up. Maybe he'll come this weekend . . .

"Saturday." Mother is giddy with joy. "He wants to see you before you leave for boarding school. And he wants to see Rian. You know how he worries about Rian's asthma. Missing school. He cares about us, my girl, but you know how things are."

Yes, I know "how things are." I am an expert in the unwritten rules that govern our family and the boundaries that can't be crossed or even mentioned out loud. I was born knowing. Mother reminds me of "how things are," on a regular basis so I'll remember that certain things in life can't be changed.

"Come." Mother grabs my arm, and we retrace our footsteps back in the direction of home. The vacant land around us rustles with sounds: secretive porcupines digging up roots, the soft pads of a house cat hunting small creatures through the bush, and a nightjar's escalating song. Mother hums "Oh Happy Day" under her breath. She used to sing in the church choir, and she has a lovely voice even now.

Car headlights swing off Center Path, and two bright beams illuminate the craggy length of Live Long Street. We automatically jump off the road and into the tall grass that grows thick along the edge. A truck speeds past, and we tuck our faces into the crooks of our arms to avoid being choked by dust. The white Ford pickup truck with a dented front fender belongs to Fergus Meadows, who lives in the house opposite ours and inherited his father's lumberyard five years ago.

A stone pings my leg, and I see that I'm cut. I wipe the blood away with white powdered fingers and step back onto the street. This is where Mother usually says, *Hooligan! His father would die twice if he knew how spoiled that boy has turned out. He saw us walking in the dark. Don't you think he didn't. Two females. Alone. Yet he doesn't even slow down. Imagine!*

But tonight is different. Instead of criticizing Fergus Meadows's manners, she flicks dust from her skirt and tucks her arm through mine. She hums and smiles at the half-moon in the sky. The neighborhood gossip and the sly glances thrown at her in the aisles of the new hypermarket on Louw Street can't touch her. She is bulletproof. She is armored by a simple fact:

He is coming.

• • •

I lie awake to the rasp of my little brother's asthmatic breath in the next room and the hard scrap of steel wool on the kitchen stovetop. Mother is cleaning in preparation for the visit. A maid comes every day except Sunday, but you can't trust them, Mother says. They don't know how to treat nice things. They are careless, and you have to watch they don't break the fine china cups or leave streak marks on the windows.

It's better to do the important things yourself, she says. That way you know they are done right. His arrival is the number one most important thing. The house has to be perfect when he walks through the door on Saturday, so Mother takes care of the details. She cleans the stove, washes the floors, and dusts the porcelain angels on the sideboard next to the settee. Tomorrow, on Friday, she will choose our outfits for his visit: a pretty dress with strappy sandals for me, and a pair of khaki shorts and a collared shirt for Rian. We will be clean and neat, to match the house.

The oven door opens, and the *scratch, scratch, scratch* of the steel-wool pad continues. To my knowledge, he has never once looked inside the oven or opened the cupboards. Maybe this visit he will, so Mother has to make ready.

I roll over and blink at the windup clock on my bedside table. It is twelve minutes to midnight.

Rian coughs and Mother cleans, and I think of the moths suspended above the phone booth, their delicate wings beating the air until dawn.

•••

Sixteen is four years too old to be sitting on his knee, but when he collapses on the lounge chair, all rumpled and sweaty from driving tar roads and gravel paths and narrow dirt lanes to get to us, I do just that. I take his right knee and Rian takes his left, and we simultaneously plant kisses on opposite cheeks: a ritual that goes back to before my memory begins. Bristles prick my lips, and I think that he is tired, that he is older than when he delivered our Christmas presents five days before Christmas Day. *He wanted to spend the holidays with us,* Mother says, *but you know how things are.*

"Look at you," he says to Rian, who is pale and exhausted from last night's asthma attack. "You'll be bigger than me soon."

That's possible. Rian is thirteen and sprouting fast while our father gets smaller each year, the black strands of his hair now overrun with gray. What he lacks in muscle and youth, he makes up for with brains, Mother says. He is an engineer. He builds the dams that hold the water that feeds the cornfields and fills the bathtubs of the people who live in town who've forgotten how to wash in rivers.

"And you." He pinches my cheek. "You are even more beautiful than the last time I was here. I'll have to buy myself a shotgun to keep the boys away."

The idea of him armed with anything but a pen and a contour map makes me laugh. He loves reading books, drinking scotch, and cutting wood-block puzzles with Rian in the lean-to behind the kitchen. And what good will a gun do when he's not here to take shots at those limber night-boys who might, one day, creep over my windowsill? He lives in faraway Johannesburg with the other children, who I imagine are red-haired and clever, with skin as white as smoke. Family friends stop them on the street corner and marvel at the resemblance. "Goodness," they say. "You certainly take after your father. It's uncanny."

The others naturally take top billing. They are classified "European," and Europeans are the kings and queens of everything. We are not European. Our skin has color. Our hair has curl, but not the steel-wool kink that's hard to get a comb through, and praise Jesus, Mother says, for that small mercy. Our green eyes shine too bright in our brown faces, as if to confirm the combination of white and black blood that flows through our veins.

When he is here, he loves to tell us the story of how they met. Him on a work trip to the land title office in Mbabane, and her, slotting ancient charts into the right pigeonholes in the map room. Mother in a blue polka-dot dress, making order of the chaos. She smiled at him. *A smile like an arrow to my heart*, he says. *Beautiful and shocking, all at once.* And how he knew in a flash that, no matter what, Mother would be a part of his life. And so she is. Not the whole part, he forgets to add, but a small, bright piece of his life that's hidden away in Swaziland. We are an add-on to Father's regular life. We are the secret well that he drinks from when no one else is looking.

Mother sits cross-legged on the flowered carpet and beams to see us perched on his lap. She'd dip the scene in amber to preserve it if she could. We are together for one day and one night, and that will have to be sufficient until the next time.

"Are you thirsty?" she asks.

"Ja . . . I'm parched. The drive took longer than I thought, and Swazi roads . . ." He shakes his head as if remembering the high mountain passes and dangerous hairpin turns. "The minute you cross the border, it's like going back fifty years. Cows and people everywhere, and more potholes than tar."

"Go get a beer from the icebox, Adele." Mother tucks a strand of freshly ironed hair behind her ear and pulls a tragic face. "Daddy has to wash the Swazi dust from his throat."

Father smiles at her comical expression, the way it distorts her features without touching her natural beauty. Whoever picks combinations of skin color, eye color, and body shape got Mother just right. She is mixed-race, like us, with golden-brown skin, flashing green eyes, and pleasing curves.

I go to the kitchen to get the beer. The maid is in the backyard, hanging up my blue-checkered school uniform and the knee-high white socks that go with it. Keeping white socks white in the blooming dust and the red earth of Keziah Christian Academy is almost impossible. I plunge my hand into the icebox, and the shock of the cold bottle against my palm shifts my thoughts from the dying days of the school break. Bowls of stiff porridge and stale toast will come around soon enough.

I shake off my bad feelings about returning to school. He is here and sulking is forbidden. When he is here, we are happy. When he is here, we are grateful and well-behaved so he'll have a good reason to come back and visit us again. *You catch more flies with honey than vinegar*, Mother says, *and don't believe what people tell you, miss. Misery might love company, but misery has to learn to shut up and take care of itself.*

I pop the cap from the beer with a metal opener, and white foam rims the lip. I step into the lounge room, and I remember to smile.

2

And the First Shall Be Last

We are late. Of all the times and places to be late, the Manzini bus station is the worst. Men drag goats through the maze of buses while women hold live chickens with their feet tied together. The women push through the crowd while the chickens flap and squawk. Children and women sell roasted corn, boiled peanuts, and bags of deep-fried fat cakes to passengers about to board the smoky buses, from pans they carry awkwardly in their arms. Passengers also buy pineapples, mangoes, and bananas from woven baskets carried on sellers' heads. Pickup trucks reverse out of narrow spaces, with their horns blaring, their worn tires flattened by the weight of the passengers packed shoulder to shoulder in their open beds.

Dust is everywhere. The purple heads of the bougainvillea strangle the chain-link fence outside of B&B Farm Supplies: YOU NEED IT. WE GOT IT. Red dirt weighs the flowers down. A million motes suspended in the air catch the early-morning sun.

Animals bleat, children cry, and bus-ticket sellers call out their destinations in singsong voices. "Quick, quick time to Johannesburg. No stopping. Best seat for you, Mama." "Smooth ride to Durban by Hlatikulu, Golela, and Jozini. Brothers, sisters . . . all welcome."

We hurry through the dust and noise to the far end of the bus ranks. My heart lurches against my ribs. We are too late. All the good spots are already taken. If Delia, my best school friend, hasn't saved a place for me, I will be forced to the middle of the bus, where the lower-class students sit dressed in hand-me-down clothing, or, worse still, I'll have to make the long walk to the very back of the bus, where the poor and smelly students group together like livestock. I walk faster, and the corner of my suitcase bumps against my knees.

"There." Rian points to a decrepit bus with a faded blue wave painted on the side.

All the buses have names. There's *Thunder Road*, *True Love*, *Lightning Fast*, and finally, the *Ocean Current*, which drops students off at Keziah Christian Academy at the beginning of the school term and picks them up again on the first day of the holidays. It's a public bus, but today the exclusively mixed-race students of the academy will take up most of the spaces. Black people with common sense wait to catch the next bus heading south to the sleepy part of Swaziland. They know that mixed-race children only stand up for white people.

On paper, we are all citizens of the British protectorate of Swaziland, but really, we are one people divided into three separate groups: white people, mixed-race people, and native Swazis. Each group has their own social clubs and schools, their own traditions and rules. Crossover between the groups happens, but it's rare and endlessly talked about on the street corners and inside Bella's Beauty Salon for All Types.

My sweaty palms grip the handle of my suitcase, and my shoulders ache from hauling its dead weight from the crossroads where Father dropped us off on his way back to Johannesburg.

"See? The bus is still here." Mother's breath comes fast. She is annoyed that I rushed us to get here. "All that fuss over nothing, Adele. We have plenty of time."

I give my suitcase to a skinny black man, who throws it onto the roof of the *Ocean Current*, where another skinny black man, barefoot and shining with sweat, adds my case to a mountain of luggage already piled there. Faces peer out of the dusty windows. I look frantically from the front row to the back. I cannot see a vacant window seat.

"Here." Mother gives me a small cardboard box of impago, food packed especially for long road trips and enough to tide me over on the eighty-eight-mile journey ahead. Inside will be boiled eggs, strips of air-dried beef, thick slices of buttered bread, and maybe an orange. Whatever the cupboard had to give.

I say, "Sorry for the rush."

The real reason I have rushed us to the bus station is my secret. Mother grew up in a shack with dirt floors, and the poor girl that she was still haunts her: the two pairs of underwear made from old flour sacks that chafed her skin, a broken comb with six uneven teeth to do the combing, and the daily walk

14

from a mud hut to Keziah Academy in shoes with more holes than leather. She never caught the *Ocean Current* to school, so she has no idea how the seating on the bus works. If she knew, she'd smack me for playing a part in keeping the rich students and the poor students apart, so I'm not about to tell her.

"Be good." She tucks a strand of hair behind my ear and blinks back tears. "Mind your teachers and keep up your marks."

"I will." I let her hug me in front of the crowded bus. Snickers come from the open windows. Hugging is for babies. I love the feeling of being held close, but I keep my face blank. Showing my emotions will get me teased by the bully boys for weeks.

I pull out of Mother's embrace and go to ruffle Rian's hair. He steps back and offers me his hand instead. Already man of the house. Rian's independence annoys me, because showing him affection in public is actually allowed. Everyone knows that Rian is sick. The last time he had a major asthma attack was smack in the middle of second term last year. May 12. I remember the date. Mr. Vincent, the white American principal of Keziah Academy, drove the dirt road from school to the Norwegian hospital in Mahamba with the high beams on and the accelerator pressed to the floor. Steep mountain passes fell away into darkness, and stones pinged the underside of the car. Death rode with us. We heard it shortening Rian's breath, willing him to surrender. To stop breathing.

Mrs. Vincent sang the *Halls of the Holy* hymn book from the first page to the last while I clutched my brother's hand and prayed—not for show, the way I do in chapel, but for real.

Please, God. Don't take him. Take another boy. Take one of the mean ones. Take Richard B, Gordon Number Three, or Matthew with the lazy eye. Please. They deserve to suffer.

The doctor at the Norwegian hospital said that Rian had severe asthma—up until then, we'd called what he had "the struggles"—and he needed a mother's care and a clinic nearby. Our house is three miles from Christ the Redeemer Hospital, where the Catholic sisters inject the sick with needles and pull rotten teeth out with pliers.

Now Rian stays home and gets his lessons via the mail. In any case, he's too delicate to survive the bullies who control the boys' dormitory, and I am secretly relieved that he has stopped coming to Keziah. Although I tell him I miss him at school, things are easier now that I don't have to defend him from Richard B, Gordon Number Three, or Matthew with the lazy eye.

"Be a good boy for Mummy," I say. "See that she doesn't get too lonely, and make sure to read all the books that Daddy brought you from Johannesburg."

"Of course!" Rian is offended by my advice, which is, after all, just me repeating words I've heard grown-ups say to children.

The ticket seller leans out of the bus with one hand clinging to the top of the chrome lip above the door. He whistles to get our attention. "*Ocean Current* to Durban, leaving now, now, now!"

I tuck the box of impago under my arm, throw Mother and Rian a last look, and climb aboard. I am sick with nerves, because I know what I will find when I reach the top of the stairs:

16

rows of occupied seats stretching all the way to the poor children at the back of the bus. Unless Delia has saved me a place, I am doomed to four hours in rough company. I buy a ticket with the money that Mother gave me and pocket the change. It's enough for me to buy one item a week from the school store.

I step into the aisle and check the first two rows. Both are taken by black teachers from the Cross of Nazareth, a native school fifteen miles from the academy. Mr. Vincent, our American principal, has told us to be polite to the black teachers and to show them respect. We do as we're told, not because we believe that natives are equal to us—they are not—but because we're afraid of being punished for our rudeness.

From row three on, mixed-race students in every shade, from eggshell white to burned charcoal, stare up at me. They are waiting for something, but I can't tell what. I start walking and see Delia in the fifth row. There's an empty seat beside her. She's saved a place for me. Praise be. I hurry toward her, ready to shimmy past her knees to claim the window seat.

I grab the metal handle on the chair back and blink in disbelief when a cinnamon-brown girl with glossy braids dressed with Vaseline pulls a bag of peppermint chews from the box at her feet and sits up in the seat that's meant for me. I don't know her, but her mint-green dress is brand-new, and the heart-shaped locket around her neck is sparkling silver.

"Oh." Delia pulls a face and makes a soft sound of apology. "Sorry, hey. Sandi got here before you. There's no room left."

Liar. Delia's not sorry at all. She is glad to turn me away in front of a busload of our schoolmates. She is the most popular girl in my year. She is the girl who all the other girls want to be friends with, and till now, she was my friend. Tears well up in my eyes, but I can't speak, because the tears are in my throat too.

"This is Sandi Cardoza." The name is velvet in Delia's mouth. "Sandi's parents met and married in Mozambique. They moved to Swaziland just before Christmas. Sandi's mother is Lolly Andrews, from the Andrews family that owns the Heavenly Rest Funeral Home in Manzini, and her father, Mr. Cardoza, owns the hypermarket on Louw Street. You know it?"

I fake a smile. "I've heard of it," I say.

A vast understatement. The hypermarket is the newest and the nicest place to shop in Swaziland. It has all the latest fashions from South Africa and an actual makeup booth. It is the place to be seen spending money. No wonder Delia is lit up. The daughter of a Portuguese businessman and a mixed-race woman whose family owns a funeral home is a big catch. Together, she and Sandi will be the queens of the school.

I've been dropped for a rich girl with a silver necklace and bag of peppermint chews in her impago box. I blush with shame at being left standing in the aisle, and I turn away to hide my face.

• • •

I hurry past the first nine rows of students, whose "sometimes fathers" and "always here fathers" have paid their school fees in advance. They wear neat, freshly ironed clothing. Their suitcases are packed with new school uniforms and new school shoes with fresh laces. They have clean faces and nails. They

18

are top-shelf, and the lump in my throat makes it hard to swallow. It's not fair. I am one of them. My "sometimes father" is a white engineer. My fees are paid in full, and my skin smells of Pond's cold cream and lavender soap.

It doesn't matter. The first-class seats are gone. No one offers to move to the back. Why would they? Giving up their prime position would be the same as admitting they are inferior. I move into second class.

Here, students with "sometimes fathers" and "always here fathers" wear a mix of hand-me-downs and new clothing of varying quality and age. Their school fees are paid in installments or whenever money becomes available. They are the middle shelf, and right now I'd give up the best food in my impago box to take a seat among them.

Claire Naidoo, a half-Indian girl with long black hair that is the envy of every student with kink or hard-to-comb curl, shrugs to say, *Sorry. I feel bad for you, but I'm keeping my place.* Other students stare at their hands, their feet, their knees. Anywhere but at me. They are embarrassed for me. Mortified by my public dumping and free-falling status.

I reach the third-class seats, where the bottom-shelf students sit with jutting elbows and sprawled limbs. Between them, they have a mix of "always here fathers," "sometimes fathers," and "many fathers" who pay the school fees whenever and however they can: a pocketful of spare change, a wagonload of chopped wood for the school cooking fires, jars of homemade jam for the kitchen, and loaves of corn bread steamed in corn leaves for the teachers' morning tea.

Third-class parents have no money. If they have jobs, the jobs don't pay well enough to afford the full school fees. Some have no jobs. Mr. Vincent and his wife raise money from overseas to help pay for the poor students' fees. I count five students wearing old school uniforms, and others with holes in their shirts and patched-up shorts. When we get to the academy, the missionaries will pick items out of the donations box for the poor students to wear on the weekends, when our uniforms are being washed.

There are two vacant seats in third class, both equally bad. One is next to Matthew with the lazy eye, who says dirty things to girls. Definitely not. My thighs will be bruised blue by his filthy fingers, and my ears contaminated by sly suggestions that involve physical acts that I've never heard of and don't understand.

"Psst . . . Adele." Lazy-Eye Matthew winks his good eye. "Come, girl. You and I can be friends."

Never! Never!

The other free seat is next to Lottie Diamond, who is half-Jewish, quarter-Scottish, and the rest pure Zulu. Lottie is light-skinned, with blue eyes and brown wavy hair that is hacked short—no doubt to help pick out the lice that live there. And even though she turned out very nearly white, she lives in a tin shack on the edge of a native reserve outside Siteki and spends her holidays washing laundry in the river and mixing with the native Swazis.

Lottie is exactly the kind of girl that Mother, because of her own impoverished background, wants me to be polite to. On the other hand, Delia is the top-shelf girl that Mother, because of her impoverished background, wants me to be fast friends with. I'm supposed to be an improved version of Mother: kind to the poor students but accepted by the sorts of snotty girls who once spurned her.

"Over here, Adele," Lazy-Eye Matthew whispers in a hoarse voice. "Come by me, Adele. Adele . . ."

The Bartholomew twins, dressed in matching blue pinafores, snort with laughter at Matthew's raspy voice. Lottie Diamond shuffles over an inch, a small gesture that invites me to sit down—or to keep standing in the aisle—while Lazy-Eye Matthew croaks my name like a bullfrog looking for a mate. I slide into the seat next to Lottie. I am humiliated and furious at being dumped in front of forty witnesses. I hate Delia, and yet I want to be back by her side, where I'm supposed to be. My bottom lip trembles, and tears sting my eyes.

No, I can't.

If I cry, the others will call me Waterfall or Sprung-a-Leak, or any other clever thing that comes into their heads, for the rest of the term. I will be an easy target for jokes, and the teasing will never get old. Lottie stares out the dusty window and ignores my red face and wet lashes.

I grab the chance to hunch over and slot my impago box between my feet. I stay hunched and press my eyes against my skirt until the cotton absorbs my tears. My stomach aches. Everything inside me hurts. I replay the last five minutes in my mind, hoping to find that my demotion to third class is the result of a terrible misunderstanding. No. The truth is simple. Delia dumped me.

I should have seen it coming. Delia wants the best of everything: the prettiest dresses, the best gossip, the most popular friends. Sandi's rich Portuguese father loved her mother enough to take her to church and make promises in front of God while my father, well, he only made promises to Mother. Mother says, *Hold your head up high, Adele. I'm as good as any church wife,* but the married women and their baptized children know they are superior. Their names are written in the official marriage registers *and* in the Great Book of Life on God's bedside table. If properly married women are diamonds, then the unmarried "little wives" and their unbaptized children are tin.

Delia has traded me for a diamond.

Now I'm stuck next to a girl from the bush, who spits and swears and fights with boys and girls. Lottie wins all her fights, but still . . . it's not nice.

"Hey." A finger taps my shoulder, and I glare at Lottie from my tucked-over position. She points out of the window and ignores my sharp expression, which says, *We are not friends. We will never be friends. Our being next to each other is a horrible mistake. A catastrophe. It means nothing in the long run.* She taps the window again, insistent.

I sit up and lean across her to squint into the swirling dust of the Manzini bus station. Mother and Rian stand on the dirt footpath, their bodies backlit by the strengthening sun. They seem unreal. Phantoms from the life that I'm about to leave behind for too many months to count. The thought of leaving suddenly terrifies me. I don't want to go back to boarding school, where I'll be alone and have to hunt down new friends. And there's a small chance that no one will even have me now that I've been dumped by the top girls. I want to get off the bus and lug my suitcase across the fields until I'm safe at home again.

"Wait . . ." Mother pulls a book from her bag and runs to the window. She reaches up on tiptoes to give it to me. "Daddy forgot this in his car. It's for you. All the way from Johannesburg."

I grab the book through the open window and glance at the title: *Jane Eyre* by Charlotte Brontë. The book is thick, which is good. Thick books take longer to read. Thick books soak up the time between study hall and dinner and help to make the long Sunday afternoon hours fly by. Books are better than gossip, though Delia doesn't think so.

Mother says, "Be good, Adele."

I force a smile and say, "Of course."

I am always good—polite to teachers, reserved with the other students, and all "hallelujah, praise his name" in chapel. That's why what just happened to me is so unfair. If there was a God, I'd be at the front of the bus, where I belong. Mother is right. God is too busy to notice the hurts of a bunch of mixed-race people in a little landlocked African country. The real gods, she says, are the white men in England who draw lines on maps and write the laws that say go here, but don't go there.

Rian steps closer. He understands everything that just happened to me. He sees it in my face and hears it in Delia's distant giggles and in the way that no one on the bus will look at me.

23

"Don't worry, Adele," he says. "She's not worth it."

"Thanks," I say quietly.

Mother blows me a kiss as the *Ocean Current* lurches from the stand and joins a line of buses snaking their way to the main road. I crane my neck out of the window to keep her and Rian in my sight for as long as possible. They grow small in the distance. The *Ocean Current* turns onto the road heading south, and Rian and Mother are swallowed by the surge of disembarking passengers and pickup trucks.

"Bet that feels nice, hey, Lottie?" Lazy-Eye Matthew snickers. "Take a mouthful while she's there."

I realize that I am leaned across Lottie with my breasts pressed close to her face. We're not touching, but you know what it looks like. Lottie stares out of the window at the native women cutting grass in the fields and ignores Matthew. She doesn't even blush at his words. It's like there's a wall around her that cannot be breached by bad words or rough hands.

3

The Road to Keziah

The journey is slow, and I am bored. Slow because the dirt road is eaten away by potholes and washboard gullies that make the wheels of the *Ocean Current* shudder and bump at twenty miles an hour. Plus, cows have the right of way, so the bus stops and starts and chugs behind lazy herds of long-horned native cattle walking from one grass patch to another.

Boring because the scenery is the same as the last trip: Mud huts sprout from fields, distant mountains loom on the horizon, and rivers scattered with stones snake through the valleys. Stray dogs and stubborn goats dot the side of the road. Barefoot black children run to a tin-shack school somewhere. Out there. We travel in heat and dust, but I can smell rain coming too.

The trip is doubly boring because I get motion sickness, so reading *Jane Eyre* is out and I have no one to talk to. I've always nodded hello to Lottie whenever we crossed paths at school, because Mother hates snobs and remembers hiding in doorways when the children with nice clothing but mean hearts came her way. Now I'm one of the nice children whose father has money for fees, and Lottie is the poor girl with worn shoes and a faded school uniform. I can see that her hem has been let down many times and the side seams let out so she can squash into the fabric for one more year.

Lottie ignores me. I don't want to talk to her either, but her silence is aggravating. If she had sense, she'd try to win me over. This is her chance to make a first-class friend who might, with luck, one day buy her a bread roll or a licorice stick from the school shop. She doesn't even try. That's the Zulu in her: too full of pride to bend with the wind and too quick to fight. Her loss.

The bus slows on a sharp bend, and the engine whines as we begin our slow crawl down the side of a mountain. A car pulls up behind us and blasts its horn. The bus conductor sticks his arm out of the window and holds up his hand to make a stop signal. He can see the road ahead while the car driver is blind to what might be waiting. When the way is clear, the conductor will wave the car through. Simple.

The driver of the car presses the horn to make more noise. As if that will clear the road or straighten the blind turns. The conductor holds up his hand with stiff fingers. *Stop*, his signal says. *Do not pass*. The car engine revs. My heart speeds up. You have to wait for the right signal. That's how things are.

The car swings wide and accelerates past the *Ocean Current*.

I suck in a breath and hold it as stones ping the side of the bus and the car engine roars.

"Idiot," Lottie whispers. "He won't make it."

The red-haired Green brothers, in second class, crane their heads out the open window and yell, "Go, man. Go!"

My jaw locks tight as the bus driver pumps the brakes to slow us down so the car has room to swerve around whatever the bus conductor saw on the road ahead. Dust hazes the air. The Green brothers cough and spit dirt from their mouths. Ernest, the older boy, shouts, "He made it! He made it!"

Thank the Lord. We are safe. Lottie was wrong. Her life is full of bad things, but the worst thing to happen today was my demotion to third class. That's enough.

Slam.

The *Ocean Current* shudders and begins to spin across the narrow dirt road. My body jerks forward, then backward, and the world outside speeds up and slows down at the same time. The mountainside flashes past the windows. Then clouds. Rocks. An aloe tree with bright-orange flowers. Terrifying blank space, and the sound of the wind tearing through the windows.

Children scream. I scream, a strangled sound that comes from deep inside my throat. We are going to die. All of us mangled together at the foot of the mountain.

"Inkosi yami." The bus driver calls to God, hoping for extra traction, and swings the wheel counterclockwise to avoid the steep drop-off on the other side of the road.

Mrs. Button, who lives in the pink house behind the mechanic's workshop, says English roads have safety rails and reflective markers sunk into the tar, no matter where you drive. In Swaziland, we only have the power of prayer and pine coffins for those who plunge down, down to the valley floor.

The *Ocean Current* groans and comes to a sudden stop. Bodies twist and turn at strange angles. My right shoulder slams into the seat in front of me, and hot pain tears through my muscles. I grunt and grab my injured shoulder. It hurts like the devil.

"Look . . ." The Bartholomew twins recover first and press their noses to the window. "Look, see?" They squeal and point. "There's the car. And a cow."

Those who aren't crying or hugging friends rush to the right side of the bus to catch the action. I squash closer to Lottie to avoid Lazy-Eye Matthew, who has pushed across the aisle to get a better view of the accident that almost killed us. Sweaty underarms and faces lit up by morbid curiosity shove closer.

My hip bumps against Lottie's, but she doesn't flinch. Instead, I notice her paler-than-normal skin and the bead of blood leaking from a cut in her bottom lip. She must have bitten down on it during our almost-crash to stop from screaming. I don't recall her making a single sound as the *Ocean Current* spun toward the drop-off.

The others ooh and aah and say, "Oh my goodness." I don't want to see what's outside, but what choice do I have? I may be seated with the bottom-shelf students, but when we get to

Keziah, reliving the screaming, the squeal of the brakes, the car, and the cow will help me fit back in with the first-class students. Besides, Lottie isn't scared. If she can be brave, then so can I. I ignore the pain in my shoulder, scoot over, and force myself to share her view.

I wish I hadn't.

A blue sedan lies on its side with its wheels spinning slow circles in the air. The front fender and the hood are smashed in to a quarter of their normal size. Broken glass covers the ground and twinkles like dewdrops in the tall grass that grows on the roadside. If the driver is alive, he's being quiet about it. Farther down the road is the cow, also tipped on its side. If its head wasn't twisted in the opposite direction to its hooves, you'd think that it had fallen asleep on the mountain pass. Mercifully, there is very little blood. Just a red crust around the nostrils.

"I hope it's dead," Lottie whispers. "Please, let it be dead."

You see, I think, *that's the problem with being poor.* Lottie could have said, *I hope it's alive. Let it be alive,* but she didn't. She lives under a black cloud: too many fathers, a mother who sells roasted peanuts on the roadside, and, according to Delia, a rusted iron cot with a corn-husk mattress to sleep on . . . so it's no wonder she can't see the bright side to any situation.

"It moved." Lazy-Eye Matthew's good eye flickers. "The car moved."

The blue sedan rocks from side to side and tilts dangerously close to the drop-off. Half a yard more and it will spill over the lip and tumble two miles to the valley floor. A bloody palm slams the cracked window, and the car rocks again. The driver

29

is alive. He's trying to get out, but if he keeps moving . . . My heart jumps into my throat.

"Stay still," I mutter. "Stop moving or you'll die."

Lottie turns her stony blue gaze onto me. It's chilling.

"Let him fall," she says. "He killed the cow and he could have killed us, because he was too important to wait. He deserves to drop."

She means it.

• • •

Lottie's harsh judgment stuns me. Nice girls don't wish death on anyone, and if they do, they keep it to themselves. They smile and stay sweet. Lottie doesn't understand the rules. She says what's on her mind . . . just like that.

There's no time to reflect on the truth of Lottie's words. The driver's bloody palm slaps the broken window again and then again. The car rocks. The bus driver, the conductor, and the teachers from the Cross of Nazareth scramble from the *Ocean Current* and run for the blue sedan. They grab a tire, a sliver of fender, a door handle: any part they can reach and hang on to. A few of the older boys from first, second, and third class rush outside to help right the car.

"Umuntu omkhulu," the bus driver calls out in Zulu.

A great thing.

"Siza naye," the ticket seller and the baggage handler respond.

We come together.

The rescuers breathe in and breathe out in time. Muscles strain. Arms tense. My stomach knots. The men and the academy boys chant, "Umuntu omkhulu. Siza naye. Umuntu omkhulu. Siza naye" in unison. The hairs on the back of my neck prickle to hear them singing together, working together. One breath. One mind. One body. I'm terrified that the sedan will slip from their hands, but another part of me is thrilled by the ancient chant that echoes against the mountainside and down into the deep valley.

Delia and Sandi Cardoza, her new best friend, cling together and sob loud enough for me to hear them all the way at the back of the bus. I will never admit to Delia or to anyone else that the native voices touch a place deep inside me. When I hear them, the dreams of England we are taught to have in school are a million miles away and I cannot imagine why anyone would leave my country's lazy rivers and the bright mountain aloes bursting orange against the hard rocks.

For a rare minute, I am at home in my brown skin, at home in Swaziland. The ceaseless chanting and the smell of rain on the wind holds me exactly where I am: caught between terror and the aching beauty of the land.

Metal groans, and the blue sedan flips toward the rescue crew. They jump back to avoid being crushed, and the wheels hit the ground. The students on the bus cheer. A pale face soaked in blood lolls against the cracked window. The ticket seller rushes back to the car with a crowbar and jimmies the door open. A skinny white man in a dark-brown suit slides onto the road like a rag the maid uses to clean the floors. The man's right eye is swollen shut, and both his legs are twisted in different directions.

My mouth opens, and a high-pitched squeal comes out. I am not alone. Lottie is frightened too. Her fingers curl around mine, and I squeeze tight. She acts tough, but underneath it all she's a sixteen-year-old girl who hates the sight of blood, just like me. I go to untangle our hands. Not in a mean way, but nicely. I don't want her to think our being close goes beyond this minute. And that's when I realize my mistake. Lottie's hands are neatly folded in her lap. I am the one who's reached out to grab her. I am the one doing the clutching, the holding.

I jerk my hand away from Lottie's, and my face flames.

4

Know Your Place

We tumble out of the bus and onto the dusty grounds of Keziah Christian Academy, hours late. The car crash affected us all differently. Most students are subdued and exhausted. Others are excited and energized. Lazy-Eye Matthew and the Green brothers can't stop talking about the accident: the roar of the car engine, the spinning wheels, and the driver's bloodied face.

"You saw it," Lazy-Eye Matthew says. "White people aren't special. They're meat, just like us."

I can't wait to get off the bus and forget the day that passed. Plus, I'm starving. In first class, I would have swapped Delia half an orange for a boiled egg, or a piece of buttered bread for roasted peanuts. But Lottie had nothing. Not a carrot or a turned-brown banana. Nothing! Eating in front of her would have been awkward, so I kept my impago box closed and starved instead. When I get to the big-girls' dormitory, I will gorge on whatever Mother packed me for the trip. It's bound to be better than the stewed meat and cabbage they serve us in the dining hall.

The skinny black man who packed the suitcases onto the roof of the *Ocean Current* throws them down to the skinny black man who originally threw them up to him. They fall into a rhythm. Grab, throw, catch, place in a row. Grab, throw, catch, place in a row. I stand back with the other students and wait for the unloading to finish. Only then can we pick up our suitcases and go to our dorms.

Matron, who lives in a green cinder-block house attached to the little-girls' dormitory, comes out to greet us. Matron is fat and brown, and wears a black wig that flips up at the ends. From her two-room house, she hears every suspicious rustle and bad word, no matter how softly it's spoken. We call her Matron to her face, and the Elephant behind her back. It's the perfect nickname for a hefty woman with sensitive hearing, and even I use the name, but only when I'm absolutely sure there are no adults around to hear me.

Matron claps her hands, and we fall into four straight lines on the side of the road that leads past the orchards, the kitchen gardens, the low-roofed classrooms, and the big-boys' dormitory built on the edge of the dried playing fields.

"Come, come," Matron says. "Quick sticks."

Take too long and Matron will single you out for public punishment. Either a flick of a switch against the back of your legs or a long lecture on obedience and respect for your elders. I prefer the switch. It's quicker.

Lines form. I move to the end of the first row and find that my usual place is taken by Sandi Cardoza. Of course. I've been dumped, and I have to find another space quickly. No way will I be the first student punished for tardiness this term. That honor is usually reserved for Richard B, Gordon Number Three, or Lazy-Eye Matthew.

I slot in beside the scrawny Bartholomew twins and three down from Lottie Diamond. At Keziah, boys and girls make separate lines. We never line up together, and from now until the end of term, the different sexes will eye each other with wary curiosity and intense longing.

"Welcome," Matron says when the last of the bags flies from the roof of the *Ocean Current*. "What will you do from now on, boys and girls?"

"Bring honor to the Lord," we respond.

"How will you behave?"

"With goodness and mercy."

"Who will you fight?"

"Temptation and the devil."

"What is your reward?"

"My reward is eternal life."

I glance sideways as the answer to Matron's question slides off my tongue with no effort and even less thought. Lottie Diamond keeps her mouth zipped shut. Every school term starts with the same call-and-response. Lottie knows the answers to Matron's questions. We all do. She simply does not care to say them.

•••

Matron dismisses the boys, who pick up their bags and march in two lines toward the male dormitories on the far edge of the school grounds. From now on, we will march from one end of Keziah to the other: stomp, stomp, from morning assembly to our classrooms, then from our classrooms to chapel, and from chapel to whatever duties we must perform to keep the school spick-and-span. We sweep the roads, pick fruit from the or-chards, wash the dormitory verandahs, weed the gardens, and do domestic chores for the staff, who don't have maids to chop vegetables and fold the laundry . . . The devil makes work for idle hands, so we are never idle.

I grab my suitcase and swallow a groan. My shoulder aches from where it hit the seat in front of me and from the weight of tinned peaches and canned meat called Spam inside, which are good for trading favors. Lottie picks up a cotton sack from the luggage line and swings it across her back like it weighs noth-ing. That's because there's probably nothing in it but a brush, a change of underwear, and a moth-eaten sweater.

"Adele." Matron calls my name. "Come here, please."

Being summoned by an adult is never good, but I can't think what I've done to get Matron's attention so quickly. I wres-tle my suitcase across the freshly swept dirt to where Matron stands in the shade of a wisteria tree bursting with purple flowers. The bus driver, the conductor, and the baggage handlers crane their necks to examine a large piece of machinery still lashed to the roof of the *Ocean Current*.

"Yes, Matron." I stand with my arms by my side and my gaze pinned to the tops of my shoes. Making eye contact with an adult is a sign of disrespect, and I always follow the rules. Ants scurry across the dirt, carrying crumbs that have fallen from the clothes of those who ate their impago on the bus. My stomach rumbles.

"Now listen, Adele. Some things have changed."

My head jerks up at Matron's overly sweet tone. "What things, Matron?"

"Well . . . Mr. Cardoza is very concerned that his daughter fit in at Keziah. He heard we had trouble with the power generator, and he donated a new one so everything goes smoothly. He wants Sandi to be comfortable, so she'll be sharing a quad room with Delia, Peaches, and Natalie."

That is *my* place.

Delia, Peaches Armstrong, and Natalie van der Sell are popular girls. They are pretty, and iron their hair straight so it falls in a limp curtain to their shoulders. A team of "pets" runs their errands and carries their books from one classroom to the other. If Keziah is a kingdom, Delia, Peaches, and Natalie are the royal princesses. And, even though their parents are properly married and mine are not, I am supposed to be one of them, sharing their space and bathing in their reflected light. Matron has chosen to keep the girls from respectable families together, and thrown me out. Now where will I end up?

"You'll be moved to another room," Matron says. "Understand?"

The baggage handlers lower the generator from the roof of the bus, careful to avoid chipping the pale-blue wave painted along the side. A pickup truck driven by Mrs. Vincent, who wears her ash-blond hair in crooked pigtails, reverses into place, and Gordon Number One, an older boy with brains, helps the bus crew lower the machine onto the flat bed.

"Yes, Matron," I say. "I understand."

My eyes sting, and I want to go home.

• • •

A row of tall Christ-thorns, covered in spikes and cheerful red flowers, separates the junior-girls' dormitory, for the little girls, from the senior-girls' quarters, for the big girls in their last three years of high school. The prickly hedge, which is planted closer to the big-girls' dorm, is nicknamed 'the silent policeman.' The school claims the thorny plants are meant to shield the windows from prying eyes, but in reality they are there to keep the naughty girls inside at night and to keep the naughty boys outside at all times. If the thorns don't get you, the poisoned white sap in the leaves will make your skin itch, and then everyone will know you're one of the bad girls who can't be trusted.

The weight of the cans and the books that Father brought me from Joburg slows me down, and my right shoulder aches as I hurry toward the long brick building that houses the big-girls' dormitory. By the time I get there, everyone in the yard is already split into groups of ten, six, and four. Some are obviously happy with their roommates, and others are sullen about who they've been assigned to share a space with for the next year.

Delia, Peaches Armstrong, Sandi Cardoza, and Natalie van der Sell link arms and lean against each other, like one tree with four intertwining trunks. They are four pretty girls who glow with pride at being themselves. I pretend they are invisible, and look for a group waiting for me to fill out their uneven number.

"Ah, Adele, there you are." Mrs. Thomas, who's in charge of the senior-girls' dormitory, looks up from the sheet of paper in her hand. Mrs. Thomas is a skinny mixed-race widow with a gap in her front teeth that makes a whistling sound when she talks, and, though she is also a matron, she prefers being called by her married name. Delia says that's stupid. Mrs. Thomas was only married for three months before her husband died in a farm accident. "Everyone to your rooms, please. Choose your beds and unpack your clothes. No fighting or you'll get a week's punishment. Supper is at six sharp."

The girls drift inside. Some lug suitcases, and others carry reused flour sacks stuffed with all that they own.

Wait, wait. My heart thunders in my ears. *Where am I supposed to go?*

Mrs. Thomas clears her throat and waves me closer. Delia and the pretties—a name that Delia herself coined for her group—hover on the front porch, desperate to see what happens next. They have money in their pockets, but gossip is also a form of currency.

"Off you go," Mrs. Thomas says to the girls in a brisk voice. "It will take a while for you all to unpack your suitcases."

Delia pulls a face when Mrs. Thomas turns away, and I realize that Mrs. Thomas just made a dig at the amount of clothes, cans, and trinkets that the top girls bring with them to school. Suddenly it doesn't feel so good to be one of them. Then I remember that I'm not a princess anymore . . . I am standing in the dirt yard with an aching shoulder and dusty shoes, waiting to be assigned a cot inside the dormitory.

"Adele . . ." Color stings Mrs. Thomas's cheeks, and I know that she has bad news for me. "Matron told you we've had to rearrange the rooms?"

Ahh.

I see the bags under Mrs. Thomas's eyes and the turned-down corners of her mouth. She's in one of her sad moods, so she's trying to be nice, but I don't want to draw the torture out any longer. "Where do I sleep, Mrs. Thomas?"

She flips the piece of paper over in her hand, and girls' names spin from one side to the other. "We've made a special room for you and one other student. When you sweep it out and wash the floors, you'll see that it's nice. I think you'll be happy there, and it's only for this term. Not for the whole school year, you understand. And maybe, in a little while, if we find another space—"

"Wait. Are you talking about the green room where Lorraine Anderson died?" That room is haunted. There's disease

40

trapped inside the walls, and the peeling paint is infected with whatever killed Lorraine. Everyone knows that.

"First," Mrs. Thomas says, "interrupting an adult is against the rules, Adele. You should know better. And, second, whatever you heard about Lorraine is not true. She didn't die in the room. She died in the Norwegian hospital in Mahamba."

That is a big, fat lie. Everyone knows Lorraine was stone-cold dead before Mr. and Mrs. Vincent rushed her to Mahamba in the back of their car. The mercy dash to the hospital was for show . . . That's why the room's been empty for three years. Nobody will sleep in it. Their parents won't let them.

"Third"—Mrs. Thomas keeps counting—"there's nothing to be done about the situation we're in. You will have to cope."

I grit my teeth to stop from yelling, *My father is white. He pays full fees. I am supposed to get first pick of rooms. My parents aren't married and my father hasn't donated a new generator but still* . . . That's how things are. Mrs. Thomas blushes, because she knows the rules have been broken. It is outrageous, and nothing she says will make it better. I grab my suitcase and drag it onto the porch.

"Adele . . ."

I turn my back on Mrs. Thomas, something that I've never done before, because nice girls aren't rude. Nice girls don't break the rules, but putting me in a dead girl's room is not nice, so I don't care.

41

5

This Is Where You Live Now

The room is small and dusty, with two cots pushed against the pea-green walls. A high window lets in slanted light, and a second, lower window lets in a breeze that stirs the dust motes in the air. I cover my mouth and nose, and try not to breathe too deeply. The dead are lonely. Lorraine's ghost is waiting for a warm body to move into so she can laugh, talk, and eat again.

I sit on the edge of the right-side cot, with my sore shoulder slumped. I could call the mechanic's shop back home in Manzini and get one of the mechanics to go and get Mrs. Button, who lives in the pink house behind the yard where scrap cars are kept for their parts. Mrs. Button is a widow with three children working in South Africa. She has time to kill, so she can walk over to our place and get Mother. Then Mother could use the mechanic's phone to call the principal's office and complain to Mr. Vincent about the room. But I don't want her to know

I've been dumped. Mother wants me to be everything that she wasn't: popular and clever with books. The truth will hurt her. Mrs. Thomas is right. I will have to make the most of it.

This is where I live now: in a haunted room that no one will come near. A shadow falls across the doorway. Lottie Diamond steps inside and throws her sack onto the cot opposite mine like she doesn't care about Lorraine's ghost or the dust on the window ledges. Of course. This room is probably a palace compared to the tin shack where she lives, and it's definitely a step up from the long room that she shared with nine other small-fee and no-fee students last year. Lottie is poor and prone to fighting, but she gets good marks and, with the help of the money that the Vincents raise overseas, she's on track to pass her final exams. That must be why Mrs. Thomas chose her to share a two-cot room.

This is the worst day of my life.

Lottie sighs like she's the one with the problem . . . like she's the one whose whole life has been turned upside down in one day.

"Are you going to help me clean the room, or are you going to sit there and sulk?" she asks.

"I'm not sulking," I snap. "My shoulder is sore. That's all."

"All right. You do the dusting, and I'll scrub the floors. We'll choke in our sleep otherwise."

"Fine." I shove my suitcase and my impago box deep under my cot, where she can't get them. I'll have to eat the food later, when she's not around. Lottie steps outside, and I follow her into the hallway. From behind closed doors, I hear excited chatter and the sound of drawers opening and closing. The girls in the other rooms are catching up on what happened during the Christmas holidays just passed. Their rooms were cleaned by an army of black women this morning. I bet the black women refused to come anywhere near our room. They know about the evil spirits the missionaries tell us are rubbish.

We walk across the dirt yard to the lavender hedge and the house where Mrs. Thomas lives. I knock. Or rather, Lottie steps back so I'm forced to knock. A yellow cat with white paws, called Socks, weaves between our legs and purrs while we wait.

"Yes?" Mrs. Thomas's brown eyes flick from Lottie to me and then back again. She expects that we've already had a fight, that we can't possibly share a room for a whole term, and she's too deep in her own sad mood to solve the problem. "How can I help you girls?"

We all know that Mrs. Thomas has mood swings. One day she's sad and soft, and the next day she's mean as a mamba snake. Delia says that's because she went from being a blushing bride to a farm widow in twelve weeks. Twelve weeks! No wonder her mind is cracked.

"We need a mop and a bucket and a dustcloth from the cleaning shed, Mrs. Thomas. Can we get them, please?" We can't just take what we want from the shed, the kitchen gardens, or the orchards. We must ask permission. We must say please and thank you.

"Of course." Mrs. Thomas is relieved. "How many buckets?"

"Just the one." Lottie promised to do the floors, and I am holding her to it. "And one dustcloth."

"You'll need a broom to sweep the room first." Mrs. Thomas unhooks the key to the main storage shed from a thin metal chain that she wears around her waist and gives it to me. "Take what you like, but be sure to put it back when you're finished."

"We will. Thank you." I take the key and walk to the iron shed under a grapefruit tree. Only the most desperate students will steal the yellow fruit to eat when they are hungry. It happens when they have no pocket money to buy food from the school shop. A situation I've never had to worry about.

I unlock the shed, and a strange feeling flips my stomach and I stop. I know why Lottie made me ask for the supplies.

If Lottie had done it, Mrs. Thomas would have made her sign the items out and then sign them back in, the way Mother makes the maid tick off the tins she takes from the pantry. The Bible says, "Ye shall know them by their fruits," which, Mr. Vincent once explained, means, "Judge a person by their deeds not by their words." Lottie is found guilty of sins that she hasn't even committed. She lives under a cloud of suspicion, and, for some reason, knowing this makes me uncomfortable.

• • •

Long after lights-out and a slow wind-down to sleep, I wake up disoriented. In semidarkness. Moonlight spills in through the high window and onto a freshly washed floor, and the smell of lavender comes from somewhere outside. I remember where I am. I am in the green room where Lorraine Anderson died, in the room that holds her ghost and magnifies the mysterious illness that killed her.

My heart sinks.

I sit up and clutch my blankets to my chest. My ears strain for the sound of her footsteps on the cement floor, the whisper of her voice in the air. Lorraine is quiet, though. I peer across the room to where Lottie's cot is pushed against the opposite wall.

The cot is empty, and, smack on top of it, right where I can see it, is my impago box. The lid is open. Lottie's thievery stuns me. She's probably so used to stealing food that she's forgotten that it's wrong.

I jump out of bed and pad across the floor to the crime scene. There's a single boiled egg in the box; everything else that Mother packed for me is gone. Lottie ate it all or swapped the contents for cigarettes or whatever else girls like her do for fun when the lights go out.

I hate her. I hate being stuck in the same room with her. It's embarrassing to be brought so low on my first day back at school. Lottie cleaned the floors well, but so what? Delia is right. Poor girls can't be trusted. They'll take your soap, your underwear, your brand-new dress—not to use, but out of pure spite. They want us to suffer the way they suffer.

Lord Jesus above. The cans . . .

I drop onto all fours and scramble under my cot to grab my suitcase. If Lottie's taken the cans, I'll have nothing to trade: nothing to help me bribe my way back into Delia's group. My hands shake as I flip the locks and drag the case into the moon-

46

light. I count four bars of lavender soap, five cans of condensed milk—a premium item—three cans of peaches in syrup, four tins of Spam, one bag of toffee chews, and two packets of short-bread biscuits and one of strawberry creams, another premium item. It's all here. Including *Jane Eyre* and three other books that Father brought me from Joburg.

I close the lid and shove my suitcase far, far under the cot. That won't stop Lottie, but it makes me feel better to think she'll have to work for what she steals. With the cans secure, I sit on the edge of my bed with my hands in fists, and I don't have to wait long before I hear footsteps picking their way through the Christ-thorns.

Lottie slides through the lower window and lands in a crouch. She's agile as a spider monkey and just as naughty. I bet she's snuck out a thousand times and never been caught. She sees me sitting on my cot, hot with anger.

"Oh, you're up," she whispers. "Good. I have something for you."

"Thief," I whisper back.

She shoves a bowl made from a dried gourd in my face. It smells, and I shrink away. Whatever it is, I don't want it.

"You stole my impago. You ate it all."

"Just the apple and the buttered bread." She has no shame. "I traded the rest for medicine."

"You think I'm stupid?" It's hard to express anger in a whis-per, but I have to whisper, because our room is closest to Mrs. Thomas's house, and while Mrs. Thomas might not have the Elephant's sensitive hearing, she's still a matron, and when her sad mood evaporates, she hits harder than the Elephant and says meaner things. "Medicine comes in bottles, not in gourds. What you have is rubbish, and it stinks."

Lottie purses her lips, annoyed, as if I am the problem. As if I am the thief who jumps in and out of windows after dark. "It's crushed nettle and aloe," she says. "I got it from Mama Khumalo, who lives across the river. It will help your shoulder heal."

It's too ridiculous. I snort.

"You swapped good food for a native medicine that some woman in a mud hut gave you . . . I was wrong. You're the stupid one."

Lottie scoops goo from the gourd and steps closer. She has a slender body, lean and muscled from hard work, and her hair is cropped too short. She looks like a boyish fairy. "Show me where it hurts. You'll thank me tomorrow morning."

"Never. Now get away from me."

Lottie blinks, and I don't see her coming till she's on me. She throws me back onto my cot with astonishing speed and pins me down with her clean hand. I try to sit up, but she's strong. Her slimy hand invades my nightgown and tugs the neckline aside to rub the stinky lotion onto my right shoulder and along the right side of my neck.

"There. It's done," she says when she's finished. "And don't try to wipe it off either. The medicine needs time to work."

She gets up and goes to her cot while I lie on mine with a lump stuck in my throat. Fights are common at Keziah. You have to fight to survive, to mark your territory, to warn others that walking over you has consequences. The rules say that I have to get up and swing at Lottie, bite her, scratch her face, and pull her hair, even if I know that she's stronger and faster than I am.

Instead, I lie limp and confused in the moonlight. The nettle mixture burns, and all the terrible things that happened to me today keep me from moving. This term will be hell, and losing a fight on my first night back will make me a weakling. If Lottie doesn't boast about flinging me down on my cot like an empty sack, then my reputation as a fighter is safe.

I crawl under my blankets and turn my back on her. The slime really stings now, but the pain has eased.

"Are you going to eat this boiled egg?" she asks of the last item in the impago box that she ransacked.

"Have it," I mumble, and hear the crack of the shell and the happy sounds she makes while she eats. The river is two miles away, and the hut where she got what she calls "medicine" is farther out still. She must be starved. I stop my soft thoughts and count all the reasons I have to hate her. Lottie breaks the rules, she fights, she steals, she has one school uniform and one change of clothing for the weekend, two pairs of underwear, a comb, a nightdress, and a tiny spinning top with strange symbols painted on the sides. She's poor. Being with her will bring me down to her level.

She slides into bed to the creak of metal springs. I stay facing away from her. I've run out of bad thoughts, and I watch the shadows flicker across the wall instead. A lightning strike. Moving clouds and then, clear as sunshine, a skeleton hand reaches out to grab me and pull me into the land of the dead. Lorraine. I gasp out loud.

"What?" Lottie says in a sleepy voice.

I look again, and the bony hand is gone. But I saw it. Right there. "Do you believe in spirits?" I ask.

"No," she says. "They don't exist."

Nonsense. Everyone, even the missionaries who finished high school, believe in good Christian spirits. Mostly the Holy Spirit, but that counts.

"How do you know for sure?" I ask.

"If they did exist, then my father would be here every night to tell me a story and to kiss me good night, but he's gone and gone. Just bones in the ground."

"Your first father?"

Delia says there have been too many to count. Some white, some mixed-race, some black.

"I only had one father," Lottie says. It's silent for a moment. Then very quietly, she says, "And he loved me."

Her words cut through me. Her father loved her. She's certain of it. She knows it from the roots of her cropped hair to the tips of her toes.

Of all the reasons to hate Lottie Diamond, that father, with his stories and his kisses, is perhaps the best one of all.

6

Surely Mercy and Goodness
Will Follow Me

We line up for Monday morning inspection, little soldiers on parade. The junior girls stand in the front rows, and the senior girls in the back. Down the road, where we can't see them, the boys do the same.

Matron inspects the junior girls for dirty fingernails, dirty necks, clean shoes, and clean underwear. Mrs. Thomas does the same, and I see from her thin mouth and glassy eyes that her sad mood has gone and that this morning she is ready to be cruel. She makes a show of inspecting Delia's shoes for dust, but we all know that she won't punish any of the girls whose parents might withdraw them from Keziah and send them to boarding school in South Africa. Sweat breaks out on my top lip when she cuts through the lines and comes straight for me. Since my demotion, I don't know where I stand in the order of things.

"Hands," she snaps.

I hold them out. She checks my fingernails and the grooves of my knuckles. This morning, I washed extra hard to get any trace of the native medicine off my skin, so I know I'm clean. She doesn't ask to see my underwear, which, in any case, is new and trimmed with lace. Mrs. Thomas moves on to Lottie.

"Skirt up."

Lottie lifts her uniform to show her underwear. The rest of us keep our eyes to the front, but some girls titter at the thought of what Lottie wears under her uniform.

"Make sure you have a fresh pair on tomorrow," Mrs. Thomas says, and moves to the next girl, this time to check behind her ears. We are checked at random, but the poor girls get extra attention because they are in imminent danger of falling into bad habits. Lottie is inspected three or four times a week. This is how we start each day, scrubbed clean and closer to God.

The view from the middle row is different from where I'd normally stand in the front row. Sandi Cardoza's braids shine with Vaseline, and a red ribbon trails down her back. Delia whispers something to her, and together they laugh.

I have to get back into the group today . . . before my being out of it becomes permanent. My reintroduction has to be natural, a return to the way things ought to be.

The Elephant claps her hands to get our attention, and her wig wiggles. It's funny, but no one laughs. "To breakfast. Nice and quiet."

"Yes, Matron." We turn and march to a long brick building that houses the kitchen and dining hall. A typical Keziah breakfast waits for us inside: bowls of stiff porridge, mugs of sweet tea, and slices of white bread with jam.

We keep to the middle of the dirt road. A dust cloud trails behind us, and the sky above us is an endless stretch of blue. We march past neat garden beds and small lawns trimmed with machetes. Behind the orchards and on the other side of a low wire fence are tall trees and a thick stand of wild bananas that grows down to the river's edge.

I think of Lottie out there at night, jumping the fence and fording the river to get medicine from Mama Whatever-Her-Name-Was. My shoulder feels much better, the pain now a dull ache that I barely notice. The medicine worked, but I didn't thank Lottie this morning. She was wrong to take the impago.

• • •

After breakfast, we march to the chapel for a beginning-of-the-January-term prayer meeting. We attend chapel three times a week, and again on Sunday, so that God is always at our shoulder.

"Right, left, right, left." Brenda, a senior girl with a permanently blocked nose, calls out the rhythm, and we fall into step. Behind us, Gordon Number One leads the boys. There are four Gordons at the academy, all sons of Scottish men who passed through Swaziland or else took up farming the land. Gordon Number One's father comes to every speech day and awards ceremony, and Delia told me that Gordon Number One will go to a university in Scotland one day.

We near the red brick chapel. It has a peaked iron roof and a small graveyard on the side nearest the school boundary fence. The five graves are decorated with artificial flowers in bubble-topped plastic containers that help to keep the colors bright. Whenever we pass the graveyard, we hold our breath, to stop the spirits of the dead from entering our bodies and stealing away our souls. The American missionaries tell us to stop believing in native superstitions and to put our faith in the hands of the Lord Jesus above, but we all know that African spirits are stronger than American spirits, so we hold our breath, and that way we stay alive.

On the near side of the chapel is a concrete baptism pit. When it rains, the pit fills with water and makes a home for the frogs. On baptism day, the pit is filled to the top by hand and the frogs are scooped up with nets. Some backsliding students have been baptized three or four times. It helps that the newly baptized get a pat on the back from Mr. Vincent and an extra helping of dessert after dinner. The devil is cunning, but the good Lord has steamed pudding and sponge cakes on his side.

In the distance, a black dot appears on the dirt road that leads though the thick bush to the school grounds. The *chug*, *chug* of an engine grows louder, and my heart sinks. It's Mr. Parns's blue tractor, and I know the ugly scene that's coming. It happens every term. Mr. Parns begs his son, Darnell, to get off the tractor and go back to school, and his son, Darnell, screams and begs to go back home, while the rest of us look on, helpless.

"To the right. To the right." Brenda directs us off the road, and our carefully arranged lines break apart. We clump together on the roadside as the tractor pulls to a stop a few yards from chapel. Mr. Vincent, the American principal, walks down the chapel stairs to talk to Mr. Parns, a short and bald mixed-race farmer with a sunburned face and a forehead cut with deep furrows from worrying about late rains and failed crops.

Mr. Vincent, on the other hand, is tall, with a smooth face and thick caramel-brown hair. He wears brown trousers, a brown sweater—no matter what the weather—a crisp white shirt, and a brown tie. His nickname is the Brown Bear, for obvious reasons. Mr. Vincent peers at Darnell through his thick glasses and welcomes him back to the academy for another year. Mrs. Vincent, his wife, smiles and nods in agreement. Americans are smilers. It suits them. They have straight white teeth, and their breath smells of mint.

Darnell, who is fifteen but can't work out simple math problems or read simple words, sits on the tractor fender with red eyes and a snotty nose. He won't look up.

"Come on, boy," Mr. Parns says, embarrassed. "Time for school."

"Home," Darnell cries. "Home, Pa. Home."

"Acchh . . ." Peaches shivers with disgust. Darnell has sloped eyes, flat features, and a broad face. Delia and all of us in the group agreed that it was bad luck and bad judgment to have a half-wit mixing in with normal students. His ugliness might be contagious.

"Quiet down, girls. No talking." The Elephant slaps a switch across her palm to show that she means business. Peaches zips it and grabs Natalie's hand for comfort.

"Take him home." Lottie's low voice comes from my right,

and I'm startled to find her at my shoulder. Did she deliberately stand next to me?

Lottie nibbles her bottom lip as Darnell clings to the tractor fender and begs his father to "Please, please, go from here." Mr. Vincent tries to move Darnell, but he won't budge. Americans think that being nice solves problems, but Mr. Vincent has to get rough if he wants to detach Darnell from his father's tractor.

Darnell throws his head back and howls, "Home. Home!"

"Gordon Number One and Barnabas. Over here, please." Mr. Vincent calls on the two biggest boys in the school for help. Both Gordon Number One and Barnabas Phillips are broad-shouldered and muscled from working their fathers' farms during the holidays, and we girls watch them walk by with bright eyes.

Mr. Parns loosens his son's grip on the blue metal while the others pull. Darnell peels away from the tractor like an orange rind. Gordon Number One holds him in a tight embrace, and Darnell will make himself sick if he keeps screaming "No, no, no" in his slurred voice.

It's a terrible scene, and I'm relieved when Barnabas and Gordon Number One drag Darnell in the direction of the big-boys' dormitory. Like always, Darnell will run away from school this week or the next, but for now, at least, the ugliness is over.

"Let him go home," Lottie mumbles, agitated. "What's the use of keeping him here?"

Lottie's rambling is none of my business, but surely she can see the use in getting an education, in learning to better yourself.

"He has to learn how to read and write," I whisper back. "It's better than staying on the farm."

"Not if he can't learn." Her jaw clenches. "He's slow. Surely even you can see that?"

"Even me?" Again, I'm the one with the problem. It's infuriating. "What do you mean, 'even me'?"

The Elephant turns, all ears, and points a meaty finger at us. "Joubert. Diamond. Come forward, please."

Lottie goes first, and I follow. My mouth feels dry. *Ba-bum. Ba-bum.* My heart slams inside my chest, and the sound magnifies inside my ears. Because of Lottie's stupid mumbling, I'm about to be punished in front of the whole school. The boys shuffle closer, to get a good look, and I wish I had sense enough to stay away from her.

Lottie stands in front of the Elephant with a blank expression. Her walls are up, and she stands behind them.

"Yes, Matron?" I am polite, even though Matron has the switch in her hands and she will use it no matter what I say.

"Tell me what you did wrong." The Elephant knows, but she needs to hear us confess.

"We talked when you said not to," Lottie says, and holds her hand out with the palm up and waits to be punished. The way she does it is almost insolent, a challenge to Matron to do her best and see how little Lottie cares. Physical punishment is a part of our education. Pain is supposed to teach us to remember the rules and to follow them; it guides us on the right path. But if the pain can be absorbed effortlessly, then the punishment is pointless.

57

The Elephant grits her teeth. She knows when her power is being challenged, and she'll take her frustrations out on the both of us. I've been hit before, but rarely. My wall is built of smiles and politeness, and it will crumble the moment the switch stings my palm. Compared to Lottie, I am a weakling, but I cannot, I will not, fall farther down the social ladder while the whole school watches.

"Sorry, Matron." I stick my hand out next to Lottie's. "We broke the rules. We should be punished."

Matron hits Lottie's palm three times, hard. Lottie blinks in time with the switch, and the cords in her neck tighten under her skin. Good. Now I know what to do. Matron moves to me, and I also get three hard hits. I blink three times, tense the muscles in my neck, and hold the sound of a gasp in my throat.

Sweat breaks out on my forehead, and three red welts cut across my palm. I hold back tears and imagine that I'm standing safe behind Lottie's wall. Matron sucks her teeth, annoyed by our closed mouths and blank expressions: our lack of contrition. It seems we've learned nothing from our punishment. She'd hit us again to teach us a lesson, but we're late for chapel, and Mr. Vincent and the senior teachers are waiting. The Elephant is ranked below the teachers, and she works to their schedule.

"In line," Matron says. "Quickly now."

We fall into place and—left, right, left, right—we march to the bottom of the chapel stairs. I lose sight of Lottie and glance backward and sideways to see where she's gone. She's nowhere close, but Delia and the pretties are one row behind me. Peaches blushes at my public humiliation, but Delia smirks. She loves to feel superior. Mrs. Thomas and the Elephant wouldn't dare hit her in public, because her parents would transfer her out of Keziah, so, in her mind, my beating confirms that she's special. She's better than me. She's better than everyone else. I've seen Delia turn on other girls for being too ugly, too fat, or just too pretty and, knowing that the same thing could happen to me, I worked hard to keep Delia sweet. I complimented her skin, her hair, and her singing voice, which is actually thin and too high. I didn't think she'd ever turn on me. My mistake.

Sandi and Natalie pretend that I'm invisible. They can't be seen with a girl who gets the switch in front of the whole school on the first day of term, a girl who shares a haunted room with Lottie Diamond. My hand clenches into a fist, and the cuts sting. I'm sure now that I've lost them for good.

• • •

After chapel, we break up and go to our classrooms. All except the really poor students, who have to report to the office to collect used textbooks with scribbles in the margins or sometimes a rude drawing of a penis that the staff missed covering up with black marker.

I take the concrete path that cuts across the central lawn and forks in the direction of the senior classrooms. A parent donated gallons of paint to the academy four years ago. Now all the classrooms are blue. The science room got two coats before the paint ran out, so it's darker. Jacaranda branches shade the corrugated iron roofs and add a dash of green to the blue landscape. Toward the end of the year, the trees will bloom purple and cover the lawns with dead flowers that pop under our feet.

Mr. Newman, a mixed-race teacher from Pietermaritzburg in South Africa, calls the roll for science class, and if Lottie doesn't get here soon, she'll be punished for tardiness. I don't care if she's late. After all, the native medicine was paid for with my impago and it was her stupid mumbling that got me hit outside of chapel. Still, my head turns in the direction of the main office, where the poor students are lined up to get their secondhand books. She's two from the front, and she won't make it in time.

We take our seats in the classroom the color of a rainy-day sky. Scarred wooden chairs and desks are ranked in five straight rows, with the teacher's desk at the front of the room, right next to the blackboard. Mr. Newman, who smells of aftershave and leans too close to girls, starts the lesson with a basic "name three planets, three trees, and three mammals" test that all but the thickest of the students will pass. Mr. Newman is lazy, and teaching us new things requires effort.

Halfway through the test, Lottie knocks on the door and asks permission to join the class. Mr. Newman picks up a ruler from his desk and raps her twice across the knuckles, the price of entry. Last night, I was sure that dead Lorraine's ghost was out to get me. But this morning, I think that maybe Lottie is right: spirits don't exist. If they did, then her father, Mr. Diamond, would take the ruler from Mr. Newman and smack him across the knuckles with the metal edge till his skin split.

• • •

Monday's lunch is boiled potatoes with boiled spinach greens and fried onions. The teachers serve themselves first and sit at the teachers' table at the front of the long dining hall with big windows that let in the light. Boys and girls in their final year go next, and then the rest of the students line up by descending grade and age. The little ones go last, which is fair because they are small and have to learn patience.

I take a plate from one of the kitchen ladies whose job it is to make sure that the food is distributed in the right amounts. Full-fee-paying students get generous helpings while the poorer students get smaller ones. Delia says that's how things are, and we can't change the situation. There are rules. If your parents pay full fees, you get a full plate. If your parents pay less, well . . . That's how it's always been, she says.

I scan the length of the girls' table for an opening close to where I need to be. There's a prime spot one down from Delia and almost opposite the other three girls in the group. Talking my way back in with them will be hard, and, once I'm back inside, keeping on Delia's good side will also be hard. But that's all right. I'm used to laughing at her jokes and agreeing with her opinions. Being on my own is uncomfortable, and I'm not ready to give up my coveted spot inside the circle of top girls.

I take a short breath and move slowly. My instinct is to run and claim the seat, but I can't appear too eager for their company. I may not be the 'diamond' daughter of a Christian marriage but I'm their equal when it comes to pretty dresses and pocket money and canned goods to trade. I am no beggar. I wander over and slide my plate down onto the table like I have nothing but time.

"How is it?" The greeting is meant for all four girls, but I speak directly to Natalie van der Sell, who is pretty but stupid and who I've let copy off my tests for years. "Were the holidays good?"

Natalie is also a boaster, so there's no way she'll ignore the question or fail to embellish all the wonderful things that happened to her over the four-week break.

"We stayed home, but guess what?" Her brown eyes bug out. She's got big news.

"What?" I say, and spoon up some potatoes. The cuts on my hands sting, but I ignore the pain and act as if this morning's punishment didn't happen.

"Daddy says that this coming Christmas, he's going to take us to Mozambique for sure. I'll get to see the ocean and play on the sand, and Daddy says we might even take a boat to an island."

"You should definitely come to Maputo," Sandi Cardoza says before I get a chance to answer Natalie. "We have a big house there, right on the beach, and sometimes we see dolphins in the water. You three should stay over during the holidays. There's room for everyone, and my father likes visitors."

Delia and Natalie and Peaches ooh and aah at being invited to stay in rich Mr. Cardoza's house, where the sand outside the door glitters with gold, and dolphins play in the waves.

"I'll have to get a new bathing suit," Peaches squeaks. "Maybe a bikini."

"If your daddy lets you," Delia says, and they all laugh at the joke, which is mildly funny but not that funny. I smile to let them know that I, too, am amused. And though Sandi left me out of the invitation list, I push on.

"Right on the beach?" I ask in the breathy voice that Mother uses when she talks to Father on the telephone. "You can smell the ocean?"

"We're like this far from the water . . ." Sandi reaches her arm across the table to indicate the distance between her father's big house and the much-dreamed-of Indian Ocean. "You can hear the waves day and night."

More oohs and aahs from the others, and I spoon the potatoes into my mouth. If my mouth is full, then I can't point out how ridiculous Sandi's calculations are. No house is that close to the water unless it is a houseboat. Next, she'll say that the dolphins eat from her hand. I chew, and force the food down my throat and into my stomach. I have to be honey. I have to smile and stay sweet, even though I hate Sandi and her rich Portuguese father.

We almost went to Mozambique once. It was all planned, the dates on the calendar circled in red by Mother, who fussed over which clothes to pack and which hat would protect her skin from the sun but leave the bounce in her hair. *Seven days to go*, she'd say, and then, *Just six days*, and that's where the countdown stopped. He canceled. His other son—older, whiter, and smarter than us—broke his leg playing rugby, and he had to stay at home. "I want to take you to the ocean," he said via the long-distance line. "But I can't. I'm so sorry . . ."

We sat in the backyard with our feet in buckets of water and pretended it was the ocean. Mother wore a pink hat.

"What will we eat?" Peaches asks. "The same as in Swaziland?"

"Better," Sandi says. "Prawn curry, grilled fish, and peri-peri chicken. Ice cream on a stick, and roasted cashews. As much as you want."

Delia makes an *mmm* sound, Peaches rolls her eyes with delight, and Natalie licks her lips at the dizzying variety of food available in Mozambique. No amount of my canned meat or condensed milk can compete with the vision of plenty that Sandi has painted for them.

7

Copycat

Later, we cluster outside of Scripture, our last class of the day. It's windy, and the girls bunch their skirt hems into their fists to stop them from blowing up. The boys hang back and pray that one of the girls will lose her grip.

Blown leaves scatter across the lawns, and Lazy-Eye Matthew reaches for the hem of Lottie's skirt. Matthew can't keep his grubby hands to himself or keep his dirty mouth shut around girls.

Lottie does what I'd do, if only I had the guts. She smacks Matthew's hand down and grabs him by the ear. "Pig," she says, and twists. Matthew's good eye rolls in the socket, and she twists harder. We laugh. He should have known better.

Miss December, our mixed-race geography teacher, is taking the path across the lawn to the senior classrooms. Miss December is in her early twenties, with a long, slender neck dotted with freckles, and huge brown eyes. All the boys are in love with her. She pretends not to notice, but I think the attention pleases her. Gordon Number One, the best of the Gordons, walks behind her with a stack of her textbooks in his arms. And behind him comes Darnell, who has calmed down since being pulled from his father's tractor in tears. Darnell copies Gordon's confident stride and thrown-back shoulders, and I blink in surprise. Darnell is an excellent mimic. He has Gordon's body movements down just right.

The other girls are too mesmerized by Gordon to pay any attention to Darnell's uncanny impersonation, because, good gracious, you should see how Gordon's muscles strain against his cotton shirt. If he flexes any more, those buttons will pop.

"Quick sticks." I turn around and poke Lottie a sharp one in the back. "Miss December's on the way."

Lottie gives Lazy-Eye Matthew a final slap across the head. He rubs his sore ear, and from the stupid grin on his face, you'd imagine that Lottie gave him a kiss. I think that Matthew always enjoys the touch of a girl's hand, no matter how rough. We quickly form lines and pretend that we are all good friends. The fight between Lottie and Matthew never happened.

When there are no adults around, we divide into different groups: some high and others low, depending on who our parents are and how popular we may or may not be. When there's a teacher around, it is us against them: children against adults, students against teachers.

"Agghh," Claire Naidoo groans. "I wish Gordon Number One carried my books to class."

The girls giggle, and the boys sneer. Gordon Number One gets too much attention. When he's around, the other boys are invisible, and it's a good thing that Gordon is in his final year. Next year, a new "best boy" will take his place, and, who knows, it might be one of them.

"Dream away," Lazy-Eye Matthew says to Claire Naidoo. "He'd rather unzip my pants than pull down your panties! You've got the wrong equipment."

There are boys who prefer boys, but the idea that Gordon Number One is one of them shocks me. What a waste. And it's wrong. The Bible says so.

"Sour grapes," Lottie snorts at Matthew. "When Gordon Number One jumps out the window at night, it's not you he goes to see."

I suck in a breath. How does Lottie know where Gordon Number One goes after lights-out? She snuck out of our room to buy the slime medicine for my shoulder, but maybe she did other things at the same time. Delia raises an eyebrow and throws me a smug look that says, *I told you that Lottie was a rough-necked slut like her mother, and you didn't believe me!*

I blush for Lottie, who doesn't understand the right way to behave. Mother taught me the proper rules to follow. Keep yourself tidy, and if you can't keep yourself tidy, keep what you do secret. Don't talk about creeping around after dark in front of a whole class of boys . . . That's the same as giving out invitations. The rules are different for boys, but still, Lottie has to learn to be more careful with her words.

Miss December stops at the head of the line, and Gordon

Number One takes her books into the classroom. Darnell strides after Gordon, still caught up in his copycat game. Lottie grabs Darnell by the shoulders and spins him around to face a classroom on the opposite side of the lawn.

"You have Health and Hygiene with Mrs. Brown, remember?" she says. "If you're late, there'll be trouble, so go quick."

Darnell hesitates, and for a moment I'm scared that he'll scream, *No, no, no,* the way he did outside of chapel. Not that I'd blame him for screaming. Mrs. Brown, the white American missionary who teaches Health and Hygiene, smells of talcum powder and sweat, and ends each lesson with the same piece of advice: *Don't forget to wash down there, boys and girls.*

Lottie gives Darnell a soft push in the right direction.

"Okay, Lo-Lo." Darnell throws her a sullen look and drags his feet toward Health and Hygiene. *Lo-Lo. He has a pet name for Lottie?* It makes sense when I realize that Lottie is the only person I know who treats him like a normal person instead of a bad-luck charm.

Darnell gets close to the classroom, and then he turns and sprints into the trees. He doesn't look back. Not once.

"Oh well." Lottie laughs. "He almost made it."

I smile despite myself. Lottie accepts Darnell with all his faults—no pursed lips or judgment. I wonder if that's because she's been judged so many times herself. Miss December claps her hands, and we file into class and take our seats. I sit in the back row. Sandi Cardoza sits in the front, in the seat that used to be mine.

A flash of movement catches my eye, and I turn to see

Darnell Parns hanging upside down from a tree branch. His fingertips tickle the long grass, and the sound of his laughter comes in through the window. Darnell might be bad at math and hopeless at reading, but right now, he's the happiest student at Keziah.

8

Ignorant

Electric lights go out at eight sharp, and we light candles for the free hour we have until bedtime. Girls visit different rooms in the flickering glow. They gossip and try on each other's clothes and shoes. The naughty girls smoke cigarettes and dabble with lipstick and eye shadow, both of which are forbidden at Keziah. They share news of the day: how Mr. Newman "accidentally" touched their shoulder in class, the moment that one of the senior boys looked across the lawn and licked his lips at them, the math test that was either too hard for some or too easy for others.

No one visits Dead Lorraine's room. Any shadow on the walls could be her ghost coming back to steal the breath from your mouth or suck the blood from your veins. I'd laugh at the girls' stupid fears, but what Lottie said about there being no spirits has got my mind ticking.

I think that Lottie is wrong. Her father may not float through the air or kiss her goodnight, but he is present. Not as a ghost, but as a powerful memory. And maybe that's what spirits are: just memories. I like that idea. And, when Mother is dead and gone, my memory of her will keep her alive, even when all that's left are bones.

I'll still hold my breath whenever I pass a graveyard, but here in the room, I know I'm safe. Lorraine's memory has no hold on Lottie or me. Besides, Lottie is a clenched fist held up against the world, and if Lorraine's ghost does appear, I'd like to see her try and haunt Lottie Diamond.

I sit on the edge of my cot and listen to the muted voices in the hall. I could go out and talk. I have news to share. Being hit by the Elephant and spilling not one tear would get me into almost any room I want. I'd show everyone the cuts on my hands, tell them how much it hurt and how hard it was to stop from crying.

I think about it. Maybe I was wrong about losing the pretties at lunchtime. Tonight could be my last-ever chance to regain a place with them. Surely, it's worth another try? But I stay where I am. I don't move, not even to scratch my itchy nose. Lottie, meanwhile, leans close to the candle flame and reads a book. We're allowed only one book a week from the novel box in Mrs. McDonald's English class, and she'll be finished with hers in no time if she doesn't slow down and ration the pages. She reads the way she eats: fast and with single-minded focus.

I open the bottom drawer of our shared dresser and take out a piece of paper and a pen. Mother expects two letters per term, mostly to let her know my test scores so she can pass them on to Father via the telephone. I place the paper on top of the dresser, where it catches the light, and I write:

Dear Father,

Does your house in Johannesburg have flowered carpets on the floor and cold beer in the icebox? Once, when you were in the bedroom with Mother, Rian and I looked through your wallet, which you'd left on the side table with the porcelain angels. We thought we'd find a photograph of the others but there was nothing. Just money. It was naughty and Mother would be furious if she knew what we'd done, but we were curious. What do the other children look like? Are they young or old? Tall or short? Do they have curly hair or straight? And what about your wife . . . is she beautiful like Mother only white and do you dance with her to the music on the radio?

I want to know all these things, though Mother says to be grateful for what we have. She says it's greedy to ask for more. What good will knowing about the others do us? We have a house, a roof that doesn't leak, beds with mattresses and blankets . . . "Stop asking questions, Adele," she says. "Be nice. Smile. Make sure that Daddy knows that you love him."

I am nice. I am grateful. I smile. Sometimes it's not enough. Sometimes you lose your friends even when

you do all the right things. I can't tell Mother what's
happened to me. I can't tell you. That's how things are
but I wish that things were different.

> *Love, your daughter,*
> *Adele Xx*

I sign the letter and put the corner of the paper to the candle flame. The page catches fire, and I watch it burn. Ash falls onto the dresser, and the color reminds me of the moths above the phone booth on Live Long Street. The flames heat my fingertips and I drop the burning letter onto the concrete floor. Lottie watches me. She thinks I'm crazy. She could be right. The fire burns out, and I crawl under my covers and turn my face to the green wall.

Ten minutes later, Mrs. Thomas rings the lights-out bell and shines her flashlight into our room to start her nightly head count. When she's done, she locks us into the dormitory and goes to her house to sit with her cat.

"You think I'm stupid," I say in the darkness. Lottie's *Surely even you can see that?* comment about Darnell Parns stings more than the cuts on my hands.

"You're clever with books," she says. "But you're ignorant."

Now what, I ask you, does that mean?

• • •

Tuesday morning is the same as Monday. The wake-up bell rings at six. We stumble from our cots in the bruised light and troop to the bathrooms at the end of the dormitory hallway.

No matter how quick you are, there's always a line for the four showers and six sinks. Plus, girls in their final year push to the front of the line, no matter what: a perk of being old enough and smart enough to sit for their graduation exams. Twelve months from now, during our final year, we'll do the same.

Lottie is right in front of me, but I ignore her, still stung by being called ignorant.

We shuffle forward in our nightgowns, the concrete floor cold under our bare feet. Andrea, an older girl, leaves the bathroom with wet hair and a bar of personal soap wrapped in a washcloth. The school provides soap, but it's the cheap kind that the natives use and it barely makes lather. Lottie moves to the front of the line.

Delia, Peaches, and Sandi Cardoza come up and stand next to her. They will cut in, and most girls, expecting a reward, will let them.

"Try it," Lottie says, "and see what happens."

Delia scoops a butterscotch candy from her pocket and holds it out the way that a child offers a dog a bone. This is new. The pretties usually leave Lottie alone, but I think that Delia is trying to impress Sandi Cardoza with her powers of persuasion. A bold move.

Lottie examines the bribe, and I hope that she turns it down. I hope that Delia, Peaches, and Sandi have to move to the back of the line. It would serve them right.

"No, thanks," Lottie says. "I don't like sweets."

Delia is annoyed by the cool way that Lottie rejects what most students, especially the poor ones, would jump at, no question. She knows that Lottie is different, but she has no idea that Lottie has built a wall around herself that butterscotch cannot breach. Not ever. An emotion stirs in my chest. It might be pride at Lottie's stubborn refusal to accept how things are.

Two girls leave the bathroom, and while I'd rather hang back and put space between Lottie and myself, I have to go in immediately or else risk losing my space. I follow Lottie in, and from the bathroom line, it looks like we're together.

• • •

We get two sinks side by side. I hang my towel on a hook, place my bar of lavender soap on the lip of the bowl, and run cold water over my washcloth. Lottie's towel is really half of a towel. The rest of it was cut to make a threadbare washcloth and a rag to clean her shoes. Mother says that her whole childhood was hand-to-mouth and "mend and make do." Lottie's is the same. I doubt she owns a new piece of clothing. Or new anything.

Lottie uses the hard-to-lather school soap, but we both follow the same rules on how to wash. There is a right way to get clean and a wrong way. First, you wash your face, careful not to get soap in your eyes. Then you scrub your neck and behind your ears to make sure that all traces of dirt are gone. Then comes your underarms and, after that, the soles of your feet and the tight wedge of flesh between your toes where a disgusting substance called toe jam likes to collect. Wipe away the soap. Last, you wash your privates. This is crucial. Imagine washing your privates and then your face. Big mistake.

After we are finished, we rinse our washcloths and wring out the water. We pat our wet skin dry, and those of us with our own soap carefully fold the bar into our damp washcloth. Now we are ready to face the scrutiny of the Elephant and Mrs. Thomas.

I finish drying, but Lottie has an extra step to go. She slips a pair of high-waisted underwear from under her nightie and washes it under the cold stream. The cotton is so thin it's practically see-through even when it's dry.

I leave her to scrub, and walk out of the washroom alone. Delia, Peaches, and Sandi have bribed their way to the front of the line with butterscotch, and I'm glad that they have to wait while I am already finished.

• • •

Back in Dead Lorraine's room, I pull on my school uniform, underwear, socks, and shoes, and open the wardrobe. The right side of the rail is mine, and the left side is hers. On my side, there are three cotton dresses, two sweaters, three shirts, and two skirts. I finger the flared skirt of the yellow dress that Mother gave me for Christmas. Father's name was on the card, but I know that it was Mother who picked it off the rack and paid for it with his money.

Lottie's side of the rail holds one green dress, with permanent sweat stains under the arms, and a thin blue sweater. She will wear her school uniform during the week and the green dress on the weekends. The same two things, all term long. It's fascinating how little she has.

I wander over to the set of drawers we share. The top two drawers are hers, and the bottom two are mine. Opening her drawers is a waste of time. I already know they are empty.

From under her pillow, I take out a small spinning top with funny symbols painted on the sides. She holds it at night before she falls asleep, but I've yet to see her spin it. It's a child's toy, and why she keeps it is a mystery.

"It's a dreidel," Lottie says from the doorway, and I jump with fright. I've been caught red-handed, and she has every right to slap me down for breaking the cardinal rule of every academy dorm room: hands off other people's stuff.

I drop the pillow like it's hot and move to my side of the room, where I should have stayed in the first place. Lottie walks in, and I don't know what to do with my hands, my face.

She drapes her wet underwear over the metal rail at the foot of her cot and picks up the pair that she left there to dry yesterday morning. I make a show of retucking the sheet corners and straightening the blankets on my cot while she dresses. Surprise room inspections by Mrs. Thomas are common, especially when she's in one of her mean moods.

My mouth opens, and words come out without my permission. "What's a *dreidel*?" I'm top of the English class, but I have never heard this word before or seen it written down on a page.

"It's Yiddish for 'spinning top.' My father gave it to me. We used to play together."

"What's Yiddish?" I hate to ask. Asking for information makes me the dumb one.

"A Jewish language," Lottie says without gloating. "I only know a few words." She places her pillow back over the dreidel. "Let's go and help the little ones," she says, and lets me off the hook for breaking the rules. Just like that.

I don't understand Lottie at all. She could have thrashed me for touching her stuff, but she didn't. At Keziah, students never let a slight go unpunished. Then again, Lottie doesn't care much for the rules. This time, I'm glad about it.

9

Hello, Jane

I crack open Charlotte Brontë's *Jane Eyre* in Tuesday study hall—not for class but for myself. On the front page is a scratched-out name, which I cover with my thumb. Father brings us books from his other home in Joburg. Some books are brand-new, and others have cracked spines and notes scribbled in the margins, like the ones that Lottie lines up to collect on the first day of school. It's stupid to compare Father's gifts with the handouts given to the poor students, though. If the two things are the same, which they're not, then Rian and I are third-class children too.

Stop, Adele, Mother's voice says in my head. *You have a book in your hands, girl. Stop fussing and be grateful. Be grateful!* She is right.

I bend to the page and read.

There was no possibility of taking a walk that day. We had been wandering, indeed, in the leafless shrubbery an hour in the morning; but since dinner (Mrs. Reed, when there was no company, dined early) the cold winter wind had brought with it clouds so sombre, and a rain so penetrating, that future out-door exercise was now out of the question . . .

Soon, I'm far from the sleepy south of Swaziland. I'm in windswept England, where the twilight is raw and Jane suffers from frostbitten fingers. Winter in Swaziland is cold but never freezing. In Swaziland, we have a rainy season and a dry season, and in both seasons there are long stretches of blue sky and sunshine. English weather is alien to me, but Jane's unhappy position inside her aunt's house is all too familiar. Jane has a roof over her head and shoes on her feet, but she'll never be a part of the "real" family, never be anyone's darling. Jane is stuck in the space between things. That's how I feel when I imagine Father and the others smiling for their family photo: their pale faces glowing with a sense of belonging. Like Jane, I am a stranger at the feast.

Another thing Jane and I have in common? Jane reads. The two of us connect across centuries and oceans through books and the escape they provide for us. While Jane hides behind a red velvet curtain with *Bewick's History of British Birds* and finds herself in a landscape—"*Where the Northern Ocean, in vast whirls, / Boils round the naked, melancholy isles / Of farthest Thule*"—I plant myself in the back corner of the Keziah Academy study hall and find myself in her world. I walk through "wet lawn and storm-beat shrub, with ceaseless rain sweeping away wildly before a long and lamentable blast." Jane and I are two girls transported into new worlds, not by airplane but by words. A strange thought. And lovely.

•••

After study hall, Lottie and I walk to the senior dorm for a short rest before dinner. Girls walk together in the late afternoons because, in Swaziland, the twilight is short. One minute the sun is balanced on the horizon, and the next minute the world is plunged into darkness—and darkness is dangerous for girls. So we walk in pairs or larger groups to ward off whatever lurks in the shadows. No girls have been attacked or kidnapped that I know of, but that's no reason to tempt fate.

We pass the little-girls' dorm and draw level with the barrier of Christ-thorns that guards our window. The shadows under the Christ-thorns move, and Darnell Parns jumps out in front of us with wild hair and a swollen black eye.

"Lo-Lo," he says, "come see."

"What happened to your eye, Darnell? Who hurt you?"

He ignores her and grabs her hand. "New pretty thing."

"You want to show me something?" Lottie says.

Darnell tugs her hand. "Now. Now. Now."

Darnell's voice gets louder on each *now*, and I suck in a breath. If Lottie refuses to go with him, he'll pitch a fit for sure. He'll scream and draw a curious crowd to the dormitory windows and onto the path, and I'd rather not be tonight's entertainment.

"All right, calm down," Lottie says. "I'll come, but it has to be quick. Understand?"

"Good. Now."

Darnell runs toward the banana field behind the little-girls' dorm. Lottie follows Darnell, and I follow Lottie. A lone girl chasing a boy into the failing light has got to break a rule somewhere. I'm also curious about the "new pretty thing." He might have found a diamond or a gold nugget, and I want to see for myself.

Darnell cuts right before he reaches the banana field, and Lottie and I keep up, careful of the uneven ground in the fading light. He stops just outside a grove of jackalberry trees and glances over his shoulder. He sees me, and he's not happy.

Darnell jabs a finger into my shoulder when I get close. "Go away."

"Mind your manners, Darnell." Lottie pulls him back, firm but gentle. "Adele is with me. Where I go, she goes."

I blink in surprise. Lottie has claimed me and, strangely, it feels good. Darnell glares at me through his unswollen eye and takes a straight path through the trees, guided by a map of the land that only he understands. He drops into a sudden crouch and points to a heap of dried grass and leaves. I hold in a sigh. So much for diamonds and gold. Lottie crouches next to him while I kneel. Crouching in a skirt is awkward, and I'd rather not flash my panties, even by accident.

"Show us," Lottie says.

Darnell pulls the leaves and dried grass away to reveal a man-made nest built from twigs and dried mud. The nest is filled with different-colored bird feathers, smooth river stones, a pair of blue butterfly wings, and more that I can't make out in the long shadows.

"Brown mamba." Darnell holds up a see-through snakeskin. "Brown mamba."

"Darnell loves animals," Lottie says by way of explanation. "Even snakes."

I nod. The mamba skin is interesting, but it's hardly pretty or new. Darnell smiles and offers me the skin. A gift. He expects me to touch it and admire it. I hesitate, and Lottie nods at me to react. Darnell has offered me the first look, and to refuse him would be rude.

I hold out my hands, and Darnell drapes the mamba skin over my palms. It weighs almost nothing. He indicates with his hands that I should lift the skin to my eyes. I hesitate again. Lottie gives me a firmer nod.

I lift the skin to my eyes, and I see the late afternoon world, different and new, through the patterned scales. Smudged tree trunks rise up to the sky, and the broad leaves turn emerald in the last rays of sunset light. My heart stills, and beauty pours into me.

"Darnell." Lottie's voice brings me out of my daze. "Tell me who hit you. Was it Bosman or one his sons? Did you steal eggs from their chicken house again?"

Darnell takes the skin from me, and I murmur, "Thanks. That was my first time holding a brown mamba."

"Good. Good." Darnell tucks the skin into his treasure nest and ignores Lottie's questions. He covers his hiding place with grass and twigs, and smiles at Lottie. It's a smile of pure joy.

"Bye-bye, Lo-Lo. Bye-bye, Adi," he says. "Bye-bye."

Adi? I guess that's Darnell's name for me.

"Where are you going, Darnell?" Lottie asks, though it's obvious that he's about to run away from school.

"Purple. Yellow," he says. "Far down and away."

The words make no sense to me. Only Darnell understands Darnell.

"Wait." Lottie grabs for Darnell's arm, but he's too fast and he runs for the river. Lottie chases him through the trees, and Darnell is halfway down to the riverbank by the time I catch up with them.

"Don't you dare go into that water," Lottie yells. "The crocodiles will get you."

Darnell kicks off his shoes and plunges into the shallow end with his shoes held over his head. He walks deeper. Water laps at his knees and then his stomach, and I hope he can swim, because one wrong move and he'll go under. Lottie and I stand on the riverbank, puffing for breath and helpless to change Darnell's course.

"Come back, Darnell." Lottie tries anyway. "You'll lose your way in the dark."

Darnell keeps walking, the river water up to his collarbones now. A long shape glides from the bank and disappears beneath the river's surface. A strangled sound comes from the back of my throat. Crocodiles take dozens of people every year, and the changeover between day and night is their favorite hunting time. Bright eyes shine in the dying light, and I open my mouth to scream but no sound comes out.

"Crocodile!" Lottie runs to the water's edge. "Hurry, Darnell. Hurry."

Darnell wades to the opposite bank, and his bare feet drag against the sandy bottom. Mother says, *The strength of the crocodile is in the water*, and Darnell has got to move fast onto dry land or the crocodile will catch him.

"Run!" My voice comes back full-force. "Run!"

Darnell hears us and vaults out of the water. He scrambles halfway up the opposite bank and reaches safety a second before the crocodile launches onto the sand and snaps its jaws at thin air. The shiny monster begins to sink back into the river, but the fear courses through me still. I press my hands to my stomach to ease the knot there. I keep my eyes on the crocodile, but it slips under the surface and disappears.

"Thank you, Jesus." Lottie breathes a prayer even though she keeps her eyes open during the meal blessing and refuses to join the Saturday Scripture club. She grabs my arm and hurries us a safe distance from the river and the submerged crocodile.

On the opposite bank, Darnell climbs to the top of the rise with the balance of a mountain goat.

"Bye-bye, Lo-Lo. Bye-bye, Adi," he yells, and runs into a field of tall grass.

"Should we go after him?" I ask. Not that I'd cross the river with a crocodile in it, but it's not right for Darnell to be out there all alone. Darkness is dangerous for boys too.

"It won't do any good." Lottie shades her eyes to search for Darnell in the fields across the river. She sighs. "He's gone and gone."

10

The Last Straw

"Fight! Fight! Fight!" The call goes out from the yard behind the little-girls' dormitory, and students run from all directions. The big-girls' dorm empties, even though we are meant to be cleaning our rooms for Mrs. Thomas's Wednesday afternoon inspection. Fights help to break up the monotony of school life, and they are must-see events. I push to the front of the mixed-race crowd with the other older girls. The Bartholomew twins face each other with flushed cheeks. Between them is a thick crop of grass, neatly braided and decorated with yellow thread. A grass doll. Highly prized.

"It's mine," the twin with the white ribbon in her hair says. "I found it yesterday."

"You stole my yellow thread, so it's mine," the twin with the blue ribbon says, and they meet each other with nails and teeth.

They roll in the dirt, scratch, and pull hair. White Ribbon holds Blue Ribbon down. Girls yell encouragement.

"Get her!"

"Throw her off!"

"Roll her over. Roll her over . . ."

The twins are evenly matched, and the fight continues, vicious and unrelenting. The crowd grows. The noise intensifies. We forget about the Elephant's sharp ears and Mrs. Thomas's sharp tongue and the rule against fighting. Blue Ribbon throws her twin off, and I step back to avoid being kicked. I collide with Lottie, who breaks through the front ranks and grabs White Ribbon by the shoulders.

"The Elephant is coming," she says in a fierce whisper, and the crowd dissolves. Some run to the stand of wild bananas at the edge of the vacant field; others slip away to the laundry room and the rear of the dining hall. I blink and the twins are gone, the grass doll trampled by the crowd. Beatrice, one of Delia's pets, is immobilized with fear. If she's caught on the scene, she will be punished, and then punished again for not giving up the names of those involved in the fight—which no self-respecting student would ever do.

I grab Beatrice and hurry her into the Christ-thorns, where we press against the wall of the big-girls' dorm. We hold our breath. The Elephant rounds the corner with her wig askew. She catnaps in the afternoons, and heaven help the person who wakes her. The closer she gets to us, the more I realize my mistake. If she glances to the right, she'll see us stuck to the wall like the insect specimens in the science room.

"Quick." Lottie holds her hand out of our window. "In here."

She pulls Beatrice into Dead Lorraine's room, and I scramble over the window ledge and slide to the floor. We crouch below the sill. The Elephant's footsteps get louder and then softer as she moves in the direction of the abandoned fight. I bite my lip to stop from giggling. I imagine her wig jiggling as she swings her gaze right to left and sees nothing but a squashed grass doll.

"Stop," Lottie whispers, and glares at me. "She'll hear."

Beatrice presses her hands to her mouth to hold in a laugh, and I do the same. Lottie rolls her eyes and zips her lips. She's good at holding still and breathing slow. Beatrice and I are amateurs. We can barely control ourselves. We can't stand the tension.

"Who's there?" Matron snaps. "Come out where I can see you."

We keep still and wait. The Elephant won't enter the Christthorns. She's too large to weave through the tall stems without getting pricked by the spikes that are meant to keep the boys away from the girls. Seconds pass, but they slow to minutes. She's out there listening for clues to our location. I keep my hand plastered over my mouth until Matron's footsteps fade and disappear. Then I collapse onto the floor and laugh till my sides hurt. Beatrice rolls on the floor with me, and we squeal and kick our feet in the air.

It feels good to laugh and forget about being dropped by the pretty girls. Lottie shakes her head at our hysterics but manages a little smile.

If I'd known what was coming, I would have stayed on the floor and laughed a lot harder and longer.

• • •

We pass the Wednesday afternoon inspection with a "Well done, girls," thanks to Lottie's talent for scrubbing floors and washing windows. It's obvious she doesn't have a maid at home to do her cleaning. Delia told me last year that Lottie and her mother live in a hut, which is really one big room with a dug-out fireplace in the middle and two cots on either side of it. I've never been in a native hut. Delia also says the native huts stink of sweat and smoke, though I don't think Delia's been inside one either.

"Keep up the good work." Mrs. Thomas ticks our names off her list and goes to the next room to search for dust under the cots and dirt in the corners. When she's finished, she'll hand out punishments to the girls who've failed. The top girls don't care if they pass or fail. They get their pets to do the sweeping and scrubbing, and if Mrs. Thomas gives the top girls a punishment, they get their pets to do that as well. I miss having pets. Cleaning is hard work, even with Lottie's help.

Lottie and I go back into our room. Late afternoon light pours through the windows, and the floor smells of pine needles. I lie on my cot and memorize three Bible verses from the book of John for Scripture class. Mother expects good grades for every subject, even Scripture. With As on my report card, she can tell Father how much I love school and how much I take after him in the brains department. I don't know why she bothers. Rian is top of his distance education class. He has a chance at becoming an engineer, but a brown girl with a contour map and a hard hat . . . who's ever seen that?

"Hey . . . Hey, Adele."

Beatrice, who hid from the Elephant with us, pops her head through the doorway. Like all the pretties' pets, Beatrice is a junior girl and she is beautiful. She has long dark hair and bright-blue eyes. She has two other pets with her . . . Ramona and Leah, I think.

"Adele," she says. "Tell them I was inside the room. Tell them that I didn't cry or run away or nothing."

I say, "Beatrice was inside the room. She didn't cry or run away or nothing."

"Trus faith?" the one that I think is Ramona says.

"Trus faith," I say, and Ramona's eyes bug out. *Trus faith* is a sacred vow among Keziah students; it means "I am telling the truth, and may God strike me dead if what I say is a lie." Nobody knows who made up the words or why we keep using them, but they are the academy's ultimate test of fidelity.

"Don't take our word for it," Lottie says. "Come inside and ask Lorraine's ghost. Maybe she'll jump out of the wall and take you to the other side. That's what you think will happen, isn't it?"

The girls nod, and Beatrice steps in first, because she's been here before. She throws the other pets a scornful glance and challenges them to match her bravery. They stay put. She walks to the window and rests her arms along the wooden sill, the queen of the room.

"See?" she says. "Easy."

Shamed by Beatrice's courage, Ramona and Leah inch inside. They stop, and start again and clutch each other's hands. Their terror is adorable, and I can't help but smile. Lottie has never had pets. Pets are expensive but well worth the extra food it takes to reward them. If you ask, a pet will go out to the laundry room when it's dark and you're too scared to go out yourself.

"Come on," Beatrice prods. "You're walking like old ladies."

Ramona and Leah screw up their courage and stride into the middle of the room. Small sounds come through the window. The distant scrape of a hoe in the kitchen gardens and the call of a dove in the grapefruit tree. Lottie says, "Shh . . . listen. I think I hear something."

The girls tense, and Lottie slams the book in her hands closed. *Bam.* The girls jump, and Beatrice screams. Lottie laughs at the sounds they make, but her laughter makes the girls scream even more. They think it's Lorraine's ghost, delighted at having three fresh girls to eat for supper. Leah spins in terrified circles, and Ramona looks like she might pee or puke or both. Beatrice makes a high-pitched squeak that travels out of the window and across the dirt yard to Mrs. Thomas's house.

"Shh . . . wait, wait, wait." I try to hush them. "Lottie is joking. It's nothing. There's nothing here."

"I saw Lorraine." Ramona hiccups. "Right there in that corner. She's got red eyes."

"And red teeth," Leah adds. If Mrs. Thomas comes to investigate, she will blame Lottie and me for corrupting young

91

minds. Talking to the dead is an offense against the one true God, and we will be punished. We might even, Lord take this cup from me, be sent to Mr. Vincent's office for a lecture and a public caning at assembly.

Lottie also understands where her innocent joke might lead, and shows the girls the book.

"See." She opens the cover and shuts it gently. "It was me. I made the sound."

The girls jump and cry harder. I scramble under my cot, pull out my suitcase, and grab the package of shortbread biscuits. Technically, feeding other people's pets is wrong, but I have no choice.

"Here. Look what I've got." I rip the package open, and the smell of sugar and butter immediately gets their attention, but Ramona and Leah hesitate, as if this is somehow a trick to poison them. I ram a biscuit into my mouth and make exaggerated *mmm* sounds. Then I give one to Lottie, who joins in the *mmm* chorus. She rolls her eyes in delight, and the girls giggle.

"One each," I say, and hand them out. Beatrice takes a shortbread finger, sits on the edge of my cot, and chews. Ramona and Leah perch on the end of Lottie's bed and take small, luxurious bites, to extend the time that it takes to finish their biscuits. Rich or poor—and pets are chosen for looks and temperament, not family money—a love of shortbread makes their fear evaporate. The silence is lovely, and I relax. Things could have ended badly, but they didn't: instead, we are five girls eating biscuits together in a haunted room.

Two shadows fall across the concrete floor. I look up, and

my good feelings evaporate. Sandi Cardoza and Delia stand in the doorway with their arms crossed and judgment written on their faces. They are furious that I've stolen their pets and fed them. I brush crumbs from my skirt and say in a brusque voice, "See? No ghosts. Now off you go."

Delia huffs, and Sandi pulls Beatrice's braids when the pets bolt through the door and hurry to the pretties' room. Lottie pretends to read her book while I make a show of memorizing John 12:46. *I have come into the world as light, so that whoever believes in me may not remain in darkness.* I already know the words by heart, but I need a wall to hide behind while Delia and Sandi Cardoza stare at us.

Peaches sticks her head between the other two and makes a clicking sound with her tongue. Then she shakes her head the way native women do when they simply do not have the words to describe the terrible tragedy they have witnessed with their own eyes. The tongue click and head shake are usually reserved for car accidents and natural disasters, but in Peaches's mind, what I've done is equally as tragic. I am a pet stealer and a breaker of the rules. I have accidentally declared war on them.

After an eternity of cold stares, they turn and walk away. I shiver. Once I was their friend. Then I was nothing. Stealing their pets was the last straw. Now I am their enemy.

11

Under-War

"Where is it?"

The next morning, Lottie checks the bottom of our shared wardrobe, the top two drawers of the dresser, and the sides of her mattress. She kneels and sweeps her hand under her cot, her breath coming in small hard gasps. Nothing. It's no use. The dry pair of underwear that hangs over the metal rail at the end of her cot, waiting to be exchanged for the freshly washed pair, is gone.

"Maybe it's under mine." I crouch and search the dark space between the iron bedsprings and the floor. My suitcase, filled with canned treasures, is pushed into a back corner. The reason that it's hidden so far from the light embarrasses me. Lottie has never touched my clothes or used my hairbrush on the sly or begged for a can of condensed milk. The incident with the impago box? Well, I may have been wrong there . . .

"Nothing." I sit up and chew the inside of my cheek. Lottie takes care of what she has. Every piece of clothing is precious, and this morning, when the bell rang and we rushed to the washroom line, her dry underwear was right where it ought to be. She didn't move it and I didn't move it and a nervous feeling grows in my stomach.

"They're gone." Bright color stings Lottie's cheeks. "Gone."

"Wait. Maybe they blew out." I scramble to the window and peek into the Christ-thorns, hoping for a miracle. Bees work the red flowers, but there's no underwear hanging from the spikes or lying in the dirt. I turn to tell Lottie the bad news and notice a black scuff mark on the spotless floor. Shoe polish. Not from my shoes, which I polish on Saturday afternoons. And not from Lottie's shoes, which she wipes with a wet rag, because, as far as I can tell, she has no shoe polish at all. The bad feeling in my stomach sharpens.

"It was them," Lottie says. "They stole the second pair."

"Who?" I ask, even though I already know.

"Delia and the others." Lottie paces the room with her wet underwear bunched in her fist. "They're paying us back for what happened yesterday."

I want to deny it, but what she says makes sense. Never let a slight go unpunished. That's another Keziah rule, and as far as Delia and company are concerned, we tried to steal their pets and we must be taught a lesson.

Lottie strides to the door with knotted shoulders and narrowed eyes. She's a fighter, and a good one. No doubt she'd win a fight against any one of the pretties, and maybe even against all four of them—she's that good—but what happens after?

"Wait." I block the door. "Let's think for a minute."

"Why?" she says. "You know they did it."

"Yes, but . . ." I get my scrambled thoughts in a row. "We have no proof that they were in the room, and Mrs. Thomas will blame us for the fight, no matter what happens. She's in a mean mood today, and she'll give us detention for the rest of term and ten cuts each for ruining her morning."

"Dinah Washington," Lottie says with a nod.

"That's right. Two nights in a row."

If you have the right key, Mrs. Thomas's moods are easy to unlock. After lights-out, we lie awake in the dark and listen to the music coming from her house across the yard. "At Last" by Etta James means that she's in a sad, soft-crying mood that leaves her tired and not much caring about who does what to whom in the dormitory. Or why. Dinah Washington's "This Bitter Earth" is the soundtrack to a bleak moodiness that makes her snappish and quick with the switch. Dinah two nights in a row means "Do not test me."

"We'll get Delia and the others back," I promise. "But not this morning. We wait for Etta James, and then we do it."

Lottie slumps onto her cot with the wad of wet underwear clutched in her hands. "Fight or no fight, it doesn't matter," she says. "Mrs. Thomas will check under my skirt at morning inspection, and she'll see that I'm wearing the same underwear as yesterday. I'll get detention, and Delia and the others will make sure that everyone knows that I wear the same pair every day."

Once the underwear story gets out, teasing Lottie will become the school sport. Undies, whether they are old, new, lace or plain, are a juicy topic, and Lottie will be poked fun at for a very long time. Little ones will snicker and point. Bold boys will lift her skirt when nobody is watching and make rude comments about what they see. Mrs. Thomas and the Elephant will seize the opportunity to lecture the morning assembly on cleanliness and how being poor is no excuse for being dirty. We will all know who they are talking about. Lottie's life will be hell. If anyone can take it, though, she can. I wish I was as strong as her.

The thing is, though, right now, sitting across from her, Lottie doesn't look tough at all. She is deathly pale, fidgeting with her fingers and frowning. She knows what will happen later this morning, and it pains her. So she sits and builds her wall higher; she cements the bricks closer and digs the moat deeper. Being impenetrable takes work. It takes effort. And the wall that shields her from the cruelty of boarding school children is not a birthright given by fairies or God above. It is earned. Lottie builds her wall one stone at a time. Time and time again.

Seeing her naked would be less of a shock than seeing her stripped of her defenses. For the first time, I notice her slight body and bowed shoulders, the glimpse of scalp through her cropped short hair and how she is smaller than I imagined her, and how, for some reason, seeing her prepare for certain hurt and ridicule makes me sad. And it makes me mad: mad enough to do a mad, crazy thing.

I rip the third drawer open and fish out a pair of blue undies with a white bow at the front. Mother bought them from the hypermarket on Louw Street, which makes them the perfect pushback against Delia and her girls. They probably own underwear just like this.

"If Matron asks, they're from the new hypermarket. The one that Sandi Cardoza's father owns." I drop the underwear into Lottie's lap and pull on my uniform. Delia will know that the undies belong to me, but right now, I don't care.

"You're sure?" Lottie touches the cotton the same way that Mother skims her fingers over jacket sleeves and dress skirts to judge the quality of the material when we are out shopping.

"Keep them."

I have six pairs, one for each day of the school week and one for Sunday when I do my laundry. Now I'll have to wash a pair midweek so I have something to wear on Sunday, but it will be worth it to see the expressions on the pretties' faces when their scheme fails.

• • •

"Scram," I tell the Bartholomew twins, who stick their tongues out at me and move to another row for the morning inspection. I claim the spot next to Lottie: the first time that I've deliberately put myself anywhere near her in public. This morning is different: I need to be close so I can see everything. Delia, Sandi Cardoza, Peaches, and Natalie throw furtive glances over their shoulders, and their lips curl in cat smiles. The joke's on them. At Keziah, you stick up for yourself and your friends. No one else. My underwear wasn't stolen and Lottie isn't really my friend, so there's no reason for me to get between the pretties and their revenge. Except . . . Lottie stood up for me when Darnell yelled for me to go away. She pulled me through the window when the Elephant came hunting and she didn't beat me for playing with her dreidel. Delia and the others think they've won the first battle in the war against Lottie but the war is actually against Lottie and me, and I cannot wait to see the change in their expressions when they realize that we have one up on them.

"Girls." The Elephant claps her hands three times to get our attention. "Eyes to the front, and hands out."

We stick our hands in front of us with the palms down, ready for fingernail inspection. Mrs. Thomas works her way from the front row to the back, on the lookout for dirt between the fingers and blue smudges of ink along the sides of the little finger. Girls flip their hands over to show their palms and flip them back again when Mrs. Thomas nods the all clear.

As usual, Delia and the other girls get only a passing glance. Mrs. Thomas reaches us. I hold my hands out and get a brusque nod. Lottie does the same, but Mrs. Thomas, as usual, lingers.

"Skirt," Mrs. Thomas says, and Delia elbows Sandi Cardoza to pay attention. Peaches and Natalie snicker in anticipation. Lottie lifts her hem. The boys are all the way on the other side of the school grounds, so showing your delicates is not a sin. Mrs. Thomas blinks in surprise and I bite the inside of my cheek to stop from giggling.

"Where did you get those?" Mrs. Thomas demands.

"My mother got my cousin to get them from the hyper-market in Manzini." Lottie stares straight ahead.

"The hypermarket?" Mrs. Thomas snorts with disbelief. "Did one of her boyfriends give her the money?"

Lottie turns bright red, and I forget that this is meant to be our big moment of revenge. This is where Delia and the others realize that their plan to get back at us for stealing their pets has failed. We've won.

Except . . .

"Well?" Mrs. Thomas spits the word out, and it's lucky that she's only lost one husband, because losing just the one man has turned her sour. "How did your mother pay for those?"

"My mother got my cousin to get them from the hyper-market in Manzini, and that's all I know," Lottie says. "You could telephone my mother and ask about the money, but we don't have a phone. Or you could call McNichols's general store and they'll get a boy to run over to our hut, and, if she's home, he'll ask my mother about where she got the money."

Mrs. Thomas grits her teeth at Lottie's subtle challenge. Long-distance calls are expensive and for serious, serious busi-ness, and what reason would Mrs. Thomas give Mr. Vincent for making the call? Checking up on who paid for underwear is a silly reason, and plus, she'd have to talk about girls' delicates in front of a white man . . . something she'd never do. Mrs. Thomas moves to her next victim.

Lottie drops her skirt, and I rock from one foot to the other, a nervous habit. I think of Mother feeding sunshine down the telephone line so Father will come back to us, and the scratch of steel wool on the stovetop at midnight, her hair ironed straight to please him. I think of the throaty sound of her laughter when he says anything remotely funny. If Lottie wants her children to have new clothes and clean shoes and six pairs of underwear, she will have to learn how to please others. She must remain soft and smiling on the outside, no matter what's going on inside her. She will have to be less like Lottie and more like Mother, who was also poor and picked on at school.

I imagine Lottie, older and in high-heeled shoes, hurrying to a public phone box at the end of a dirt road, and my heart hurts.

12

Moonlight Shadows

Luke 3:22. *And the Holy Spirit descended on him in bodily form, like a dove; and a voice came from heaven, "You are my beloved Son; with you I am well pleased."*

I tick Luke 3:22 off my "to memorize" list and move on to the next Bible verse.

1 Corinthians 6:19. *Do you not know that your body is a temple of the Holy Spirit within you, whom you . . .*

The words vanish from my mind, and I stare at the ceiling in the dark. My heart beats fast. I'd rather be reading *Jane Eyre*, but I need to memorize a minimum of ten verses to make it into the finals of the Scripture competition. My mind is too busy to focus on Bible verses, though. I'm worried about Jane Eyre going to Lowood Institution. That Mr. Brocklehurst who runs the school? He has it out for her. I can tell. He'll make her life difficult—just you wait and see. Jane is jumping from the frying pan into the fire.

On top of Jane, I'm also worried about myself. Knowing where I stand with Delia and the others gives me a surprising feeling of relief. But it's also frightening. I'm not sure what comes next or whom I should make friends with. Loners do not do well at Keziah.

Lottie's bedsprings creak, and her bare feet slap the floor. She waits a minute to make sure that I'm asleep and then creeps to the window. What she does after Mrs. Thomas locks us in the dormitory is none of my business, but I have to ask:

"Are you going to meet Gordon Number One?"

She jumps with fright and spins to face me.

"No! Of course not. I need to pee."

The girls' toilet block is across a grass field and hidden behind a screen of trees for privacy. When money comes available, three indoor toilets will be added to the washroom but, till then, peeing after dark is a nightmare.

Bold girls use chamber pots and empty them behind the banana field the moment the wake-up bell rings. Most of us cross our legs and pray for dawn. Some don't make it, and washing wet sheets in the middle of the week is a worse humiliation than having to carry your own waste across the field and dump it in broad daylight.

"Why don't you hold it like everyone else?" I ask.

"Mama Khumalo says it's bad for you. When your body wants to go, you should go."

"Mama Khumalo who made the slime?"

"Yes, her, and I really have to pee." Lottie moves to the window, and I follow her. My bladder stings, and a night pee would be an adventure and a relief. Plus, maybe she's meeting Gordon Number One after all. I'm going out with her to see things for myself.

"I have to go too," I say.

"All right," she snaps. "Follow me and be quiet."

We climb over the windowsill barefoot and drop down into a crouch when we hit the ground. Moonlight falls through the Christ-thorns, and spiked shadows play across our nightgowns. It might be a warning to go back inside. I ignore the omen and wait for Lottie to lead the way.

"Quick to the corner." Lottie runs in the tight space between the towers of tall thorns and the dormitory wall. She waits at the corner of the building and spies ahead. "We go from here to the banana field. No matter what happens, don't stop. Understand?"

"Yes."

Lottie sprints across the wide field behind the little-girls' dorm, and I follow her. Wind tangles my hair, and my mouth goes dry. I cannot believe that this is me, Adele Joubert, running shoeless across a field at midnight in my nightgown. Nice girls stay in bed and have no interest in what bad girls do in the dark. Maybe I am not so good after all.

We reach the edge of the banana field. Lottie slides between the trunks of the banana trees, and we squat under a green canopy of leaves that branch over us. It's a lovely night. Moon-light shadows stretch across the empty field, and spent banana flowers drop to the ground at our feet. The dormitories are small dots on the land, and the whole school is just a small thing under the enormous sky full of stars.

"It's nice out here," I say to Lottie, who swings her head to the left and puts her finger to her lips. She tenses.

"Shh . . . Stay down."

I freeze. I wait for the Elephant's hand to grab my shoulder or for Mrs. Thomas to tell us that we are bad girls and do we know what happens to bad girls who steal out of the dorm windows at night? Disaster. Lives ruined.

Footsteps creep through the banana field, and small animals scuttle through the leaves. Luckily, I have already peed. Some-one passes close to us, and I could reach out and touch a trouser leg or an arm if I wanted to, but I don't. A man stops at the edge of the banana trees and checks in all directions. He's cau-tious.

Something in the width of his shoulders gives me pause. And his stance is familiar, the taut body and loose arms. *Could it be? No, that's cracked. Set your mind on higher things, Adele.* The man turns, and the moonlight finds his face. I gasp. Lottie glares, and I tighten my jaw, my stomach, and my buttocks as Gordon Number One searches the rows of banana trees for the source of the noise. It's hard, but I manage to stay small and still when what I want to do is jump and run.

When he's satisfied with the silence, Gordon takes off across the vacant field and sprints in the direction of the senior-girls' dorm. Once there, he crouches in the shadows of the Christ-thorns, and I stretch to see which window he crawls into. Or will someone crawl out to meet him?

I flick through the likely suspects, but the girl most likely to break the rules is squatting right next to me. Who could keep a tumble with Gordon Number One a secret anyway? If it was me, I'd want to tell everyone, especially since Gordon is so elusive. He keeps to himself, but he's not considered a loner, only independent and mysterious.

Lottie yawns and rubs her eyes, ready to go back to bed. She has no interest in Gordon or his final destination. Then it hits me. She knows what happens next. She's seen this before.

"Where's he going?" I say.

"Watch and see."

Gordon detaches from the shadows and moves quickly in the direction of Principal Vincent's house, which makes no sense.

"Mrs. Vincent?" I squeak in amazement. "It can't be."

"You're right. It can't be." Lottie hands me dry leaves to wipe with. "Mrs. Vincent loves her husband, and he gives her everything that she needs."

"Who then?"

"Think." Lottie stands to stretch her legs. "What else is over there?"

"The Vincents' house. The rose gardens. The overflow hut where the new teachers live during their yearlong probation. And . . ." *Oh my goodness.* I jump up and grab Lottie's arm harder than I intend to. "Miss December!"

Lottie grins.

"But . . . but she's engaged. She has the diamond ring and everything."

"So?"

"She's engaged to someone else!" Lottie's dismissive *So?* shocks me more than the idea of Gordon Number One crawling through Miss December's window to kiss that long giraffe neck of hers. And, truth be told, the thought of Gordon naked in bed thrills me, though I will never tell Lottie that. "Miss December is a teacher, and sleeping with a student is wrong. Plus, she's engaged, which means that's she's cheating on the man she's going to marry, and that is also wrong."

"Your father is married, and he sleeps with two different women," Lottie says. "Why is it okay for him to do what he likes but not Miss December?"

I am speechless. My face stings. Father takes care of us. He does what he can in the time that he has. He pays for all the things that Lottie doesn't have. Like underwear. Plus, in Swaziland, a man can have many wives but a wife cannot have many husbands. That's how things *are*. Father lies to his other family to be with us but he hasn't broken the rules, not like Miss December, who sees Gordon Number One on the sly. When Father visits, he parks in front of the house and Mother kisses him in the doorway. Lottie's wrong but I still have a knot in my stomach.

I take a deep breath, cool my temper, and hit her back with, "Is that what your mother told you? That you can swap one man for another, and on and on, until you're shriveled up and nobody wants you anymore?"

107

Lottie clears her throat like it's blocked and walks away. I have no choice but to follow her across the wide field behind the little-girls' dorm and then into the bristling Christ-thorns. She climbs through our bedroom window, gets into her cot, and turns to face the wall, the way that I do when I don't want to talk. What a baby. She was the one who dragged my father into the discussion. She got what she deserved.

I throw back the sheets and climb into bed with noisy movements. I fold my arms across my chest and glare at the ceiling. If Lottie thinks I'm going to apologize to her, she's got a long wait. Her cot springs creak as she turns one way and then another, restless. I imagine the tiny spinning top with the Jewish symbols clutched in her hand as images of her father loop through her head.

"My mother told me that falling in love is the best thing in the world but it's also dangerous." Lottie's voice is thick in the darkness. "My father loved her and she loved him, and when he died, he left her with a sadness that won't go away. When a new man comes around, she thinks that he will take away the sad feelings and give her back what she had with my father. It never works out. She gets sadder, and they leave. That's why you have to take care of yourself, she says. Finish school. Be a nurse or a teacher or a secretary in an office, so that, no matter what happens, you'll have a job and a roof over your head. Don't . . . don't ever give your happiness to a man to take care of, because when he's gone, where will you be?"

I lie awake, stunned. In my imagination, her mother is a creature with her blouse hanging off her shoulder and a hand-rolled cigarette in her mouth. She does not talk about love and staying in school and sadness. Now Lottie's put new thoughts in my head. She's made me worry for the future.

What would happen to Mother, to Rian and me, if Father died or left us? Fear of being deserted preys on Mother's mind and, if I'm honest, it preys on mine too. Mother's job is to keep Father coming back to us and, when I'm home for the holidays, I walk to the telephone booth with her because I, too, have a part to play in keeping Father close. When he visits, I am all honey. I smile and laugh and keep my problems to myself. I give him every reason to visit again. Mother can't afford to take Father for granted and neither can I.

Men leave women every day for brighter faces and warmer welcomes. Take Tandy Lewis. She had a cement-brick house with a lawn and a maid, and a dog that slept inside; now she lives in a tin shack behind Delgardo's Liquor store. Now the dog sleeps in the yard, and she has no electricity. Everyone says it's a shame. Her Irishman left her with nothing. And there are others . . . and that's how things are.

Worse than a possible disaster waiting for us down the road is an unsettling question for which I have no answer: Does he love Mother and does Mother love him? He is mostly a voice on the other end of the phone and a face during brief visits at holiday times. He can't know her—her inner feelings, how clever and sensitive to slights she is—any more than she can know when he'll walk through the door next.

I glare at the green walls, the half-open window, and the lumpy shape that Lottie's body makes under her blankets. I am furious at her for pushing my mind where it doesn't want to go and for pulling images to the surface that ought to remain buried where they can do no harm: there's Mother in the public phone booth, the white moths, the cracked glass, the ache in my jaw from smiling too hard for too long when Father comes to visit, and the three of us sitting in the backyard with our feet in buckets of warm water. I love Mother's voice, but now, because of Lottie's stupid comment about him having two wives and why can't Miss December do the same, the memory of Mother singing "Oh Happy Day" under the night sky makes me want to cry and pull my hair out.

The even in-and-out sound of Lottie's breath reaches me, but I'm not fooled. She's wide-awake, just like me. I can tell. I have spent long hours tuned to Rian's asthma attacks and to the quiet that comes when he finally falls sleep. Lottie's breath is too hard and deliberate. She's faking sleep, and I think that my unkind words about her mother have dug up memories of the time that her father gave her the spinning top and her mother was happy. Bet she wants to cry and pull her hair out too.

"Good night," I whisper across the room, and she's got to know that my saying good night is an apology, but that I will never tell her sorry to her face, because that would put me in the wrong and make me weak.

"Good night," she whispers back.

We lie awake with our memories until sleep takes us away.

13

Goliath

Why, I ask you, does a dirt road on the southern border of Swaziland have to be swept? Chores keep us busy outside of the classroom, but I'd rather use the time to learn more Bible verses for the Scripture class competition. First prize for the most verses memorized is a spool of white satin ribbon if the winner is a girl, and a penknife if the winner is a boy. Lottie says the knife is worth more, which is typical of her and, I suspect, true.

She works across the road from me, bent over at the waist, her broom sweeping in wide arcs that leave a fan pattern on the ground. Last night, she hurt me and I hurt her back, and instead of hating each other and planning revenge, we got out of bed and got on with our day. We are not friends, but we're not enemies either.

She lifts her head at the sound of a car engine and looks across the cattle grid that marks the entrance to the school grounds. Engines are rare at Keziah, and most students within earshot will stop to check the make and model of the vehicle.

"White bus," Lottie says, and moves to my side of the road. "I thought it was Mr. Parns bringing Darnell back to school. He's been gone for more than two days already."

"Darnell will show up," I say. "He always does."

"True enough," Lottie says. "But that black eye of his gave me a bad feeling, and God help him if he's making trouble on Bosman's farm."

"Darnell is gone and gone," I say. "And what can we do about it?"

"Nothing," Lottie says. "We just have to wait and see, and hope that he's safe."

The engine noise grows louder, and I catch sight of the "white" bus. The bus is actually blue with a silver grille covered with dead insects, but the people inside it are white, so that makes it a white bus. If the people inside it were black, it would be a native bus.

The bus is packed with white South African children on their way to an outdoor "Praise Jesus camp" somewhere near Hlatikulu. They come through Keziah in the late afternoon on the first Friday of the January term, every year, sure as rain. We know the blue bus by sight and try to avoid being near when it cuts through school. Everyone on the blue bus thinks that mixed people are inferior, but the road that runs through

Keziah is smoother than the main road, so the driver makes a detour to use it.

The bus slows and rumbles over the cattle grid. The gears shift lower, and the wheels make a mess of our smooth brush-strokes. Now we'll have to start all over again or risk getting more work tomorrow. I step back and bump against the fence that guards Mrs. Vincent's rose garden. We should move farther away from the bus. Mother says that poor white people are the most dangerous. Some of them have less money than we do, and they hate us for it. From the moment we slide into the world with our mixed blood and mixed features, we live below them, no matter how stupid or hopeless they are.

The bus draws level with us. An ugly boy with freckled skin sticks his head out of an open window. "Hey, monkeys," he yells. "Stay in the bush where you belong!"

"Go climb a tree." A pale girl with messy red hair joins in. "Where are your bananas, crinkle-heads?"

"*Oh ha ha ha.*" The boy imitates a monkey, leans out of the window, and spits. A wet glob hits my cheek, and I squeal as if I've been slapped across the face. I wipe away the spit with the back of my hand, which trembles. My reaction makes the boy laugh, and I shrink. This is my fault. I asked for it. We should have run away while we had the chance.

"Yeah . . . good aim." Lottie grabs a stone and clenches it in her fist. "But you'll die ugly, bum-face."

The boy's cheeks flame. He is shocked that a brown girl, that any girl with color, would insult him out loud and in public.

113

His cheeks puff with another mouthful of spit, and Lottie raises her arm. She flicks her wrist, and the stone whistles through the air, hits the boy above the eyebrow, and splits the skin. Blood leaks from the cut.

"Spot on!" Lottie says under her breath, and smiles at the boy's expression, the faint glimmer of tears in his mud-brown eyes. He cannot believe that a colored girl got him back with such perfect aim. That a colored girl is David to his Goliath. But Lottie's not finished. "Hottentot! Bush monkey . . . Bet your pa has a face like a toad. And your stupid, fat, cross-eyed ma too!"

"Shh . . . What if the bus driver hears?" I grab Lottie's arm and pull her toward the side of the Vincents' house. From the backyard, we can run and hide in the bush if the bus slows down. "What if he stops?"

Lottie pulls away. "That boy got what he deserved, and I'm glad. Aren't you?"

"Yes, but . . ."

"You're scared of everything," she says, exasperated.

"That's not true." I scramble for a reply. "It's just . . . we should have left before the bus got here."

She turns on me. "He spat on you, and we're the ones who have to run and hide? He's the one who ought to be ashamed of himself. Not us. Him."

Words stick in my throat. Lottie's face is bright red, and a vein throbs on her forehead, so full that it might burst. She is furious at me for shrinking instead of fighting back. She picks up a stone and shoves it into my hand. I open my fingers to let it drop, but she forces my fingers closed and holds them there. She is stronger than I am.

"Throw it," she says.

I shake my head.

"Throw it," she repeats.

The bus is farther down the road now and almost at the long rows of orange and mango trees planted in the school orchards. No way I'll hit it, even if I throw it as hard as I can. Still, I hesitate. Bad girls throw stones, scratch and bite, and talk back, and I am Adele Joubert and I am trying as hard as I can to be good.

"Do it." Lottie pinches the soft flesh behind my upper arm. I gasp in pain, and she leans closer with glazed blue eyes. She had that exact look when she said that the driver of the crashed sedan deserved to die because he caused the accident. She was right. He killed the cow and almost killed us, and he got what was coming to him.

"Do it or, trus faith, I will pinch again, till you scream."

I lift my arm and I throw. The stone falls well short of the bus, which will stop to disgorge a stream of angry white boys any second. And the girl with the pale skin who told us to go climb a tree . . . She'll hit us harder, because our neat uniforms and our combed hair enrage her.

The bus keeps going: the wheels churn dust into the air.

"Do it again. Just for fun," Lottie says, and she is the devil whispering temptation into my ear. My fingertips tingle. The bus is way past the orchards now and well beyond reach.

I grab a stone, and the weight and the shape of it fits naturally into my palm. Sunlight hits the dried spit on the back of my hand, and I tighten my grip. That ugly white boy spat on me. My stomach knots, and Mother is right. They hate us. They treat us like animals. And Lottie is right. Why must we be polite when they are not? Sweet when they are sour? My fear leaves me, and anger rises in its place. I raise my arm, ready to throw.

"Girls," Mrs. Vincent's voice says. "Come here, please."

• • •

Lottie and I swivel to face Mrs. Vincent, who is right there on her porch with her cheeks flushed from working in the garden. She saw everything: the white bus, the spit, the stone, and the blood. The mixed-race teachers and matrons who patrol the students are God's soldiers, but the five white American missionaries who've come from across the ocean to bring us to righteousness, they are God's captains.

I let the stone drop from my hand. Too late to pretend I was clearing it off the road. Lying is our first way out of trouble at Keziah, but now that option is gone.

"Over here," Mrs. Vincent says. "It's all right."

Lottie opens the garden gate, and we walk through the pink and white blooms. Bees nose the petals, and the air smells sweet. I go slow. Being invited closer by the white staff is a badge of honor, but being punished by them is a badge of shame.

Lottie and I stop at the bottom of the porch steps. Children must keep their place, and our place is below adults. Mrs. Vincent wipes dirt from her hands and says, "Come on up. I won't bite."

Lottie hangs back so that I'm forced to take the steps first.

I am her shield. She hopes that my politeness, which she hates and thinks of as weakness, will help soften whatever happens next.

Mrs. Vincent stands with her hip against the porch rail. She is lean and tan from living under the African sun, and wears her skirts below the knee, despite the new fashion for short shorts and minidresses. Compared to Mother, Mrs. Vincent is plain, but she is white and foreign and belongs to a world we can only dream about. Lottie and I duck our heads and stare at our feet.

"What that boy did was wrong," Mrs. Vincent says in her American accent. "But the Gospel tells us to repay unkindness with kindness, and hatred with love. Do you understand?"

"Yes, Mrs. Vincent," Lottie and I say in unison, because our job is to agree with adults.

She sighs. "Look at me, please."

We raise our heads, but I concentrate on Mrs. Vincent's chipped front tooth, a strange imperfection in an otherwise perfect American face. She purses her lips, thinks for a moment, then says, "What does the Bible tell us about loving our enemies?"

I wait for Lottie to contribute, but she keeps stubbornly quiet, so I say, " 'But I say to you, love your enemies and pray for those who persecute you.' Matthew 5:44."

"That's right." Mrs. Vincent smiles. "Violence begets violence, so tell me what you should have done instead of throwing stones."

" 'We . . .' " I go to quote another Bible verse, but Lottie cuts in.

"Adele should have turned the other cheek and let the boy spit on her a second time. Then, amazed by our humility and goodness, the boy would have come to love and appreciate us."

Mrs. Vincent seems to struggle to say something but finds nothing.

"In time," Lottie adds in the silence.

"Yes . . ." Mrs. Vincent draws the word out because Lottie gave the right answer, but Mrs. Vincent doesn't know how to tell me straight to my face that, yes, I should have smiled when the boy called us "monkeys." That I should have let him spit on me again. That God loves to see his children endure, because it teaches them strength.

Would she give her two young daughters the same advice?

Her silence makes me bold, and I look straight at her. She's bright red, and the cords in her neck stick out under the skin. I wait for her to do something, say something, anything. But Mrs. Vincent is quiet, and it strikes me that she doesn't know what to do or what to say to Lottie's perfect reply.

My boldness makes Lottie bold. She sticks out her hand, with the palm up, and says, "Punish us, so that next time we will be kinder and gentler to white boys who hate us."

Mrs. Vincent blinks, and the cords in her neck stretch so tight I'm afraid they'll snap and her head will collapse on her shoulders. She turns away from us and grips the porch rail with both hands. "Go," she says. "You're dismissed."

Lottie moves fast, in case Mrs. Vincent changes her mind and sends us to ash the toilets. I move slower, and when I reach the bottom of the stairs, Mrs. Vincent says, "Be careful of where your anger will lead you, Adele."

"Yes, Mrs. Vincent. I will."

I hurry through the roses, grab up my grass broom, and catch up with Lottie. We walk the road to the senior-girls' dorm. Halfway there, I stop and look over my shoulder at Mrs. Vincent standing alone on her porch. We escaped, but I'm not elated like I should be.

"Come on." Lottie tugs my arm. "She doesn't know anything about us. She's white and American. How can she?"

It's true. Mrs. Vincent will never know what it means to live in the space between black people and white people. The spitting boy will keep her up tonight. And while she struggles with the challenge of spreading God's love, Lottie will lie awake and remember her dead father and her broken mother.

And I will lie awake and imagine my own father in his house far away, surrounded by children that I will never meet.

14

The Lord Giveth

Saturday is set aside for "healthy body, healthy mind" activities: soccer for the boys, calisthenics for the girls, and track-and-field training for all students who've shown athletic talent. After lunch, we get a choice of activities. I work in the gardens while Lottie goes on an organized walk to the Matula Gorge. The gorge is to hell and gone, so I stay on school grounds, and when the gardening is done, I join the Saturday Scripture club to learn more Bible verses.

Sunday is our day off. On Sundays we get to sleep in for an extra hour, and after breakfast and church, we do whatever we want. Girls iron their hair straight with hollow-bellied irons filled with hot coals while others knit, do puzzles or laundry, and walk hand in hand to splash in the river . . . so long as a senior girl is there to supervise them.

I wash my school clothes first thing and hang them over an out-of-the-way bush to dry. Then I find a shady indoni tree to sit under and read *Jane Eyre*. I was right about Lowood. Jane has gone from being a virtual prisoner in her aunt's house to being the prisoner of a boarding school that is similar to Keziah but far, far worse. We get Sundays off. We eat roasted sweet potatoes and curried beef and bread-and-butter pudding with raisins. It's plain food made from cheap ingredients but warm and spiced. Jane eats cold or burned porridge, toast, cold meats, and brown bread, with a single mug of coffee. All the food is served in small portions, "scarcely sufficient to keep alive a delicate invalid."

Keziah students do die. Mostly, they die at home in farm accidents and car accidents and by drowning in rivers. Lorraine Anderson and Billy Bernard are exceptions. A mystery fever took Lorraine in the night, and Billy dropped dead, just like that, on the sports field.

Billy died before my time, and I have only a vague memory of Lorraine, an older girl with brown hair and brown eyes. The death of Helen Burns, Jane Eyre's best friend, affects me more than the deaths of real students who walked where I walk and might have sat under this exact same tree. I wipe away tears to think of Helen and Jane shivering together in the cold stone hall of Lowood Institution.

Helen was sweet and kind and turned the other cheek just like Mrs. Vincent told me to do with the white boy. Helen died. Jane can see when adults are wrong and greedy and cruel, and she resents them for it. She has a temper. Her mouth doesn't hurt from smiling.

She's the one who gets to live and write the book.

• • •

Near sundown, when the shadows creep across the valley floor and the trees ring with the sound of nesting birds, I collect my dry uniform from the bush behind the native servants' quarters, hang it on my side of the wardrobe, and slide *Jane Eyre* under my pillow. Jane's gaunt face shadowed by a black bonnet, with a black ribbon tied under her chin, promises to share her next adventure with me when I get back. I hurry to the dining hall. If I arrive early, I'll avoid the long walk past the groups of girls sitting together and the boys who throw food to get my attention.

I collect my plate and find a seat in the middle of the table. That way, the spaces on either side of me fill up and I disappear into the noise and the chatter. Lottie arrives late, with red cheeks and her hair sticking up. She disappeared straight after church, and by the wild look of her, she's been out in the bush all day. I'll bet money that she spent her free time searching for Darnell Parns in the fields and farms that surround the school. She worries about him, and, even though she tries to hide it, I've caught her staring down the length of road that leads to Keziah with a fierce concentration, as if willing Mr. Parns's tractor to appear. It is strange. Darnell ran off on Tuesday at sunset and now it's Sunday afternoon. His father should have brought him back to school by now.

Lightning strikes outside the tall windows, and the little girls jump. The big girls laugh to prove they aren't afraid, but we all fear the lightning. It kills in a flash. Last year a bolt hit the man who owned the Skonkwane Stock and Feed Co., outside of Hlatikulu. He died. And the year before that, lightning hit three cows in the Ezulwini Valley, and they died. When lightning strikes the ground, it can spark fires that destroy villages and farms. We give lightning the respect that it deserves.

Lottie walks past me with her dinner plate and squeezes next to the Bartholomew twins at the far end of the table. The boys watch her pass and, infuriatingly, say nothing. She interests them, but they keep their mouths shut because she's been known to clout rude boys who say rude things. Just ask Lazy-Eye Matthew.

I eat slowly, the same way that I take small bites of *Jane Eyre* so the story lasts longer and the suspense over what Jane will do next builds. Lottie, meanwhile, is forced to read *The Oxford Dictionary* from A to Z, because the students in Mrs. McDonald's English class have put a temporary hold on Lottie raiding the novel box. They want first pick of the titles, and Lottie's read all the books anyway. Most of them twice.

"Are you going to eat that?" Claire Naidoo points to a burned crust on my plate. I shrug, and she scoops it up and throws it into her mouth before I change my mind. When I was with the pretties, we gave our scraps to our pets and we felt good about it. Sharing my scraps with Claire Naidoo is different. It doesn't feel good at all. Just the opposite. I think of the canned peaches and shortbread biscuits hidden in the suitcase under my bed and how Mother, who was poor, most likely ate the scraps from other people's plates. She was always hungry, she says, her stomach hollow with need. I'm embarrassed at having so much where Mother had so little.

•••

After dinner, I brush my teeth in the washroom and sit on the edge of my cot in the dying light. I wish the remaining nine weeks of term were over. I wish that I was anywhere but alone in Dead Lorraine's room with my unsettled feelings about sharing scraps and hoarding food. Life was easier when I was with the pretties. The pretties cared only about themselves and they had rules I followed: Never look Darnell Parns in the eye, or your mind will turn slow. Don't make friends with the poor girls; they'll steal from you. Give scraps to your pets only; it makes them feel special. Dress perfectly and keep your hair beautiful so that the others can see, with their own eyes, just how top-shelf you are. Now I'm free to make my own rules, and it's hard because I'm not sure what makes me *me*. Am I happy in and of myself, or do I smile and keep my voice low because that's what nice girls do?

I don't know anymore. I blame Lottie. Her lax attitude towards Miss December's cheating is wrong. The way that she challenges adults is also wrong. And throwing stones at a white bus is very wrong and yet . . . I can't help but think that she is right to stick up for herself and right to follow her own rules. In the time that I've shared the room with Lottie I have been hit by the Elephant in public. Talked to Darnell Parns. Peed in the moonlight. Thrown stones at a filthy white boy and looked Mrs. Vincent in the face. Lottie is a bad influence on me for sure.

I lift my pillow so that Jane will distract me from my thoughts. Jane will take me to a place where the naked trees shiver in the wind and where rivers freeze in the winter.

Wait one second . . .

I shift position to make sure I'm exactly where I was when I put Miss Eyre to bed. If I'd been in a hurry, the way that Lottie's always in a hurry to find the right page and dive into the story, I might not have noticed that someone has moved my book.

She walks in and makes a sound that is half surprise and half apology. I'm furious. First, my underpants, which I gave to her to spite Delia and the others, and now my book, which I did not give her permission to touch, and at the rate that she reads, she might already know if Jane has left Lowood. Without me.

"Where are you up to?" I snap.

"I stopped where you stopped. Trus faith."

"And how did you keep up with me?"

"I read while you were asleep and when you went to Saturday Scripture club to learn more Bible verses." Lottie lets out a deep breath. "And just now, when you were in the washroom."

"You stopped where I did?" That's a big, fat lie. Once Lottie is inside a story, she reads till the end. She's greedy that way.

"I did. Honest. It would be rude to go past where you are, to know what happens before you do." Lottie throws herself onto her cot with a groan. "I can't believe how slow you read. It's excruciating."

She's the one who did wrong by touching my things, yet somehow I'm the one in the wrong? I am clever but ignorant.

I read too slow. And now, thanks to reading through *The Oxford Dictionary* resting on top of our shared chest of drawers, she has new and better words to describe my faults and life in general. Homework is *laborious*. Mr. Newman, our lazy leans-too-close science teacher is a *degenerate*, and the sunset sky is *suffused* with color. Show-off.

"It's excruciating how fast you read," I say. "You miss all the details, and the story ends too quickly."

To prove the point, I open the book and carefully set aside the bookmark. Lottie sits up: a bright-eyed puppy who might, if patient, be given something from the dinner table. She's too proud to actually beg, though.

I like that about her.

I shift closer to the pillow, the same way that she moved closer to the window of the *Ocean Current* when Lazy-Eye Matthew croaked, "Adele. Adele," to get me next to him in third class. Lottie accepts my silent invitation. The cot springs creak, and we lean our backs against the wall. I find my spot and, afraid that Lottie will race ahead and get to the good bits first, I read out loud.

"*I tired of the routine of eight years in one afternoon. I desired liberty; for liberty I gasped; for liberty I uttered a prayer; it seemed scattered on the wind then faintly blowing. I abandoned it and framed a humbler supplication; for change, stimulus; that petition, too, seemed swept off into vague space: 'Then,' I cried, half desperate, 'grant me at least a new servitude!'*"

"Thank heavens," Lottie breaks in. "Jane is ready to make a move. I was afraid she'd stay at that school till kingdom come."

"Same here," I say. "Imagine being stuck at Keziah forever? I'd go crazy like Mrs. Thomas, for sure."

"Me too. But 'a new servitude' sounds dull. I want Jane to have excitement in her life."

"Maybe she will." I think about Jane's future for a moment. "Jane's got no money, so she has to find work, but work that's new and different from what she knows. It's the same for us. We'll have to find jobs when we graduate from Keziah after next year. Just like Jane."

"True," Lottie says. "What are you going to do?"

If I was still with the pretties, I'd know the right answer to give, right away. It would go like this: *I want to marry a good-looking man with money. We'll live in a big house and spend the summer holidays in Durban or Mozambique.*

It's different with Lottie. With Lottie, there are no right or wrong answers—just the words that come out of your mouth. I close my eyes, and I search for a vision of my future that comes from my own mind and not from the ideas of others. After a moment of terrifying blankness, images flicker to life: stone buildings and snowcapped mountains, ocean waves rolling under a slate-gray sky and lazy rivers winding through a hot green jungle. A pang of longing blooms in my chest and spreads across me. For the first time, I know what I want from the future.

"I . . . I want to travel to all the places I've read about in books. Scotland and India. England and America. The Swiss Alps and Canada. Maybe study overseas." My eyes fly open, and I glance at Lottie, afraid that I'll find annoyance or, worse, ridicule written on her face. Daydreams are for children. And my daydreams of traveling overseas and studying in an ancient university hall covered in climbing ivy are . . . impossible. I'll be lucky to get as far away as Joburg. Lottie's expression is warm and curious with no trace of annoyance or ridicule. She takes me at my word.

"And you?" I throw the spotlight back onto her. "What do you want?"

She shrugs. "A small farm with cows and goats and a view of the mountains. I'd leave the trees for the birds, and the fields for the wild animals. There's a river to swim in, and I have . . . uh . . ." Lottie leaves the sentence hanging and motions to *Jane Eyre*. "Enough about us. How's Jane going to find a job and get free?"

I'd love to know the secret word that Lottie left off the end of her sentence, but now is not the time to push. The two of us speaking honestly to each other is wonder enough. I give her *Jane Eyre* and say, "Your turn."

Lottie licks her lips and clears her throat. Reading aloud in class is indeed excruciating. Mistakes aren't allowed. Mispronunciations are greeted with the whack of a ruler across your palm if the teacher is being kind, and a rap across the knuckles with the metal edge if the teacher is not.

"Go slow," I say. "We've got plenty of time till lights-out."

"Here a bell, ringing the hour of supper, called me downstairs." Lottie begins reading where I left off, and I am Jane Eyre and I am also Adele Joubert, a mixed-race student at Keziah Christian Academy in the British protectorate of Swaziland, where

lightning strikes outside the windows and wind tugs at the red flowers of the Christ-thorns. I am here, and I am there— balanced between two worlds.

It's wonderful.

I forget that the Lord giveth and . . .

15

The Lord Taketh Away

A bell rings from far off, and the sound grows louder as another bell near the dining hall dings. Outside the high window that faces Mrs. Thomas's house, a third bell joins the chorus. Footsteps hurry across the dirt yard. The dormitory door flies open and hits the inside wall, and *bang* . . . I am 100 percent back in Swaziland.

"Fire," Mrs. Thomas shrieks. "Fire!"

Lottie drops *Jane Eyre* on top of my pillow and jumps up to open the wardrobe. She pulls my sweater from the hanger and throws it across the room.

"Put it on."

"But fire is hot," I say even as I shove my arms into the sleeves and do up the buttons with shaking hands. Alarm bells ring from every corner of the school grounds. Lottie shrugs on her thin sweater and drags me into the hall, where dozens of frightened girls gather. Mrs. Thomas stands in the doorway and rings the alarm bell for all she's worth. Her arm shakes from the weight of swinging an actual brass bell with the word *alarm* written across the handle in blue pen.

"Where's the fire?" Brenda, the student with the nasal voice, yells over Mrs. Thomas's clanging. Everyone knows that Brenda has a brother with a limp, and that it's her job to take care of him in a flood or, like now, in a fire.

"In the bush near the sports field," Mrs. Thomas says. "Everyone pair up. We'll collect branches on the way."

I inch closer to Lottie. I make her mine, because fire doesn't care if your father owns the hypermarket on Louw Street or if he lives with his other family in Johannesburg. It eats what it can and spits out rich and poor children just the same. Lottie is used to fighting, so I'll stick with her. She leans closer and whispers in my ear, "Ask her for machetes to cut the branches."

I hesitate, and Lottie pokes me in the side. "Please, Mrs. Thomas," I yelp. "Can we have machetes to cut the branches?"

"Good thinking, Adele." Mrs. Thomas unhooks a key from the chain she wears around her waist and gives it to me. "Hurry now. Meet us at the sports field."

I run outside with Lottie and unlock the equipment shed. Again, she let me do the talking. If she'd asked, Mrs. Thomas would have turned her down, because who knows what a poor girl with a machete might do. We grab two pangas, what the natives call the long cutting knives with stout wooden handles, and I make sure to lock the door behind us. I push the key into my sock for safekeeping, and we hurry to the sports field at the far end of the school grounds.

A funnel of black smoke reaches into the sky at the bottom of the dirt road that leads past the classrooms, the staff houses, and the boys' dormitory. Lightning forks through the low clouds, and the air crackles with the sound of burning brush and the shrieks of panicked birds. Senior boys run from late study hall, and we run with them, our pangas held stiff against our thighs so we don't accidentally slice off an arm or a leg if we trip.

Students swarm the sports field. Smoke billows from a hundred yards into the bush on the opposite side of the field from the boys' dorms. The air vibrates with sound: adults yell, the fire crackles, a distant alarm bell rings. The little ones are mute as they watch the seniors and staff assemble. Mrs. Vincent drives the school pickup truck onto the field with her hand pressed to the horn. Mr. Vincent jumps out and blows his emergency whistle. We can see, back in the bush, the fire start to climb up the trees. Suddenly, three antelope run out of the scrub and bolt past us. The senior teachers blow their whistles in short, shrill blasts, and a nervous silence settles over the crowd. It is important that we follow instructions and do as we're told. Our lives depend on obedience now more than ever.

Students form into ranks. Gordon Number One and two other boys help Mrs. Vincent roll water barrels from the back of the pickup truck and store them against the walls of the little-boys' dorm in case the fire jumps to the buildings.

"Quick." Lottie pulls me from the field to a stand of trees to our right. She hacks at a branch and cleaves it straight from the trunk. "Cut off the branches with green leaves and make a pile."

I lift my panga and bring the blade down onto a branch. My muscles quiver when the metal meets the wood, and it takes me five blows to cut the branch loose. I move to the next branch and the next till I'm wet under my arms and shaking.

"Give the branches to the senior boys," Lottie says, and keeps cutting. I drag the branches onto the field, where Mr. Vincent and Mr. Moses, the dorm master, organize the students into firefighting units.

Mrs. Button, who lives behind the mechanic's workshop, says that in England, fires are put out by specially trained firemen who drive big red trucks with powerful hoses, and ladders that reach to the tops of buildings. In Swaziland, we have water barrels and students armed with wet flour sacks and green tree branches.

"Four lines," Mr. Vincent says. "Boys in the front two rows, and girls in the back two."

I dump the branches near a stack of wet flour sacks, and the senior boys grab whatever is closest. The piles disappear, and I run into the trees to collect more. Lottie has a stack ready, and I run a relay between the field and the trees till each of the boys in the front line has a branch or a dripping flour sack to beat down the flames. Lottie and me stab our panga blades into the ground so they are ready for quick use, if the need arises.

"Shoulder-to-shoulder. Keep close together," Mr. Moses tells the firefighters. "If it gets too hot . . . back out. I don't want no dead heroes tonight."

"Yes, sir," the boys reply.

Mr. Vincent, Mr. Moses, and the front-line boys move toward the fire in the bush. Burned leaves float to the ground at my feet. Flames wink deep in the bush, and my heart drums inside my chest when the second row of boys fades into the shadow of the forest.

"Here." Lottie hands me a crooked branch, and we join the end of the girls' line. "With luck, we'll get to go in next," she says.

"With luck?" I say. What an odd phrase to use, and her with a fresh list of *Oxford Dictionary* definitions to draw on. "You'd rather be with the boys than here where it's safe?"

She shrugs her bony shoulders. "It's better than waiting."

Behind us, the junior boys and girls form a human cordon around the little-boys' dormitory. Each of them holds a wooden bucket, which Mrs. Vincent fills with water siphoned from the ten-gallon drums. I pray that the big boys and the male teachers keep the fire well away from the dry field and the tiny bodies standing in defense.

Brenda with the nasal voice goes over to Mrs. Vincent and whispers in her ear. Mrs. Vincent nods, and Brenda pulls her lame brother, Leon, from the junior line. He fights her. He kicks and bites. She grabs his ear and twists.

"Please, let me," he begs. "Let me stay."

"I promised Pa." Brenda pulls him to the road, and his pleas grow faint the farther away he gets from danger.

"Poor thing," Lottie says, and strangely, I understand what she means. Leon wants to be part of the fight. I wouldn't want to be anywhere else either. The school generator turns on, and light from the boys' dormitories floods the sports field. Mrs. Thomas shifts her weight from one foot to the other and makes soft clucking noises that are meant to soothe us, but they only heighten our fear. If the grown-ups are afraid of the fire, how are we meant to be brave?

We wait for what seems like hours while the boys tackle the flames out of our sight. More lightning bolts pierce the sky, and I swap my branch from one hand to the other, agitated and bored.

Mr. Vincent stumbles out of the bush with wild hair and a red face. He blows his whistle to get our attention. "The main blaze is under control, but we need to put out the spot fires." His voice is hoarse from shouting orders. "Bring the wa-ter buckets!"

"One bucket each, girls." Mrs. Thomas is calm now that the fire is beaten. "Careful. And no spilling."

"Finally," Lottie whispers. "A little fire is better than none."

A third-class girl offers Lottie her bucket.

"Adele and Lottie," Mrs. Thomas says. "Take the pangas back to the shed and return the key to me, please."

"But . . ." Lottie is outraged. I am outraged. We've been

135

dismissed from the best part of the crisis, and tomorrow the others will tell us what we missed in full detail. Tall trees alight . . . A burned snake curled around a rock . . . Towers of flame and smoke, and the smell of sweaty boys. *Where were you? Oh, that's right, you missed it.*

"Now," Mrs. Thomas snaps. "No arguments."

16

Fire, Fire, Burning Bright

Light from the boys' dormitory fades, and the road ahead is dark. We drag our branches with us so we'll be ready to fight the fire the moment that we get back. Butcher, a Rhodesian ridgeback who killed five chickens last term and almost cost the night watchman his arm, barks in Mrs. McDonald's yard. Butcher is cracked in the head, but Mrs. McDonald doesn't have the heart to put him down, so she keeps him chained to a metal spike under the mango trees. I'm sure that Lottie thinks chaining an animal is cruel and that Mrs. McDonald is wrong to do it.

"I wish Butcher would shut up," I say. The staff houses on either side of us make black shapes against the night. "The generator is on. How come there's no lights?"

"Nobody's home to turn the light switches on. Everyone's at the fire." Lottie is sullen. "Everyone but us."

"It's all right. We'll go when we get back from the shed." I loop my arm through hers to let her know that she's not alone in her disappointment. We're more than just roommates. We shared our dreams for the future and read *Jane Eyre* together and we might even be friends, though neither one of us would say it out loud. Friendship with Lottie Diamond seemed impossible at the beginning of term but now, well, here we are, arm in arm, and not one part of me is shocked by how easily we fit. Strange thumping sounds break through my thoughts and I go still.

"Hear that?" My heart leaps into my throat.

"No," Lottie says.

"Shh . . . listen." Another thump comes from our left. Butcher goes berserk. His metal chain rakes across the dirt as he chases whatever's back there. I grip the wooden handle of my panga and squeeze Lottie's arm. The ground shakes, and a vervet monkey leaps over the front fence of Mrs. McDonald's house and runs across the road with a baby on its back. A troop of monkeys follows, and their howls make the skin on my neck prickle. They disappear into the vacant land between the big-boys' dorm and the woodworking shed, and the monkey run happened so fast that I wonder if I dreamed it, except that Butcher is mad with barking and Lottie is wide-eyed.

"See that?" she says. "Something scared them. We should go look."

"No." I grind my feet into the ground. "We have to take the pangas to the shed and join the others."

"Fine." Lottie pulls away from me. "When you get back to

138

the sports field, tell Mrs. Thomas that you lost me. I'm going to see what made those monkeys run."

She hurries toward the classrooms and doesn't look back.

I look toward the faraway shed. Then I look at her vanishing in the dark. I chase after her. "Wait for me!"

I'd rather follow her into the darkness than walk alone on a deserted road where nobody can hear me scream if Butcher gets free.

•••

We move between the school buildings in the direction we think the monkeys came from. It's dark, and all we can hear is the sound of our shoes on the gravel path and Butcher's distant barking.

"Look," Lottie says suddenly, and points toward an orange glow coming from behind the school shop, where the neat school grounds meet the bush. We run toward the glow and turn the corner.

The bush behind the school shop is ablaze. A lightning bolt must have hit here while we were on the sports field. Fire starts to climb the trees, and the embers float down and spark on the tall grass. Lizards and black beetles run between our legs and over our feet to get away. That's what we should do. Run. Run for help. Run for water. Run for our lives. The fire is big, and we are two girls with green branches and pangas.

"Fast, Adele!" Lottie beats the flames back with her branch. "Before the shop burns down. And then the classrooms. Now. Now."

I run toward the fire instead of away from it, because Mother

139

says that only cowards run away from trouble. I run toward the fire instead of away from it because the school shop food is precious. It is the grease that makes the wheels of student life go round.

I beat back the flames with my branch. Sparks rise. Smoke stings my eyes, and the roar of the fire is terrifying. Lottie yells something at me in Zulu, but I don't speak or understand Zulu.

"Umuntu omkhulu!" Lottie takes up the native chant that the senior boys and the bus driver used to pull the crashed blue sedan from the lip of the mountain.

I know what to say. "Siza naye!"

Together, we chant, "Umuntu omkhulu! Siza naye! Umuntu omkhulu! Siza naye!"

We speak it, and we become one body, one mind, one purpose.

The spirits of our African ancestors—whom we refuse to talk about and never acknowledge in public, because our black blood is shameful and ignored—these sleeping spirits find a home in us. Our mixed blood does not matter: Portuguese, Zulu, French, Scottish, Jewish, and English, the percentage of white blood to black. In the face of the fire, we are Swazi.

Hot cinders burn through the sleeves of my wool sweater and leave small blisters. I'm glad Lottie made me put it on or the cinders would have hit my bare skin and the burns would have been far worse. I grit my teeth against the pain and fight on. Lottie is relentless. Her strength and determination are double mine, and I will only stop when she stops. I will only give up when she does, and not before. Not one second before.

A loud crack makes me look up. Flames and sparks spit into the air. A burning branch breaks free from a tree and falls toward me. Hot wind tears through my hair, and a scream freezes in my throat. I have to move, jump, run—but my feet won't budge. The flames are beautiful as the branch falls toward me.

I hope that Mother knows I did my best.

• • •

"Adele! Adele!"

Lottie's voice breaks the spell of the flames, and I step back in time to avoid being scorched. My shoulder slams into the school shop wall as the branch lands a foot to my left. Fires lick at the grass. I can feel the heat on my ankles, and the storage shed key that I slipped into my sock burns. The branch is too near me, too near the buildings. Suddenly, the branch pops, and flying embers billow out and up, and some of them land on Lottie's skirt. Without thinking, I throw myself against her to smother the sparks before they become a flame. My weight throws us both off balance, and we hit the ground hard. Lottie groans, but a hurt spine is nothing compared to being roasted alive. I quickly check her skirt to make sure the embers are dead, and feel the hot breath of the fire on my back. The blisters on my arm throb a warning. Lottie saved me and I saved her, and now we have to save the shop from catching alight.

"Get your branch," Lottie says, and grabs hers.

We struggle to our feet, weary but determined to defend the blue buildings and the branching jacarandas that shade them from the bright summer sun. We lift our branches and slam them down in unison. Up and down, a hundred times and more. Together, we fight the flames till the tree branch smolders and the blackened grass on the edge of the bush blows a thick gray smoke that stings our eyes. The wind holds its breath long enough for us to move into the bush and kill the last of the flames.

When we're done, we slump against the shop wall and breathe. Just breathe. The hot bricks warm our backs, and a sliver of moon peeks through the smoke haze. Our fingers refuse to let go of our branches even though we have nothing left to give. We are empty.

"You come back right now!" Brenda, the final-year girl with the nasal voice calls from the other side of the shop. "When I find you, you're in for it. You hear me, Leon?"

Her brother fast-limps around the corner and stops when he sees the smoke and the black trees. Red coals blink in the burned grass, and we need water to finish the job properly. "Ohhh, my goodness," Leon says with wide eyes.

Lottie sits with her knees tucked close to her body, and her shoulders shake like when you're in chapel and have to hold in a laugh or else get the cane for disrespecting the Word. Only Lottie's not laughing. She's crying. Tears stream down her face, and her bottom lip is caught between her teeth to stop her from making a sound. She's trying to hide her sorrow but the fire has burned down the internal wall that she's built inside her.

"Leon. Go get Mrs. Vincent." I take charge of the situation when I realize that Lottie can't speak, let alone give orders. "Tell her to bring water. Quick sticks, now."

"Sure. Sure." Leon hobbles away, happy to be of use in an

emergency. He disappears, and soon, his sister and her threats move in the direction of the dining hall.

I pull my legs to my chest and wrap my arms around my knees. Maybe the smoke made Lottie cry, but even I'm not ignorant enough to believe that. If the fire had destroyed the school shop and then ripped through the classrooms, there'd be no Keziah Christian Academy for this term and for the rest of the year. School is the best part of Lottie's life. She has three meals a day and bread with apricot jam for morning and afternoon tea. She has shelter and, most importantly, she has books.

Lottie wipes her nose on her sleeve, and I want to tell her to cheer up. We did it. We saved the school shop, and now's not the time for tears. *Be happy. Be grateful. Smile.* Mother's voice inside my head tells me how to behave and what to say. This time, I ignore it and lay my cheek against my knee. My throat tightens, and my eyes water. I cry in small, hard sobs that rack my body. I cry for more than the fire. I cry for Mother and Rian and Father so far away, and how close Lottie and I came to dying.

•••

Mrs. Vincent backs the pickup truck around the corner from the school shop, and students of both sexes jump from the tray with brimming buckets of water. They extinguish the remaining embers, and thick smoke billows from the burned woods. Lottie and I make a half-hearted attempt to get up and help, but Mrs. Vincent shoos us away.

"Find clean air and have a rest," she says. "You've both had enough fire for today."

She's right. We are dazed and hollow, and I want to lie down and sleep for a week. Maybe two. We rescue our abandoned pangas from the edge of the woods and drag our way toward the senior-girls' dorm. Images of the fire churn through my mind, but I'm too tired to make a sound or leak another tear. Lottie walks beside me, pale and listless. I doubt she cries very often, and maybe she's embarrassed by her tears now that we're out of danger.

I want to know what she's feeling: Does the cut on her bottom lip hurt? How long will it take to rebuild the wall inside her? A day, a week, or a month? I keep my mouth shut and hold the silence. There's a strange comfort in our shared exhaustion, and fighting the fire has moved us beyond words. Together, we experienced what it was to stand before the towering flames. And beat them.

The school grounds are empty, and lantern light from Mrs. Thomas's house guides us through the darkness. Behind us, students help put out what's left of the fires behind the school shop and near the sports field, so we are alone. When we reach the storage shed, I crouch by the door and roll down my sock to find the key while Lottie holds the pangas.

It's heat-sealed to my skin, and I wince as I peel it away to reveal a key-shaped imprint seared onto my ankle. The fire has marked me inside and out. I unlock the shed door and move aside to let the light from Mrs. Thomas's living room shine into the interior. Lottie stops and tilts her head. She listens.

"What?" I whisper, and she hands me my panga. My heart nudges my ribs, and I hold still. I listen. Soft sounds come from the Christ-thorns, and Lottie lifts her panga, ready to strike down whatever's hiding in the shadows. I do the same, except my hand shakes and the panga blade twitches from side to side like it's dancing.

A brown rabbit shoots from the aloes and runs between us with its ears pinned back. The rabbit's white tail flashes bright in the darkness. Another victim of the fire. I jump back with a squeal, and Lottie laughs at the sound I make.

"You were scared too," I say when my heart rate calms.

"Ja, but not like . . ." She imitates my shaking hand and fearful yelp, and it's so funny to see myself so perfectly mimicked that I laugh, too, instead of hitting her a good one, which is the rule when being made fun of by another student.

A twig snaps in the direction of the little-girls' dorm, and our laughter stops. The fire might have flushed a bigger, meaner animal out of the bush. A wild dog, for example, can tear a chunk out of your leg and give you rabies. Lottie lifts her panga again, and we listen to the night. Small sounds find us: the wind in the trees, crickets, an owl hoot in the distance.

"Darnell?" Lottie suddenly calls. "It's Lo-Lo and Adi. Come out. We won't hurt you."

We wait and wait and get nothing back from the darkness. If Darnell is out there, he's happy to stay quiet. Lottie's shoulders slump in defeat. Like her, I'm sad no one answered.

Female voices, high-pitched with excitement, reach us from the dirt road. Lottie hangs the pangas on their hooks, and I lock the shed door and slip the key back into my sock for safekeeping. Mrs. Thomas leads a gaggle of girls into the yard, and everyone has a story to tell, a close call to report, and a good reason to chatter loudly as they make their way back to their beds. Lottie and I have the best story of all, but neither of us says a word about the troop of monkeys or the flames eating away the trees behind the school shop. We know what we did. And if there's a God and he turned his head to our dead corner of Swaziland for even five seconds, he knows it too.

"Inside, ladies." Mrs. Thomas herds us into the hall. "The generator goes off in twenty-five minutes, so there's enough time for the older girls to take a shower. The rest of you will have to wait till tomorrow."

The younger girls groan. We collectively stink of sweat and smoke, and now our sheets and our pillows will stink too. It's no use complaining. Graduating students get first go at everything, and the rest of us have to wait till morning to get clean. Lottie and I perch on the edge of our cots, exhausted.

Normal sounds come from outside Dead Lorraine's room. Showers turn on in the washroom, and girls get ready for bed. Our room is exactly as we left it, with my hairbrush on top of the chest of drawers and *Jane Eyre* still flipped open on my pillow. Lottie sighs and throws herself back onto her mattress to enjoy the bustle of the dormitory settling down for the night. My body softens, and I relax. I miss Mother and Rian and the comforts of home, but tonight the distance between Keziah Christian Academy and Manzini seems to matter less than usual. Lottie and I survived, and that is a good enough reason to enjoy a quiet moment of happiness.

17

New Rules

We climb into our beds with ash under our fingernails and the smell of smoke in our hair. The generator is down for the night, and the dormitory is pitch-black. Mrs. Thomas has banned candles for tonight, because open flames inside the buildings will tempt fate, and how could she sleep knowing that we're still in danger of being burned alive?

"You can manage without light for one night, my dears," she says. "Better safe than sorry."

I close my eyes and wait for sleep to take me. My blistered arm aches, and the two aspirin that Mrs. Thomas gave me from her personal medicine supply have done little to blunt the pain. I'm exhausted, but my mind is wide-awake, and when I close my eyes, all I see are flames roaring in the trees and embers sparking the grass.

Mrs. Thomas shines her torch into the room for her nightly head count, and Lottie and I simultaneously turn so that our faces are visible in the spotlight. Stuffed pillows under the blankets don't fool Mrs. Thomas or the Elephant.

"You two can have a candle for an hour," Mrs. Thomas whispers. "You've earned it, hey?"

Lottie strikes a match and lights the wick. We've been granted a special privilege by an adult, and to refuse it would be rude. Mrs. Thomas lingers. We wait, made nervous by her attention.

"A little bird tells me that Mr. Vincent wants to give two special girls a Golden Sun Award for bravery," she says. "There'll be a presentation night, and Mrs. Vincent is sure to take pictures for the Missionary Foundation newsletter. People in America will know your names and your faces. Imagine that. You'll be famous."

"A Golden Sun?" I'm in awe. "For certain?"

"For absolute certain." Mrs. Thomas edges farther into the room, the bringer of good news. "Plus, your parents will be notified, and they'll get a special letter to frame and hang on the wall so everyone knows how clever you are."

Mother will be pleased. Golden Sun Awards are rare, and she'll be sure to tell Father how many have been given out and how few are chosen for the honor.

"Tell me your favorite food and I'll make sure the kitchen girls cook it for the celebration dinner," Mrs. Thomas says. And to look at her, you'd think she was the one about to receive an award.

Lottie throws me a frown, surprised to be asked for her personal menu suggestions. We eat what we're given, and we're grateful for it.

"Roast beef," I say off the top of my head. "And corn bread with butter."

Simple food, easy to make. Anything more complicated might seem that I'm taking advantage of Mrs. Thomas's goodwill, and that might, in turn, bring out her spiteful side.

"Sponge cake with apricot jam and fresh cream." Lottie knows what she wants, and grabs it. Mrs. Thomas smiles at her request, and I have to admit that her boldness yields better results than my "be humble" strategy.

"I'll pass on your requests to the kitchen staff." Mrs. Thomas reluctantly moves to the door to finish her head count. "Sleep well, and good work, girls. Be proud."

Lottie and I lie awake in the semidarkness as Mrs. Thomas's voice echoes in our minds. *Sleep well. Good work. Be proud.* At school, it seems that the job of adults is to magnify our faults so that, burdened by shame, we learn to be better. Mrs. Thomas, in particular, has a history of putting girls in their place. Something has changed in our world.

"Well." I blink at the ceiling, disoriented. "That was . . ."

"Abnormal." Lottie finds the correct *Oxford Dictionary* word to fit Mrs. Thomas's unusual behavior. "But it was nice, hey?"

"Yes," I say. "It was." And I mean it. Our parents send us to Keziah to get an education and to toughen us up for life's challenges, except school itself is a challenge that many of us will never conquer. School is a battlefield. The teachers and the other students are our enemies, and we learn to endure the slings and arrows alone.

Lottie turns to face me. "Tonight she'll switch from listening to 'This Bitter Earth,' to 'At Last.' Wait and see."

"For how long?" I ask. "A night or two if we're lucky?"

"I don't know, Adele. That's why we have to enjoy it while it lasts. Tomorrow will take care of itself, but tonight . . . tonight we are heroes."

The way that Lottie says "heroes" fills me with a sensation of strength and power. I stretch out and, when my eyes close, a wall of flames roars to life in my mind again. A burning branch twists and falls, and showers me in sparks.

"All I can see is the fire," I say to Lottie, who lies on her cot and stares at the ceiling, wide-awake.

"That's normal," she says. "When a bad thing happens, your mind goes over and over it, till one day, it stops."

"How long will that take?"

"A week, maybe more. Some things never go away. With the fire, at least, we won. We beat it. We made a difference. The other hurts will fade or not, but there's nothing we can do about that."

The seriousness of Lottie's voice tells me that she speaks from experience. I hate to think of an older version of me with a key mark still visible on my wrinkled skin, still visited by dreams of fire and ash, decades from now.

"I wonder what's in that letter that Jane Eyre picked up from the post office?" Lottie says, and she's a genius for asking.

England is far, far away from our small piece of Africa, and Jane's problems will help to push our own worries away.

I slide Miss Eyre from under my pillow, wrap my blanket around my shoulders, and sit in the circle of candlelight that pools in front of our shared chest of drawers. Lottie sits next to me, also wrapped in her blanket, and I flip to the place where she left off when the fire bell rang. The words are hard to read in the flickering light, but I know how to make the situation right.

"Hold the book, Lottie." I dive under my cot and drag out a suitcase. The weight of it makes my shoulders bow, and heat flares in my cheeks. Lottie is poor, but she's no thief, while I am a first-class skinflint, a word that Lottie read aloud from *The Oxford Dictionary* on Friday night.

Skinflint: a person who spends as little money as possible. A miser.

Replace the word *money* with *food* and you have me right there. Lottie's choice of word wasn't personal, though. She also read out *saber* and then *salacious*, the definition of which had us both rolling with laughter.

I scoop an extra candle from the open suitcase, and Lottie's eyes bug out at the sheer amount of bounty that I've kept hidden. It looks bad, I know, but there are rules to follow when it comes to using food. Food buys favors and pays bribes. Food keeps your pets sweet. Food gives you power, and you don't give it away without getting something in return.

I light the second candle and keep my mouth shut about the rules. The rules are stupid. Food, I decide, is for eating.

"Choose something," I tell Lottie, and sit down next to her.

"These?" Lottie points to a box of strawberry-cream biscuits, nervous. Strawberry creams buy a lot of favors.

"Fine," I say. "Eat as many as you like."

We settle against the chest of drawers and scoff down a strawberry-cream biscuit each before I start to read.

"'If J.E., who advertised in the —shire Herald of last Thursday, possesses the acquirements mentioned, and if she is in a position to give satisfactory references as to character and competency, a situation can be offered her where there is but one pupil, a little girl, under ten years of age; and where the salary is thirty pounds per annum. J.E. is requested to send references, name, address, and all particulars to the direction:—

"'Mrs. Fairfax, Thornfield, near Millcote, —shire.'"

"She'll get the job," Lottie says with confidence. "Then she can leave Lowood. Is thirty pounds a lot of money?"

"I don't know, but Thornfield sounds big. Unfriendly."

"And isolated. Look here, it says 'near Millcote, —shire,' which means Thornfield is out in the boonies."

"Like Keziah . . ."

"Keep reading," Lottie says. "It's the only way we'll find out where Jane ends up."

I find our spot and read on. The scratched-out name at the front of the book doesn't bother me anymore. Father's other children and Mother's anxious cleaning have no power inside Dead Lorraine's room. Inside these pea-green walls, only Lottie, Jane, and I exist.

18

Liars and Thieves

The morning bell rings for the second Monday of the school term, and I wake up on the floor with a pillow under my head and a blanket over my body. Lottie lies beside me, with *Jane Eyre*, the empty box of strawberry creams, and the Jewish spinning top tucked between us. Last night's hour of grace turned into two hours, and then Mr. Rochester turned up on his horse and almost killed Jane, and although he's a proper white man with money and Jane is only a servant, it's obvious that he's attracted to her and that she's falling for him. But that house, Thornfield Hall . . . Something's wrong there, that's for sure. We kept reading until the candles burned down and we fell asleep to the sound of "At Last," played over and over again. Mrs. Thomas will be in a soft, don't-much-care-who's-wrong-or-right mood this morning.

"What?" Lottie says when I shake her from sleep.

"Move it. We have to get one of the showers or we'll stink for a week."

We grab our towels and washcloths, and rush to join the bathroom line, which is already long. I snag a spot behind Claire Naidoo, and Lottie falls in behind me. The fire is the main talking point, and the atmosphere is festive. We're alive, and standing in line is better than being consumed by fire, which would mean we'd have to have closed caskets at our funerals, and wouldn't that be a shame?

A door slams, and Delia, Peaches, Natalie, and Sandi Cardoza come out of their room with flushed faces. Sandi's hair sticks up like porcupine quills, and something disastrous must have happened for her to show her natural kink in public. Delia walks straight toward us like she's on a mission, and I can't imagine what she wants from Lottie or me.

"Here. Take it." Delia throws a wad of material in my face. "Now give it back!"

"Give what back?" I'm in shock. Delia just threw Lottie's stolen undies in my face. In front of everyone!

"Don't play dumb," Delia snarls. "Give it back."

"I don't know what you're talking about," I say, exasperated. "Give back what?"

"My silver necklace." Sandi Cardoza's eyes are red from crying. "The one my father gave me for Christmas. That one. It was in my top drawer, and now it's gone."

Lottie grabs her undies from the floor and crushes them in her fist. "Who says we took the necklace?"

154

"It couldn't have been anyone else," Delia says. "The two of you came inside and stole the necklace while the rest of us were at the fire."

"We were also at the fire!" Lottie says.

"You stole the necklace when Mrs. Thomas sent you back with the pangas."

My stomach clenches. Stealing is a serious accusation, and if just one adult believes Delia's lie, we'll be expelled for sure.

"Are you calling me a thief to my face?" Lottie stands nose-to-nose with Delia and bristles with impending violence. The bathroom line breaks to form a semicircle around us. There might be a fight, and nobody wants to miss that. "Are you calling Adele a thief too?"

"You're in it together. You took the necklace to spite us, because you're jealous." Delia is certain that what she says is true, and in her righteous fury, she's forgotten that Lottie can move faster and hit harder than she'll ever be able to.

The girls in the semicircle ooh and aah, because Lottie has to pay Delia back for the insult immediately. Defending your honor is part of the school code, and the only way to do that is to fight. The strange thing is, I haven't thought about Sandi Cardoza in the four days since the underwear theft, or tried to scheme my way back into the group, but in Delia's mind everyone wants to be her. She's too vain to notice how little I care anymore.

Lottie grabs Delia by the hair. She twists, and the audience gasps. That was fast. Delia didn't see it coming. Lottie turns Delia's head so she can look right into her face. "Call us thieves again," Lottie says with cold-eyed calm. "I dare you."

155

Sandi Cardoza steps back and bumps into Natalie and Peaches, who are also suddenly nervous. I love their fear. It's a guilty thrill. I know violence doesn't solve problems—except it does.

"Girls!" Mrs. Thomas's voice breaks the semicircle that shields us and everyone melts back into a straight line. "What's going on?"

Lottie and I take our original position behind Claire Naidoo and keep our mouths shut. If Delia wants to accuse us of stealing, she can do it herself.

"Well?" Mrs. Thomas goes straight to Sandi Cardoza, with her stick-up hair and puffy eyes. She's obviously involved. "Tell me what happened."

Sandi sniffles. Delia darts us a savage glance and says, "Lottie Diamond and Adele Joubert stole Sandi's silver necklace while the rest of us were at the fire."

Mrs. Thomas sighs. Girls and their problems, she must be thinking. She'd rather be with Etta James than standing in a concrete hallway with vain little creatures who make it impossible to figure out who's lying and who's telling the truth.

"Now"—Mrs. Thomas turns on Lottie and me—"tell the truth, and shame the devil: Did one or both of you steal the necklace?"

"No, Mrs. Thomas," I say in a firm voice that carries the length of the hallway. "Lottie Diamond and I did not steal Sandi Cardoza's necklace."

"She's lying. They did it!" Delia's voice makes Mrs. Thomas flinch. Her fragile mood makes her sensitive to sharp sounds and bright lights.

Mrs. Thomas raises her hand for quiet. Delia's father pays

156

full fees and Sandi Cardoza's father donated a new generator to the school, so she has to make an effort to investigate. She asks the bathroom line, "Did anyone see Adele and Lottie steal the necklace?"

Silence.

"Does anyone know where the necklace is now?"

The line remains stubbornly quiet. If a girl steps forward to say that, yes, they saw Lottie and me with the necklace, they'll be rewarded by Delia and Sandi, but how sweet will that chocolate bar taste after Lottie's given them a cut lip and a black eye for lying about us?

"Check our room," Lottie says. "We've got nothing to hide."

Moments later, Mrs. Thomas strides into Dead Lorraine's room and pulls open our drawers. She checks the pockets of the clothing hanging in our wardrobe and strips our beds to find what might be hidden under the sheets. Then she hauls my suitcase from under my cot and rifles though the contents. Heat stings my face. The bounty of cans and unopened biscuits is embarrassing but no longer shameful. I shared with Lottie last night, and together we'll make quick work of eating what's left. The cans and boxes prove that I have no reason to steal.

"All clear." Mrs. Thomas's mouth softens into a smile. She's relieved that we're innocent and still eligible for the Golden Sun Award. Her happiness is selfish. Stealing in the dorm casts a shadow over her reputation. If we're good girls, then by extension, so is she.

"They stole the necklace and hid it," Delia huffs. "They knew you'd search the room."

Mrs. Thomas blinks and her jaw clenches, and for a moment it appears that her soft mood has evaporated and, with it, any shred of patience or kindness. Delia steps back, expecting a lashing.

"Now, now," Mrs. Thomas coos. "You've got no proof that Adele and Lottie are the thieves, so my hands are tied. I'll list the item in the lost-property book, and if it doesn't turn up in a week, I'll make a report to Mr. Vincent."

Delia bites her tongue. Mrs. Thomas won't make the report this week or next week or the week after, because she's afraid to admit her failures to a white man. She'll write the items into the lost-property book, knowing full well that what's lost at Keziah is never found.

"Get washed and dressed for chapel and take your mind off earthly things," Mrs. Thomas says. "We have much to be thankful for this morning."

She drifts out of the dorm and back to her house, where she'll take the plastic rollers from her hair and style it into the elaborate victory rolls that were popular during WWII, but are way out of style in 1965.

Delia sucks air through her teeth to let us know what she thinks of Mrs. Thomas's handling of the situation, and I shut the door to Dead Lorraine's room in her face. It's no use talking. In Delia's mind, Lottie and I are liars and thieves. She's got the wrong girls.

Somebody stole Sandi's necklace. Not us.

19

Praise Be

After breakfast, we march from the dining hall to the chapel for a special Monday morning "give thanks" service. Boys sit on the right side of the aisle, and girls on the left. Senior teachers take the row closest to the pulpit, and junior teachers sit at the end of the student rows to make sure we behave. Mrs. Thomas, the Elephant, and Mr. Moses, the dorm master, sit in the very back row, where they get a good view of who passes notes and who whispers through the sermon.

Mr. Vincent takes the pulpit. "Let us pray," he says, and we bow our heads and thank the Lord for the branches that beat the flames and the water that doused the embers. We thank Him for our salvation. We thank Him for our lives.

Then Mr. Vincent says, "We are God's instruments, and last night God worked a miracle through Adele Joubert and

Lottie Diamond, two girls who embody the fighting spirt of Keziah Christian Academy. Together, they faced the fire and, with the Lord at their side, saved the school shop from burning down."

Heads turn in our direction, fingers point, and voices whisper, "That one's Adele, and that one's Lottie."

We are the center of attention, and I've imagined this moment a hundred times in my daydreams: me with windblown hair and glowing skin, every detail of my face made beautiful by the heat of envious glances. Instead, my heart lurches in my chest. I feel exposed. One of Mother's favorite expressions is "The higher a monkey climbs up the tree, the more you can see of its bum." I am that monkey. The more the others stare, the more I'm certain they can read my thoughts and see the sins of envy and greed written across my forehead.

Our rapid elevation to top girls is breathtaking and confusing. I've been high and fallen low, and, strangely enough, being low isn't so bad.

Mr. Vincent continues. "To acknowledge their bravery and courage, Lottie and Adele will receive a Golden Sun Award at a ceremony next Friday, and well deserved. Following the Golden Sun Awards, there'll be a special dinner to thank you all for the hard work that each of you did in keeping Keziah safe from the flames."

Excited voices break the silence. Golden Sun Awards are scarce, but nothing compared to a special dinner of roast beef with gravy and slices of corn bread smothered in butter. One of the younger boys claps his hands and says, "I want second helpings!" Everyone laughs . . . a rare sound in the chapel, where we usually try to maintain silence and holiness. Mr. Vincent and the senior teachers let the chatter die down on its own. After the fire, we have all earned the right to make a little noise, and two hours of rest and contemplation before lunch.

We sing the final hymn, "To God Be the Glory," and Lottie and I leave the chapel with little girls gathered around us like bridesmaids. It's sweet. We have pets, and it didn't cost me one piece of impago. Boys stare at us, and final-year girls, who are usually standoffish, acknowledge our existence with quick nods. If there's a place above the top students, then that's where Lottie and I now sit. Delia, Peaches, Natalie, and Sandi Cardoza smile stiff smiles and pretend they love us, too, but I see right through them.

"Sour grapes," Lottie says of them, and I understand their resentment. It's hard to fall all the way down to ordinary. It feels like failure: a small death that wipes out the old you and replaces her with a cheaper version. I can't find it in me to care, though. Despite our temporary status, Delia and the others still have pocket money and rich parents and pretty faces. I was pushed off the top shelf and forced to share Dead Lorraine's room with lower-shelf Lottie Diamond. I survived. Delia and her girls will recover soon enough.

●●●

Lottie and I find a pool of shade under an indoni tree with a distant view of the river. I open a bag of toffee chews and crack open *Jane Eyre* to where we left off reading in the early hours of this morning. I give the book to Lottie. She'll read too fast, as usual, but she saved my life last night, so it seems like giving her the first turn is the least I can do.

She clears her voice to start. "*I both wished and feared to see Mr. Rochester on the day which followed this sleepless night: I wanted to hear his voice again, yet feared to meet his eye. During the early part of the morning, I momentarily expected his coming; he was not in the frequent habit of entering the schoolroom, but he did step in for a few minutes sometimes, and I had the impression that he . . .*"

"Hey. Hey, Adele . . ." A voice interrupts Lottie's reading, and I look up in frustration. Surely, Rochester will come and see Jane soon—especially after she saved him from that mad servant with the mad laugh.

Beatrice and the other girl, Ramona, stand side by side in the circle of shade. I'm certain Delia has warned them against talking to us, and I'm curious to know why they are taking the risk anyway.

"Is it true?" Beatrice asks.

"Is what true?" I say.

"That you and Lottie started the fire behind the school shop."

Lottie and I exchange glances.

"Who told you that?" My shoulders go tight, and Lottie's fingers grip *Jane Eyre* so hard that I'm afraid she'll rip a page.

"No one." Beatrice bites her thumbnail. "It's just . . . it's just we heard that no way could the fire have spread from the bush near the sports field to the bush behind the classrooms. Unless . . ."

162

"The two of you started it by yourselves," Ramona says, finishing for Beatrice. "That's what we heard."

"From Delia?" Lottie demands, and the pets flush red.

I'm angry, too, but it's bad manners to ask Beatrice and Ramona to name names. Lottie is all fists. She doesn't know that this situation calls for soft words.

"Why did we start the fire?" I ask in the sweet voice I use when Father comes to visit and I'm the loveliest daughter in all of southern Africa. The girls hesitate, and I say, "Tell me what you heard. No hard feelings, hey."

"Well . . ." Beatrice looks over her shoulder, nervous at being caught talking to the enemy. "You've got nothing that makes you special, so you started the fire to get attention . . ."

"Plus," Ramona pipes in, "both your mothers are squint-eyed sluts who got no class and—"

"Shut up." Beatrice slaps Ramona's arm.

"It's all right." My smile does not waver. Inside, though, I am ashamed that I said similar things about Lottie's mother once. We gossiped about the dirty hut she lived in, the endless parade of men, and the irony that she, of all people, had a fair-skinned daughter who could pass for white. We also used to say that Lottie was more native than mixed-race, and wasn't that a shame? Joining in the gossip made me feel a part of the group; an almost diamond. I could, and often did, secretly list all the things that made me a top-shelf girl. Mother is unmarried but she has one man, not many. She lives in a nice house with carpets on the floor instead of a mud hut. She has paper money in her pocket instead of loose coins. In my mind, my mother was

163

better than Lottie's mother and, therefore, I was better than Lottie and all the other illegitimate students. I shudder now to remember the poison that came out of my mouth.

"How did we start the fire?" I shift the conversation to safer ground. "With a box of matches, or by rubbing sticks together to make a spark?"

Ramona and Beatrice shrug, and Beatrice says, "We didn't hear about that part."

I grab a handful of dried leaves and a stick from the ground near me and offer them to the girls. "Here," I say. "Start a fire with these. Go on. Try."

They stare at the leaves and the stick.

"What do we do?" Ramona asks.

"How do I know?" I say. "Do I look like a bushman?"

They giggle, and I push the leaves closer. "Go on. Take these to whoever told you that we started the fire and ask them to show you how we did it. And then you can show us."

The girls grab the fire starters and run in the direction of the senior dorm. I laugh to imagine Natalie—and, hand to Bible, it will be Natalie—sweating over the fire stick with her cheeks puffed as she tries to get a spark.

Lottie glares at me. She thinks we should retaliate against the girls for lying about us and our mothers, but she doesn't realize that we just struck a blow against them without raising a finger.

• • •

For one minute, we were lost in Jane's story, and now we're back in Swaziland and standing under the branches of a tree that Jane Eyre would find extraordinary and mysterious. Maybe it's just as well. My blisters sting, and I want to be all here when Jane and Rochester meet again.

"Let's go to the river," Lottie says, and we walk down a steep slope that leads to the sandy shore. I hold my blistered arm to my chest, the way a child holds an injured bird. I'm terrified that if I fall, the blisters will burst and fill with sand, and Mrs. McDonald, who keeps the school first-aid kit between the brown sugar and the allspice on her kitchen shelf, will give me an aspirin for the pain and a smelly homemade poultice, donated by one of the poor parents, to fight an infection.

"Does it hurt bad?" Lottie asks, and I'm embarrassed that she sees my weakness, but last night's aspirin has worn off, and Mrs. Thomas is stingy with her medicine. She hates to waste it on whining girls who are yet to make the acquaintance of true and deep pain.

"Not too bad." I stare across the river to the fields of wild grass, but no amount of soothing scenery can distract me from the pain.

"Put your arm in the water and keep it under for a while." Lottie snaps a leaf off an aloe plant and squeezes drops of pale juice to the surface.

I hold my arm in the powerful current, and the cold water numbs my skin and makes me shiver. When I've air-dried, Lottie rubs the cut aloe leaf over my blisters, and they shine in the sun. The aloe juice soothes the pain, and we walk along the bank of the river as swallows skim the water's surface. It's peaceful, and but for the charred leaves and ash speckling the rough sand, the fire might have happened a hundred years ago.

We walk for twenty minutes, hardly talking, till we reach a wide stretch of water with bulrushes growing along both sides. Hundreds of woven nests cling to the bulrush stalks and bend them closer to the water. Noisy weaverbirds come and go from their colony, and the air seems decorated with the song they sing.

"See that rock?" Lottie points farther downstream.

"I see it." The rock is flat and slender, and cuts the river almost in two. Rusted red streaks make a pattern on the surface. It's almost wide enough to lie on.

"Never go past that rock," Lottie says. "No matter what."

"Why?" I notice the unfamiliar hills and the strange trees around me. "Wait . . ." A thought jolts me from my walking daydream. "Are we out of bounds?"

"Not yet," Lottie says. "This side of the rock is Keziah, and the other side is Bosman's farm. Don't go there. Bosman and his sons have guns, and they hate mixed-race people . . . especially anyone from school."

"How do you know?"

Lottie sighs. "Take my word for it, Adele. Past that rock is trouble."

The land on the other side of the rock is serene and beautiful, and that's the problem, Mother says. One moment, it's sunshine and beauty and happy songs, and the next moment, you are in inescapable danger, hurt and scared. When God made Africa, she says, he cut his thumb by accident and bled all over the land, every hill and valley soaked. Now the earth is stained with blood. Now violence and beauty live together forever in Swaziland, she says. It can't be helped. It's how things are.

"You mentioned Bosman before." I suddenly remember when. "You think he's the one who gave Darnell the black eye."

"Ja, Bosman is the kind of mean that makes animals and children run for cover," Lottie says. "Me and Mama Khumalo have warned Darnell away from Bosman's farm, but Darnell doesn't listen to anyone. You saw him at the river, how impetuous he is."

Impetuous. Another Lottie word, meaning "acting or doing quickly and without thought or care."

"You think Darnell is in trouble," I say.

"Yes, I really do," Lottie sighs. "Darnell runs away and his daddy has him back at school in two or three days. He's never been gone this long. Ever. Something is wrong, Adele. I can feel it. That's why you have to steer clear of the rock and Bosman's farm. One missing person is enough."

Lottie is worried about me, and I'm touched that she cares enough to warn me away from danger.

"To the rock and no farther," I say. It's an easy promise to make. I will likely never come this way again, and certainly not alone. Lottie is the adventurous one. She lives on a native reserve out past Sisteki. The countryside is her backyard. Yet she somehow gets herself from the sticks to the Manzini bus station at the beginning of every term. That's how much being at Keziah means to her. Me? I'm a town girl. I prefer cracked pavements, and windows lit from the inside.

A dull clang breaks the weaverbirds' song, and we turn from the dividing rock. It's the lunch bell. We have to get to the dining hall before the head teacher says, "Let us bow our heads," or we'll miss lunch. No one gets to eat if they miss grace. Not even Golden Sun winners.

"Make tracks, Adele." Lottie runs hard to close the gap between our empty stomachs and food, and, driven by pride alone, I keep up. We climb the steep riverbank and gouge the soil with our fingers to find handholds and pull ourselves up. Red dirt stains our clothes and dusts our hair, but dirt is a short-term problem. If we miss the roast chicken legs and gravy, they'll be gone forever.

We make it to the dining hall in time. The big girls are already seated with their meals, and we push into line ahead of the little girls. They don't complain. Lottie and I get extra-large helpings, and vacant seats magically appear at the table when we turn to find a place.

Boys follow us with their eyes, and if this was a week ago, I would have happily walked the entire length of the dining hall to soak up the attention.

Delia smirks at us, and Peaches shakes her head like she's witnessed a fatal car accident. I see Lottie and me through their eyes: filthy shoes, sunburned faces, and clothes covered in red dust from our expedition. We are a disgrace.

Old Adele kept herself neat and sweet. New Adele is a mess and doesn't care. Fighting the fire and eating strawberry-cream biscuits with Lottie by candlelight has changed me. I live in a different country from the pretties now, a country where I hear my own thoughts and share my food, because eating and reading at the same time is wonderful.

I snag the seat next to Lottie and take a bite of my green beans. Lottie is oblivious to the stares. She falls on her roast chicken with soft *mmms* and licks her fingers. She's in heaven, her lips slick with gravy, which she laps up with her tongue.

Mother roasts a chicken on the maid's day off, and afterward Rian and I have a cup of sweet tea with a jam biscuit. But I'll never replicate the pleasure that Lottie finds in eating what I take for granted. She's got nothing, yet her experience of the world is richer than mine. It makes me jealous and annoyed and grateful, all at the same time.

Ramona, Beatrice, and the other pet, whose name I can't remember, sit directly across from us. They ought to know better. Delia, of course, notices their act of treason. She and Sandi are seated five down from us and across the table from Natalie and Peaches. Now, on top of stealing Sandi Cardoza's necklace and disgracing the female sex with our dirty clothes and flyaway hair, we have also let their pets sit with us. Delia's attention is so intense that even Lottie feels it.

"Should we move?" she says through a mouthful of mashed potatoes.

"No. If we move, we'll insult the girls who are already here. We have to stay. Might as well make the best of it."

"How do we do that?"

"Watch." I ignore the pets and smile at the younger girl sitting next to me. I ask her name and what does she do at home on a Sunday? Church and then a visit to Grandma? "Lovely. Me too." That's a lie, but no harm done. Mother hasn't been to church since she got pregnant with me, but Nuttie, my small lunch companion, doesn't know that. Lottie copies me, and soon we know who lives with their mother and father, who loves English and hates math, and who likes ice cream. Everybody, it turns out.

"We got the sack," Beatrice blurts out during a lull in the conversation.

"All of us," Ramona says.

"What happened?" I drop my voice low. The pretties are close enough to hear and it's better to keep any conversation we have about them private. I don't want to give Delia and the others ammunition to use against the pets later.

"We took the leaves and the stick to the dorm, and Natalie tried to make a fire," Beatrice says in a loud whisper. "She tried and tried, and it was funny to see her cheeks puffed out, so we laughed. I mean, you'd have laughed, too, but Natalie didn't like it. We each got a smack, and then Natalie told us to leave and don't come back, and it's a shame, because we had it good and then we spoiled it."

Oh, Natalie. Of course she was the one who tried to make fire with a stick. Just like I guessed she would when I sent the pets back to the pretties with the fire-making kit. Natalie's under the impression that being popular also makes her clever, which she is not.

"Natalie's not the boss," I say. "Wait a day or two and pretend that nothing has changed. They'll take you back."

There's a limited amount of smart little girls to choose from, and Ramona and her friends are already trained. They'll be fine.

Beatrice leans across the table with bright eyes. More news.

Any pet worth their salt has the latest gossip memorized and ready to spill.

"Guess what?" she whispers. "Sandi Cardoza found her necklace. It was hidden in her underwear drawer all along. She put it there before the fire and then forgot about it."

Of course . . . The mistake makes perfect sense. Drama is the glue that holds Delia and her circle together. Stolen pets and missing necklaces and envious lower-class students scheming against them out of pure spite and envy: those outside threats are what keep the group together. They live to be offended and, not so long ago, so did I.

"Well . . ." Lottie gnaws her chicken bone and sucks out the marrow, the way Mother does when Father is in Johannesburg and too far away to witness her country ways. "At least I got my undies back."

I laugh. What she said is funny, and, instead of walking over to Delia and pushing her face into her mashed potatoes to get her back for falsely accusing us of stealing, Lottie finishes her lunch.

20

The Search

On Tuesday morning, the graduating girls let us into the front of the bathroom line, and the Elephant and Mrs. Thomas sail past us during the morning inspection. Afterward, a troop of little girls carry our textbooks from classroom to classroom. Boys whisper when we draw near, and even Mr. Newman, the science teacher from Pietermaritzburg who stands too close to check your notes, keeps the sharp end of his ruler away from us.

The attention is exhilarating and unrelenting. It is tiring too. By morning teatime, I'm exhausted. Being popular is a drain. I want the Golden Sun ceremony over with so Lottie and I can go back to being normal, unremarkable us.

"Walk to the cattle grids by the chapel?" Lottie asks after Scripture class. Being the center of attention is extra hard for her. She's used to the freedom of anonymity, and now everyone looks at her all the time.

We split off from the group of little girls who beg to walk with us to the chapel. The Swazi laborer digging a ditch beyond the cattle grid chants a work song. The sky is enormous and blue, and dotted with clouds. We take in the scent of Mrs. Vincent's garden: dark earth, cut grass, and, of course, roses. The smell, the sky, Lottie standing beside me, and the rhythm of the workman's shovel in the dirt . . . I am present in my own skin, full of the world, as if all of it is inside me.

A car turns off the main road, and the sound of the engine interrupts the peace. It's Mr. Moses's white Volkswagen Beetle with the silver rack on the roof for when he goes camping during the holidays. Cars are a rare sight on school roads, and it's the custom for drivers to smile and wave—or, better yet, beep their horn to greet the students. Mr. Moses does neither. He parks in front of the Vincents' house, opens the door, and takes the stairs two at a time, which is against the rules for students. Mr. Moses is in a hurry.

"Something's wrong," Lottie says when Mr. Vincent opens the door and Mr. Moses shakes his head no before Mr. Vincent speaks a word. The men huddle and talk in whispers, and the topic of their conversation comes to me in capital letters.

My heart drums. "They're talking about Darnell Parns. He's been gone a week today."

Lottie nibbles her bottom lip. "It might be that Darnell's father is planting the fields late. He needs Darnell's help, and that's why he hasn't brought Darnell back to school."

When the summer rains fall, the *Swazi Times* prints a "plow now" roster for each region in the country. I'm a city girl but I take notice of what happens around me. For example, Mrs. But-ton, who grew up in the shadow of the Lebombo Mountains, loves to garden. She plants her corn and melons in September, and Mother throws tomato seeds out of the kitchen window in early November.

Lottie lives in the sticks and dreams of one day owning a farm with trees for the birds and fields for the wild animals. She knows explaining Darnell's disappearance with late planting is wishful thinking.

"Farmwork for sure," I say in my "sunny voice," and pre-tend that Lottie is right. Late planting is the reason that Dar-nell's daddy hasn't dragged him back to school on his tractor. But my heart's not in it, and I add, "Maybe . . . um . . ."

"Maybe what, Adele?" Lottie snaps, and turns on me. "For once in your life, say what's on your mind instead of what you think other people want to hear. Go on. Try it!"

Her attack lands a blow, and I hit her back with, "It's the first week of February, Lottie! The fields are already planted. No way is Mr. Parns so far behind."

"Idle speculation, Adele." She uses her superior vocabulary to put me in my place. "You don't know anything for sure."

"And neither do you, Miss Oxford Dictionary!"

She leans in with balled fists and glazed blue eyes, spoiling for a fight. We were close, but once we've exchanged blows we'll be enemies, and that's a shame because all I did was speak my mind when she told me to. My scalp tingles, anticipating a vicious tug by the roots, a favorite Lottie move.

Instead of brawling, we stand face-to-face, and the heat goes out of the moment. Lottie's lips quiver, and I understand why she yelled at me. She's angry because she's scared that Mr. Moses is talking to Mr. Vincent about Darnell and the news is bad.

"You're right," I say. "I talked out of turn." Lottie being scared makes me scared, too, so I take back my rash words. "Mr. Parns might be planting his fields late, and I have no idea where Mr. Moses has come from or where he's been."

Lottie accepts my semi-apology with a quick nod, and we stand in awkward silence. Neither one of us knows what to say next.

"Adele Joubert. Lottie Diamond." Mrs. Vincent's voice breaks the quiet, and we turn to face the verandah. "Please tell Mrs. Thomas to gather the senior girls in the quadrangle. Go now. Quickly."

"Yes, Mrs. Vincent," we answer in unison, and hurry in the direction of the cement-brick house guarded by Socks the cat and a dry lavender hedge. On the way, we pass a group of little girls playing pickup sticks in the vacant lot beside the garden sheds, and a group of big girls gossiping in the shade of a jacaranda tree. Delia stares daggers at us, and Peaches loops her arm around Sandi Cardoza's waist to prove how close they are. The necklace glitters around Sandi's neck, and I shake my head with a wry smile.

Their "for show" behavior makes them look silly in my eyes. They are caught up with small dramas: which hair straightener works best, which boy is the most handsome, and how short is too short for a summer skirt? That was me before Lottie's straight talk about sad mothers and the future. Lottie and I have hit deeper ground, and our being chosen for an urgent mission by Mrs. Vincent feels right.

"It's true what you said." Lottie knocks on Mrs. Thomas's door. "The planting is done. Darnell should be back by now."

● ● ●

Male and female senior students form a line that stretches from Miss December's probationary hut to the sports field on the far side of the boys' dormitories. They stand an arm's length apart to make a human chain, and wait for Mr. Moses to blow his whistle to start the search.

"Hurry . . ." Lottie drags me to the far end of the line. On our left is a stand of trees and on our right, a tall boy with sweat patches under his armpits. A whistle blows, and, as instructed, we comb through the land with slow steps and call out, "Darnell. Darnell. Darnell."

The trees on our left grow thick, and Lottie edges under the branches and away from the main search party. I catch up to her, annoyed at how easily she is able to pull me off the normal path.

"Where are you going?"

"To find Darnell." She weaves through the grove, marking her own course. The call "Darnell, Darnell" grows faint in the distance, and Lottie grunts in annoyance. "He won't come just because he's called. He hates school. The noise will make him hide deeper."

"What then?"

"We're going to search a place I don't want to go."

• • •

Behind a barrier of dried branches is a cave, and inside the cave is a primitive home decorated with bleached animal skulls, and chalk pictures of guns and knives and naked girls with large breasts and unruly pubic hair. "Raise Hell" is written above the pictures, and the air inside the snug space stinks of sweat, wood-fire smoke, and pee.

I cup my palm over my mouth to stop from gagging. The cave disgusts and fascinates me. Boys, in greater number than Darnell Parns, found this hideaway and furnished it with a long log to sit on and a dug-out fire pit filled with ash and the bones of tiny birds. A stack of canned food and a metal can opener rest against a wall, no doubt stolen from boys like Rian, who are too small or weak to defend themselves.

"No Darnell." I slowly circle the cave, drawn to the rude pictures and the damp section of wall where boys pee. It really is foul, and we ought to leave immediately. "Did he tell you about his place?"

"The boys who use this cave buy their home-brewed beer from Mama Khumalo. I followed them one day, just to see where they'd end up. They disappeared into the hillside and I knew, for sure, that there was a cave hidden somewhere."

"You were right," I say and step around a pile of bloody chicken feathers. What the boys did to the chicken, I do not want to know.

"Look here." Lottie wanders over to a hand-drawn map on the back wall. Father says that maps help us make sense of the world. They tell us where we are and which direction to go in to find what we're looking for. If you're lost, a map can save your life.

"That's Keziah." I recognize the square shapes that represent the chapel, the classrooms, and the girls' and boys' dormitories. Trees drawn with stuck-out branches mark the orchard and the bush that grows down to the river.

"And that's Mama Khumalo's hut," Lottie says. Of course, she knows what lies beyond the school boundaries better than I do.

"What do these mean?" A dozen white crosses are scattered across the map at odd intervals and make no sense to me. Lottie tilts her head and squints. She overlays her mental map of the lazy river bends and the blue distant hills and, after a moment, her eyes go bright.

"I get it. The white crosses are food." She jabs a mark near Mama Khumalo's hut. "That's a fig tree, and these baby crosses here are a stand of bananas right on the border of Bosman's farm. The fruit is still green, but in a few weeks it'll be good to eat."

"And the red line around the bananas?"

"A warning," she says. "Bosman. He has guns, and his three sons have guns, like I told you. It's better to stay away from him and his farm."

"Oh . . ." Hunger makes people do strange things. One day, one of the poor boys who helped set up the cave might ignore the red warning lines and risk an encounter with Bosman and his sons to grab a handful of ripe bananas. "Let's go."

I hurry to the entrance, ashamed to remember tiny Eoin Colfey, with his shaved head and snotty nose. Eoin, Alan Brownlow, Janice Pistorius, and Melody Pine come from the Fairview Orphanage, a long concrete building with a tin roof weighed down by bricks and car tires. Mr. and Mrs. Vincent raise money from overseas to cover the cost of their education, because Fairview orphans have no parents to pay their school fees and no parents who wish to claim them. No-fee students get smaller portions of food. Their stomachs are always empty, and that's not how things should be. I wish there was a way to make things different.

"Follow me." Lottie ducks through the low entrance and stands awhile to breathe the clean air. The cave is on a high ridge, and far below it is the river. A line of girls and boys wades through the water, calling out, "Darnell, Darnell" in flat voices; the novelty of searching for him is already starting to wear off. Soon, one of the bad boys—Lazy-Eye Matthew or Richard D, who lives with his uncle in Manzini and rides his rusted-out bicycle from one end of town to the other with a slingshot stuck in the waistband of his shorts—one of them will change Darnell to Dumbbell or Bumsmell, and the others will laugh.

"Should we catch up with them?" I block the entrance to the cave with the dried branches.

Lottie says, "There's one more place that Darnell might be."

Of course there is.

21

The Village

A group of grass huts sits in a stony field, and stray goats wander across our path. Lottie is sure-footed and confident where I am nervous and slow. As we approach the native compound, my bravery deserts me. We walk up a slope into the sun, and the silhouettes of ramshackle huts rise against the sky. A tall boy lopes across the path. A dog follows him, stops, turns to bark at us, then trots away. It was a mistake to accompany Lottie on her personal search for Darnell, but I will not give in to fear. I realize something about me is different since the fire.

Don't stray from the road, Mother warns me when we leave our house in Manzini, and I never have. Till now.

"That's Mama Khumalo's place." Lottie jerks her chin in the direction of a hut built in a clearing. A tall, dark-skinned Swazi woman with angular features and a wide, smiling mouth stirs a pot of maize beer in the dirt yard. She greets Lottie in a familiar way and points to a grass mat under the shade of a corrugated iron lean-to attached to the hut. The lean-to is made from rusted iron sheets and wooden planks held together with mud.

A group of Swazi children dressed in traditional animal skins and cast-off Western clothing stand outside the stones that mark the boundaries of Mama's yard. They point and whisper at the stranger in their village: me. Lottie they already know. Far off in the distance, a woman sings in a field, and the sound tugs at my insides. The song reminds me of a favorite doll that I lost on the trek home from the markets in Manzini when I was little.

Mama beams at Lottie, and they talk in Zulu, easy in each other's company. I sit with my legs tucked to the side, as Lottie instructed, and wonder what they're saying. I know just enough Zulu to tell the maid to wash the dishes and scrub the floor, but even then, I mime the actions so she understands.

"Darnell comes and goes from the village, but Mama hasn't seen him for days." Lottie translates Mama's words into English for me. "He's not here."

Mama leans closer and becomes animated. She makes the shape of a gun with her fingers and pulls the trigger. Boom. One of the children, a girl with cornrowed hair, clutches her chest and falls to the ground, where she twitches her arms and legs while the other children shriek with laughter. Mama smiles, amused by their antics.

"There was trouble on Bosman's farm last night," Lottie tells me after the girl gets up and dusts herself off. "Mama doesn't know what started it, but they heard a gunshot blast and the dogs barked all night. She's not worried for Darnell. Bosman and his sons shoot at shadows and Darnell knows every inch of these hills so he's probably fine. We should go back to school, where it's safe. She says to stay away from Bosman's farm."

Good advice. It's time to rejoin the main search before Mr. Moses discovers us missing and sends out a second wave of students to call our names into the wind.

"That's that." I tell Lottie. "Time to go back."

"We can't pick up and leave the moment we get what we want!" My suggestion horrifies her, as does my ignorance of the niceties of Swazi society. "It's bad manners. We have to stay and talk. Take our time."

Mother says that our maid works on "Swazi time," which has no relation to the chime of the hours on our clock in the lounge room. Swazi time is fluid. It shifts and flows, and often stops altogether. That's why ordinary tasks take so long. It's not the maid's fault, Mother says. It's how life unfolds in the country.

"All right . . ." I tuck my legs close to my bottom so the soles of my feet don't face Mama, which, Lottie earlier explained, would be an insult that implies the person sitting across the mat from me is a patch of dirt for me to walk over.

Mama Khumalo stares at me a long time, and I smile to show that I'm comfortable in her presence and not a little bit afraid of being here. She makes a comment, and Lottie throws me a sharp look.

"What is it?" I ask.

"She says you have your mother's eyes," Lottie says.

Mama adds something else, and Lottie translates again: "A darker green but the same shape."

"What?" I either misheard Lottie or she got the translation wrong. Even Lottie is surprised. "How does she know my mother?"

Lottie relays my question, and I hold my breath while I wait for the answer. Lottie and Mama have an animated exchange. Then Lottie turns to me.

"Your mother's mother was Agnes Dlamini from near the 'Cross of Nazareth' school," Lottie tells me. "Your grandmother and Mama Khumalo's mother were cousins. You're related!"

Years of training my face to hold the right expression fail me. The muscles in my face go slack. Heat stings my cheeks, and the tension in my throat makes it difficult to swallow. I'm shocked, and it shows. Mother is, in her own way, as mysterious to me as Father. I have never heard the name Agnes Dlamini before in my life.

"My grandmother died a long time ago," I say. Then I think about the information parceled out to me in isolated fragments over sixteen years: throwaway sentences on long walks into town, vague references to *the place I was born*, and how *nothing is too big a word to describe how little we had*, Adele. Our mixed blood was never a secret, but whenever I showed an interest in digging up our family history, Mother would say, *My parents are dead, Adele. There's nothing left to tell.* Eventually, I stopped asking. Mother's silence kept me silent.

"Mama says, one day your granny Agnes was hoeing the

cornfields, and the next day she was too sick to get out of bed. Your mother paid a doctor from the Norwegian hospital in Mahamba to come to the hut, but it was too late. That was fourteen years ago." Lottie plucks at the hem of her school uniform, uncomfortable with giving me my own family history. "You were at your grandmother's funeral."

That can't be true. Mother would have said. I would have remembered. I am surprised to feel tears sting my eyes.

Mama Khumalo shakes her head and makes a soft sound of apology for causing me distress. She can't have imagined the depth of my ignorance, the ocean of not knowing that she's thrown me into without warning.

Mama continues her story, and Lottie tells me, "She says she's sorry. Of course you don't remember . . . You were young when Granny Agnes died, and your mother never returned to visit after the funeral. She chose to leave her cousins and the land. Now you are here, and it makes her happy."

Mama is pleased to see me, a long-lost relative, but I'm still reeling. Mother, Mummy . . . how many secrets have you hidden from me? How many memories have you kept bottled inside you? And why?

"Are you all right?" Lottie asks, and it takes a long moment for me to answer.

Polite Adele finds me. I smile and say, "I'm fine. I'm fine, really. I'm just . . . Tell Mama that I didn't know about the funeral or Granny Agnes. Mother doesn't talk about the past."

Lottie speaks for me and then gives me back Mama's words. "She wants to know . . . is your mother still beautiful?"

184

"She is," I say. "And she sings beautifully."

Mama nods yes—she remembers Mother's lovely voice—and I see in my mind's eye a vision of my mother, young and barefoot under the same bright sky I sit under now. Mother, who now walks in high heels and wears short skirts, belongs to this valley and these hills, to this mat pulled into the shade of a lean-to.

If I'd listened to my mother and stayed inside Keziah's boundaries, her secrets would have remained hidden. Perhaps that's why she warned me to never stray from the marked roads. I know a secret now, and the knowledge has shifted something deep inside of me.

"Is your mother well?" Mama asks through Lottie.

She's done well, I want to say. We have carpet on the floors, and curtains on the windows, and when the bills come due, Mother has the money to pay them. No begging the landlord for an extension or fighting the hypermarket for a discount. When Father visits us, he walks through the front door as if he made promises to Mother in front of a preacher. That's why the church ladies hate her. She sins boldly, and if those matrons "closer to the Lord" throw her a sour look across the pavement in town, she tells them to their faces, *See what I have? Two lovely children and a man who comes back to me rain or shine. God doesn't take sides. He loves you and me the same.*

Instead of saying all that, which is complicated, I tell Mama Khumalo that, "Mother lives well."

That makes Mama happy, and my smile relaxes, becomes more natural. Mother left her Swazi family behind, but Mama is, I think, proud of her cousin's rise from deep in the country to the big town.

"Of course, yes," Lottie says, translating. "Mbali always had her eyes on the hills and what lay beyond them. And by God's good grace she has arrived safe at that other place."

"Mbali?"

"It means 'flower.' That was your mother's Swazi name."

Manzini is eighty miles or so from where we sit in the shade, but the journey from a grass hut to a house with running water and porcelain angels on the shelf is much greater than any number of miles on a map. Some days, when the sun hides behind the clouds, Mother, who goes by the English name Rose, stays in bed till afternoon. Now I think I know why. How hard must the journey have been from here to there?

"Mama has oranges." Lottie's happy to change the subject. "Will you stay a while and eat with her?"

"Of course." Seen from inside the window of a car or bus, Swazi compounds are remote, alien places that I thought I'd never visit and, if God be good, never eat a single mouthful of food in because breaking bread with native Swazis is the fastest way to backslide into blackness. Now I am here, face-to-face with the ghost of my mother's past, and the new information has thrown me off balance.

"I didn't know. About your grandmother." Lottie apologizes when Mama disappears into her hut to fetch the oranges. The children on the edge of the yard sense the appearance of food and inch closer.

"I didn't know about her either," I say, and Lottie laughs.

It's funny. Me, stumbling into a Swazi relative two miles from a school that only enrolls mixed-race children who refuse to stand up for natives on the bus. Swaziland, a speck on the map of the British Empire, is not one country, but many, and even I have to laugh at how neatly each world excludes the other.

"Here." Mama Khumalo places a bowl of oranges in front of us, and a plate of "fat cakes," glistening balls of deep-fried dough that children, including me, love to devour. "Eat."

I fall on a fat cake: a favorite food of bus drivers and maids, and white ladies with skinny lips and thick waists. Food is a bridge between worlds: it connects all Swazis. The fat cake is gone in two bites, and I lick my fingers, satisfied. Lottie peels an orange and asks Mama a question. Mama's answer—a brisk nod—brings the children running to the mat.

They swarm over us, hands out for pieces of orange and greasy fat cakes. A girl reaches over my shoulder, her warm body pressed against my back. Two boys slot between Lottie and me while another leans a hip against Lottie's arm. The children eat and laugh, and brush against us like eels. Together, we are one hungry animal with speckled brown, black, and white skin.

Mother left this closeness behind and I wonder if she's tried to reproduce it in her own small way with Rian and me. When I'm home for the holidays, she combs and braids my hair every morning and tucks Rian and me into our beds every night. The tips of her fingers trace the line of an eyebrow and the tip of a nose before she kisses us good night. And when Father visits, she straightens his collar and keeps

187

a hand on his knee or brushed lightly against his shoulder—
always in physical contact.

In the morning, Rian and I bring them breakfast in bed and
climb under the warm sheets with them. Our clumsy movements lap the milk tea over the sides of the mugs and spill sugar
from the bowl. Mother says that Father loves the way we all
squash in together, with crumbs on the blankets and jammy
fingerprints on the cutlery.

Now, sitting in Mama Khumalo's crowded yard, I realize
that our family breakfasts in bed might be the closest thing that
mother has to being back in her village.

In Manzini, she has Rian and me and the weekly sound of
Father's voice on the end of the long-distance telephone line.
Here, in the bush, she was part of a tribe.

But it's the wrong tribe if you live in Swaziland.

22

Deep Valley

Covered in curious children and filled with fat cakes and oranges, I momentarily forget about Darnell and the shotgun blast on a strange man's farm. This is my first proper visit to a Swazi village, and Mother would die to see my glorious backslide from an almost-European girl to a very-nearly-Swazi girl. I imagine Mother sprawled in the shade of the lean-to. My mother . . . who ate cold porridge with her fingers and washed in rivers. My mother . . . who now brings light into our house with the flick of a switch.

"We can go now," Lottie says when the last piece of orange is gone and the afternoon sun is high overhead. "If we get into trouble, we'll say that we got lost."

"All right." No one will believe that Lottie Diamond got lost in the bush, but they'll believe it of Adele Joubert, who hates flies and mud, and always stays on the path.

The children run to their games, and Mama holds both my hands in hers. I look at where we touch, her skin dark and mine lighter.

"Hamba kahle." *Go well*, she says in Zulu, and I mumble, "Sala kahle, Mama," which means "Stay well," and is one of the few non-English expressions that I'm able to speak with any confidence.

Lottie takes us on a different path out of the village, and steep hills bank against the horizon in every direction. I swear that we came from the far side of the cornfields.

"School's the other way, isn't it?"

"This is a shortcut." Lottie veers right onto an overgrown path that's two hands wide. I hesitate, and she grins at me over her shoulder. "Trust me, Adele. We'll be back at Keziah in fifteen minutes."

I don't trust her. That's the problem. She lacks my inbred fear of what might be hiding behind the rocks and in the tall grass. The land dips sharply, and I slip and slide behind Lottie, who is, like Darnell, part mountain goat. Stones kick from under my shoes, and the sun beats down on our heads. I keep my eyes on the ground, careful of snake holes and grass roots that might trip me and send me rolling down the incline into a narrow gorge. Time ticks by, and I lose track of it.

"Almost there," Lottie says. I don't believe her. We're in the boonies.

The land evens out, and a grove of banana plants heavy with bunches of green fruit appears ahead of us. Lottie slips into the shade of the banana field and drops into a crouch. My jaw goes slack. I suddenly know exactly where we are. From the map. We are in danger.

"Get out," I snap. "Get out of there right now!"

"Shh . . . the whole valley will hear you squealing." Lottie holds out her hand to me like we're at a church picnic and she has the only shady spot left for us to sit in. "Quick, before someone sees you."

I'm furious. Mama said that Darnell knows every inch of these hills and that he is probably fine. She told us to stay away from Bosman's farm. The red lines on the food map in the cave also warned us, yet here we are, exactly where we are not supposed to be. Typical Lottie. And typical Adele . . . always the follower, never the leader. Just like when I was in Delia's group. I am ignorant and gullible, and other choice words that Lottie read aloud to me from *The Oxford Dictionary*.

"Come on, *Adele*." She pours sugar on my name. "It's safer in here. We won't stay long. Just a quick look for Darnell. Cross my heart."

I snort in disbelief. What a liar.

"And what happens if we find that Bosman has shot Darnell? Have you thought about that?"

"We tell Mr. Vincent and Mr. Vincent will call the police constable."

"That is the stupidest plan in the world! I'm going back to school right this minute. I'll tell Mr. Vincent about the gun-shot blast and he'll get the constable to check Bosman's farm. You can do what you like." I turn and show her my back, which is held stiff and tall in an effort to reclaim my dignity. Enough is enough. There are limits to my stupidity. Lottie Diamond can stay and reap the whirlwind of her own mischief. One of the children from the village will show me the fast way back to Keziah.

I take quick steps on the craggy path, furious at Lottie and furious at myself. New Adele is brave but not foolish. Grass roots catch my right shoe, and I throw my arms out to keep my balance. Too late. The sky tilts at a strange angle and I tumble off the path and down the incline. The world spins in violent circles. Dirt. Mountains. Bright-orange aloe flowers. Yellowed grass. I flip head over heels and come to a hard and painful stop. I taste blood in my mouth.

•••

It hurts to breathe, to move, to do anything but stare up at the perfect blue sky above me. No clouds or wind break the stillness of the valley floor. It is eerily quiet. Then noises return. The thump of my heartbeat. A cricket's chirp. Birdsong and the muffled sound of Lottie calling my name from far away.

"Adele. Adele. Say something, Adele."

My back aches, and I pray to heaven.

Please, Jesus. Let me be whole or walk with a limp, but no more than that. I beg you.

Mrs. Button's niece, Charlotte Button, survived a head-on collision outside of Lavumisa two years ago. A miracle, the preacher said, except that now Charlotte's a cripple. Now Charlotte sits on the front porch of her daddy's house in her wheelchair and watches people walk to wherever their two legs wish to carry them. Mother has Rian and his asthma to take care of. I'd rather die than add to her burden.

Stay with me, Jesus. The sky remains still, pale blue, and empty. Mother is right. Jesus is in London, working on more important matters.

I turn my head from one side to the other, anticipating a cracking sound, or worse still, no movement at all. The sun beats down. Sweat stings my eyes. I'm in a narrow valley, surrounded by wild grass and smooth stones. Aloes stand sentinel on the ridge above me. My tongue swells in my mouth, but I'm alive: hurt, but all here.

I sigh with relief, and there in the dirt is one of my shoes. It must have come off when I fell from the path and hit the ground. Except . . . I blink into the hazy light. The shoe is wrong. It's two sizes too big, and the leather is scuffed and worn. My shoes are brand-new from the Bata shoe store. I wiggle my toes and feel the new leather stretch against them. That shoe is not mine.

"Adele. Hold still," Lottie calls. "I'm coming."

I sit up slowly and realize that the shoe is attached to a foot, and the foot is attached to a pale leg with an ugly blue bruise on the right knee. Pressure builds in my throat. My mouth opens, and a long scream comes out. Flies scatter from Darnell's face, and my scream goes on and on, till the valley echoes with the sound of my terror.

"Shh, Adele." Lottie arrives and covers my mouth with her hand. "It's all right. I'm here now."

I try to shake her off, but she holds me down with a fierce expression. "Not all right." My muffled words escape from between her fingers. "Darnell. Over there."

"I see him, Adele," she says. "I see him."

"He's . . . he's . . ."

"I know." Lottie's voice is still and flat. "We need to get Mr. Vincent and Mr. Moses, but first you have to be quiet. Remember where we are."

On a crazy white man's farm. Or on the edge of it. I don't know.

"Are you ready?" She waits for me to catch my breath and slowly lifts her hand from my mouth. The pressure inside my throat builds, and I press it down inside my body. I keep it there.

"We have to go and find help." Lottie pulls me to my feet, and Darnell is close enough for me to reach out and touch. I try not to look, but the stillness of his limbs and the strange way his eyes reflect the sky breaks my heart.

Lottie makes a soft sound, and the pressure inside me moves from my throat to behind my eyeballs. Tears roll down my face, and I cry in small, hard sobs.

"Stop," Lottie says. "Crying won't bring him back."

"It's just . . . he reminds me of when Rian is sick and there's nothing we can do to help him. Only be here."

What I say is silly. Rian is clever and fits wood-block puzzles together for the fun of it. Darnell was simpleminded and always behind. They both hated school, but Rian escaped. He got away. Now Darnell is stuck on the border of Keziah forever, and that makes me beyond sad.

194

"Come." Lottie grabs my hand and hauls me up the steep rise. She forgets that I'm hurt, and I think that's because she's hurt too—just in places I can't see. That wall inside her is strong, and with Darnell dead on the ground, she's focused on what to do next. "We'll go back to the village. Mama will send a runner to Keziah with the news. Mr. Vincent will need two or three senior boys to help bring up the body."

We reach the top of the rise, damp with sweat and puffing for breath. I wipe away tears, embarrassed that Lottie, who knew Darnell and was his friend, hasn't leaked a single tear.

"Hey . . ." A voice calls from the mountainside, drawn by my endless scream. It's the little girl who pretended to fall over dead from Mama's pretend gun. She waves at us and shouts a question in Zulu, afraid to come closer.

Lottie answers the girl, and I make my own translation. *Dead boy. Go to the school. Bring the white man. Tell him to bring others.*

The girl disappears, and I go to follow her. Lottie grabs my arm and holds on. "We can't leave Darnell alone," she says. "We have to stay with him and tell him where he is and what's going to happen. If we don't, his spirit will stay trapped here forever."

"But you said there are no spirits. Just bones in the ground."

"We can't leave him, Adele. He needs us."

"But he's dead . . ."

"Go then." Lottie waves me off with a flick of her hand. "I don't need you to stay with me. I'm all right by myself."

Except that she's not. The muscles in her neck strain against her skin, and her eyes have the glazed blue expression that signals her rising temper and fear. I spoke half a dozen words to Darnell when he was alive. But he was Lottie's friend, and Lottie is the only friend I have left at Keziah. I won't leave her crouched all alone, behind that wall of hers.

"Do we have to go down there?" I pray that she'll say no. From the ridge, Darnell's body is a dark smudge in the landscape, and that's how I prefer it.

Lottie nods and mumbles, "Once more unto the breach, dear friends. Once more," and I believe that she has gone mad.

• • •

Lottie leads the way back to Darnell, and I shuffle after her, scared of falling off the path again and terrified of what's waiting to greet us at the bottom. Wind stirs the wild grass, and a cloud of butterflies lifts into the air. Yellow circles on their purple wings shimmer in the afternoon light. I grip my hands into fists. It's almost insulting to see such extravagant beauty so close to a dead boy's body.

"Darnell," Lottie calls as we approach where he lies. "It's Lo-Lo from school. I'm going to stay with you till Mr. Vincent and the others come and get you."

Lottie turns around and sees me nibbling my bottom lip, and she glares at me, having already explained what we have to do and why we have to do it. Darnell, she said, hasn't been dead very long, and he is confused by the sudden change. Lottie's mother has taught her that we must keep his spirit calm so that when the time comes, he'll leave this place with us.

We arrive at the body. Darnell lies spread out on the ground, his uniform dirty, faceup. My stomach is in knots.

Lottie kneels beside him and tries to close his eyelids. All by themselves, his eyes half open again, to stare at nothing.

"Hello, Darnell. It's me. Adi. You showed me the snake skin, remember? It was lovely and . . ." My voice fails. I swallow a lump in my throat and crouch opposite Lottie with Darnell between us. Two girls at the bottom of a hill, speaking to the dead. What we're doing is insane. Maybe even unchristian.

"It's a beautiful day," Lottie tells him. "The sun is bright, and the air is fresh. You picked a nice place to rest for . . ."

She stops to grab a breath, and I realize that every word she speaks is painful for her but she stays strong for Darnell, she holds her tears back for Darnell, for the sake of keeping his spirit safe from harm. African beliefs mean nothing to me, but Lottie believes, so I take up where she left off.

"And butterflies," I add. "Clouds of purple butterflies with yellow circles are all around us. If you listen carefully, you can hear their wings beating and the birds singing in the brush."

Darnell's mouth is slightly opened, and for a moment, I think that he might sit up and speak to us. Contrary to what the old aunties say after every open-coffin viewing, Darnell does not look as if he's fallen asleep. He looks startled, as if he had other plans and can't believe how he's landed in the grass looking at the sky. The faded bruise under his eye, for some reason, makes my heart ache.

"The valley's nice, but you can't stay here," Lottie says.

"Your father is waiting for you to come home, and your mother's waiting for you in heaven. When we take your body, your spirit has to come with us all the way back to your daddy's farm. I promise we'll get you there, safe. All right?"

Lottie falls silent. I count to thirty, half a minute gone, and I tell Darnell about the aloe plants and the smooth white stones scattered across the ground; the sun above us; and the heat. I talk *to* Darnell, but I talk *for* Lottie—to lighten her sorrow.

We crouch together next to the body. Lottie starts to cry softly. I put my hand on her shoulder. It's not enough. I shift position and put both my arms around her, and her body shakes with grief. I feel her tears on my neck.

"Oh, Darnell . . ." Lottie says.

23

I Know You

It takes Mr. Vincent, Mr. Moses, and two senior boys an hour to haul Darnell's body up the slope to the where the land is flat. The stand of green bananas is below us, and all around is dry grass and a wide, flat sky. Mountains loom in the distance. We lay Darnell in the shade of a marbled rock, and Lottie and I go and sit under a scrawny indoni tree. After two hours of close contact with the corpse, I'm glad of the break. Grateful for the silence. The childish injuries on Darnell's body still tear at my heart: the scrape on his knee, two broken fingernails, and the bruise under his eye. Small hurts. Easy to fix. Death can't be fixed.

Mr. Vincent sends Gordon Number One and Barnabas Phillips to see if Mrs. Vincent is back from picking up supplies in Howard's Halt. "Tell her to put sheets and a blanket in the back of the pickup truck, and to park in the field just inside the Bosman farm," he says. "I don't care whose land she has to cross to do it."

"Yes, sir." Barnabas and Gordon take off at a sprint, and I think tonight Gordon Number One will visit Miss December's probationary hut to try and forget the weight of Darnell's body pressed to his shoulder and the low murmur of Lottie Diamond's voice whispering comfort to the dead.

Lottie and I huddle in the thin shade and wait for Mrs. Vincent to arrive. I curl my hands in my lap to stop them from shaking. Outside I'm calm, but inside I'm filled with dread. No matter how many times Lottie and I shower or douse ourselves in talcum powder, the stink of death will stay with us.

A faint machine noise comes from far off and Lottie sits up straight. She peers across the field.

"What is it?" I ask. Mrs. Vincent is fifteen minutes away.

"Pickup truck." Lottie scans the horizon. "Driving fast."

Mr. Vincent wipes his glasses on the tail of his shirt, and Mr. Moses points at a dark speck that quickly takes on the shape of a rusted red truck with a cracked headlight.

"Bosman." Lottie pulls me to my feet. "Those are his sons in the back."

Mr. Vincent and Mr. Moses pass a look between themselves as the truck speeds straight toward us, the tires churning dirt into the air. "Stay where you are, girls," Mr. Vincent says. "I'll handle this."

Lottie sighs. Americans think that the whole world is America, but this is the British protectorate of Swaziland, with its own guns and warring tribes. Smiles don't fix anything here.

The truck screams to a stop a few yards from us, and I cough up dust. Three white boys, scrawny teenagers in grubby clothes, sit on the edge of the truck tray with rifles balanced across their knees. A sandy-haired girl crouches between them with her face hidden in her hands. The driver's door opens, and a tall man wearing khaki pants and a blue work shirt gets out. He grabs a rifle from the dash and swings it onto his shoulder, the way hunters do before they set out.

Mr. Moses whispers, "Stay calm, ladies, and keep back."

Four armed white men: Lottie and I already know well enough to steer clear. We eye the boys with their guns, and the man with his. The father, Bosman, spits on the ground and walks straight up to Mr. Vincent. White man to white man.

"Mr. Bosman." Mr. Vincent smiles his wide American smile and goes to shake the farmer's hand. "I'm Edward Vincent."

Bosman ignores the greeting and growls in Afrikaans: "This here is my land. What are you doing on my land, kaffir-lover?"

I blush for Mr. Vincent. *Kaffir-lover* is the worst insult that one white man can call another. Not that Mr. Vincent understands. Missionaries mostly speak English, with a smattering of Zulu words thrown in to prove their commitment to being here in southern Africa. Afrikaans is another matter.

"What did he say?" Mr. Vincent asks Mr. Moses, who shrugs. Mr. Moses is from Durban, where decent mixed-race people speak English and poor whites speak Afrikaans.

"Go and help, Adele." Lottie gives me a shove even though she takes Afrikaans classes and speaks the language too. It's only fair, I suppose. She translated for Mama Khumalo and talked Darnell Parns's soul out of the valley with her words.

I reluctantly go over to Mr. Vincent, and Lottie follows, two steps behind. Bosman takes in Mr. Vincent's dirty clothes and flyaway hair with contempt, and I'd turn back and hide behind the rock with Darnell except that Lottie is right behind me. Then she's right beside me, and somehow her presence makes me feel safer, even with the rifles so close.

"You two belong to him?" Bosman motions to Mr. Vincent with an ugly smile, and my cheeks burn at the insinuation. Lottie huffs out a breath. If she had a stone, she'd throw it.

"He's the American principal," I say before Lottie has the chance to tell the man to shut his fat mouth and go home to his fat, cross-eyed wife, or whatever insult comes into her mind. "Mr. Vincent doesn't speak the tongue."

"Bad luck," Bosman says. "This is my country. My farm. We use my language."

"What's he saying?" Mr. Vincent asks, frustrated.

"He wants to know what you're doing on his land," I tell Mr. Vincent. *Kaffir-lover* is an insult that I can't bring myself to say out loud in front of adults. And the sly suggestion that Lottie and I are Mr. Vincent's girlfriends is too filthy to repeat.

"Tell him that we have an emergency." Mr. Vincent combs rough fingers through his hair and peers at the sunburned farmer standing with a rifle hitched onto his shoulder like he was born with a notch in it to fit the gun. "We'll be off his land soon."

I translate from English to Afrikaans in a shaky voice. The wounds on Darnell's body scare me, but Bosman's lopsided grin scares me more. He is full of hate, this one. He enjoys being mean.

"What emergency?" Bosman makes a show of scanning the empty field. "I don't see nothing here but a foreigner and his half-castes walking on my land without permission."

"Mr. Bosman wants to know what the emergency is." I change Bosman's ugly words to nice ones, but Mr. Vincent isn't fooled. Bosman's scorn is obvious.

"There's been an accident." Mr. Vincent's American accent takes on a sharp edge. "A Keziah student died in the ravine below. We're here to retrieve the body."

Bosman rubs sweat from the back of his neck while I translate. His eyes are a peculiar shade of green flecked with yellow, which reminds me of Socks the cat when she hunts lizards in Mrs. Thomas's garden.

"And where's this dead coon?" Bosman asks.

"He's in the shade of the rock over there, Mr. Bosman." Polite Adele throws pearls before swine, hoping to make things nice. "We've sent for a pickup truck from the school to bring him home."

"Well, now." Bosman pretends to think, an excruciating sight. "A dead colored on my land is bad luck. You've got to move him."

"We will," I say. "The pickup truck is on its way. Ten minutes, tops."

"No," Bosman says. "Now, now."

Now, now means right away, this minute, no delays. I don't understand.

"What?" Lottie demands in Afrikaans. "You heard what she said. The truck will be here in ten minutes."

"Not my concern," Bosman replies with grim satisfaction. "I don't want no dead coon on my land. Move him."

"Are you befoked?" Lottie demands, and the boys on the back of the truck go still. *Befoked* means "fucked in the head," a stunning insult coming from the mouth of a mixed-race girl. *Lottie, Lottie . . . what have you done?*

Bosman swings his rifle from his shoulder and fires a shot over our heads. The crack makes me jump and my ears ring. Birds fly from the indoni trees, and the girl in the truck screams in short, sharp bursts, a human siren. Bosman laughs at my terrified expression and Lottie's pale face. He likes that we're afraid of him.

"What happened, Adele?" Mr. Vincent grabs my shoulder and pulls me away from Bosman, who really is befoked. "Tell me."

"He . . . he, uh . . ." I stop to clear my throat. "He wants us to move Darnell off his land right away. I told him that a pickup truck is coming, but he doesn't want to wait for it. We have to go."

"And the gunshot?" Both Mr. Vincent's feet are planted in Swaziland now, a country where "Love thy neighbor" is an almost impossible commandment.

"Lottie wanted to know why we had to move Darnell." I tell half the truth. "He shot the gun to hurry us up."

"God help me." Mr. Vincent flexes his fingers open and shut, open and shut. "What difference will ten minutes make? Ask him."

A waste of time. Those of us who are from southern Africa know Bosman's type. We meet them at police roadblocks, in stores, and standing guard in their front gardens to protect their personal kingdoms from the jealous eyes of natives and half natives who dream of taking everything they have. They are obsessed, Mother says, with white ruin and black revenge.

"He won't listen to reason, Mr. Vincent." Mr. Moses breaks the standoff. "Between you, me, and the girls, we'll be able to move Darnell across the border. It won't take long."

Bosman's finger lies across the trigger guard, and something like hate wells up inside me. Voices from the past echo inside my head. *Rules are rules! That's how things are! Keep sweet and avoid trouble!* I'm sick of how quickly the laws of this stupid world roll off the tongues of teachers and aunties and parents, off my tongue. Things could so easily be different if the serving ladies gave the poor students an extra portion of mashed potatoes. If Bosman chose to be kind instead of cruel. Or if Father lived with us instead of splitting his love between two families.

If.

If only things were different.

"Adele." Lottie tugs my sleeve, and I wake from my daze. Bosman stands a half yard in front of me, with a searching expression that turns my stomach inside out. He scans my face, trying to place me.

"I know you, girl," he finally says. "You were born to sell yourself to a man with money."

My heartbeat drums so loud in my ears that it might actually send me deaf. I have never, ever been talked to with such loathing and contempt. My skin crawls, and I want to spit and scream and run, to hide my face from the ugliness of Bosman's words. This filthy man actually thinks that he knows me.

"Come." Lottie grabs my hand and squeezes tight. "We have to fetch Darnell."

"He . . ."

"I heard him." Lottie pulls me back from Bosman and the red pickup truck with its load of sullen white boys. The girl stays crouched between her brothers and hums a broken tune, which softens the sharp feeling of hatred that I have toward her father and the way things are.

I will leave this farm.

But the girl, she has to stay.

• • •

The men shuffle-step Darnell across the open field, with Lottie and me walking beside them like pallbearers at a country funeral, our straight-backed bodies and our silence adding dignity to an undignified parade. We pass the red pickup, and the girl starts to cry with body-shaking sobs. The dead body, now stiff-limbed and unnatural, scares her.

Bosman snaps, "Shut her up before I do."

The girl continues to wail, and I wish she'd button it. She

has to swallow her tears and suffer in silence, because otherwise, sure as Jesus rose from the dead, she'll get the stick when she gets home.

The youngest and skinniest of the boys reaches out and pats the girl on the back. He murmurs soft words, and I'm surprised by the tender gesture and relieved when the girl drops her cries to a hoarse whisper.

We gain a small, hard-won distance from Bosman and his family. Mr. Moses slows his step and says, "Watch yourself, Mr. Vincent. There's a trench right here."

A zigzag scar cuts the length of the field, deep in some parts and wide and shallow in others. Erosion. The land is too exhausted to grow crops, and I bet food is scarce in the Bosman house. No wonder his children are scrawny.

"Hear that?" Lottie stops and cocks her head to one side.

"I hear it." I shade my eyes to block the slanting sunlight and pick out a white speck on the horizon. The school pickup. Mrs. Vincent, who usually drives at ten miles an hour, races across the rough ground at high speed to close the gap with us.

"Thank you, Lord." Mr. Vincent's faith is instantly renewed.

"Hallelujah," Mr. Moses adds.

They lay Darnell on the ground and wait to be rescued.

Bosman's work boots crunch the grass as he strides over to us. We are still on his land, and he wants us off it, no matter what.

Lottie walks out to meet him, with her chin raised. She stands directly in his path, and no mixed-race girl in her right mind stares openly at an angry white man with a gun the way she is right now. We are supposed to look at the ground. We play dumb. We try to disappear. That's the way we survive.

Instead of becoming invisible, Lottie pins Bosman with a cool stare. I run to her.

"Come . . ." I tug her skirt to warn her to behave, but she shakes me off. She's Swazi. She knows the penalty for daring to challenge a white man, but she does it anyway. Lottie is insane. She wants Bosman to know that she finds him loathsome.

"What you looking at, coon?" Bosman demands in Afrikaans.

"You," she says in a loud, clear voice: another challenge.

Bosman spits on the ground, and the girl in the truck stops crying. She huddles close to her brother, her muscles tense in the strained silence that must always come before her father loses his temper. I step closer to Lottie, and freeze when Bosman's fingers grip the butt of his rifle. I don't move. I'm scared of dying before my life has properly started, but I stick by Lottie's side.

"Leave," Bosman says. "Get off my land."

"We will." Lottie stands her ground while Gordon Number One and Barnabas Phillips help the grown men roll Darnell onto a blanket and lift him onto the back of the school truck. The boys climb on board, and Mr. Vincent slams the back shut with a loud bang.

The sound starts Bosman's daughter off again, and this time, her brother's soothing words go unheard. She throws her arms over the side of the tray and clutches at the air with her fingers, trying to hold on to something invisible.

The girl's face is exposed for the first time; she's around fourteen, with slanted eyes and flat facial features that are so like Darnell's that I take a sharp breath of wonder. The girl is white and Darnell is mixed-race, but they are the same. They are both simpleminded. The girl's wild, clutching fingers suddenly make sense. She's reaching out to Darnell, trying to hold on to him by magic.

A bright lightning bolt of what Lottie would call "divine intuition" hits me. Bosman's daughter and Darnell knew each other. They were friends.

"Get," Bosman says in a tone reserved for farm dogs. "Get off my land."

"Gladly," Lottie says, and Bosman vibrates with rage at being looked down at, and not for the first time, I'm sure. Mother says that poor white people are dangerous because only a thin layer of skin makes them kings of the land, but it's not enough to save them from the pity of other whites or the silent contempt of natives who must suffer their cruelty.

"Come." I snatch Lottie's hand, and now it's my turn to drag her away from Bosman.

Mr. Vincent boosts us onto the back of the pickup truck. We squat at Darnell's feet, Swazi guardians of the dead.

The girl's fingers clutch the air over and over again, and the sound of her weeping contains all the sorrows of the world. It's wrong for a white girl to cry for a brown boy, but Bosman's daughter doesn't understand the way things are. She's simple, and her ignorance sets her free from the rules. There's a lesson in that for me if I could grasp it through the pain in my heart.

Mrs. Vincent starts the engine, and the truck bumps over the washboard corrugations in the eroded field.

"I'll remember you two." Bosman points his gun barrel from Lottie to me and marks us out for special attention should we ever meet again. "You better believe that."

24

A Dark Wind

The sun is hot, the hole is deep, and the coffin is made of pine. Three days after finding Darnell, leather-skinned farmers, from the surrounding area, and their wives bunch together around the grave. The men grip their hats in their hands, the women hold hankies to their eyes. Two Swazi farmworkers crouch in the blazing sun with shovels balanced on their knees, waiting for the ceremony to end.

Darnell's father, Mr. Parns, stands at the foot of the freshly dug hole, dressed in a clean shirt and khaki pants ironed for the occasion. His face is pinched tight with a grief that burns my eyes.

Darnell's father knows true emptiness. With the loss of his only child and with his wife passed away, too, he's all alone to face the future. I do not know how he can bear it. I think of the days after Father leaves us to return to his other family in Johannesburg. Mother cups my cheek and strokes Rian's hair at every opportunity and murmurs the same soft words: *What would I do without you? Tell me that.* What will Mr. Parns do without Darnell? With no family at all?

A dark wind lifts dirt into the air. The land absorbs the sobs of the women and the flinty silence of the gravediggers. The long fields and tall hills swallow us all. If I could be anything as I stand beside the empty grave, I'd choose to be a mountain, or the river that flows year after year, its course unaltered, free from pain eternal.

Darnell was almost a stranger to me, but his death has shaken me, and only the heat of Lottie's body pressed against my shoulder keeps me from running away from the grave.

Mr. Vincent opens his Bible and says the words " 'By the sweat of your face you shall eat bread, till you return to the ground, for out of it you were taken; for you are dust, and to dust you shall return.' "

Four senior boys lower the pine box into the ground, and I swear I can't breathe. I can't find the oxygen to feed my lungs. I am afraid the pressure that began to build up inside my throat three days ago, when I found Darnell lying in the valley, will tear me apart. Mr. Parns is silent, but I want to scream on his behalf. I want to scream till the hills ring with the sound of it. My heart aches, and my throat burns.

Lottie grabs my hand, and my fingers will break if she holds on any tighter. The pain brings me to, and I feel her shoulder slump against mine. I grind my feet into the dirt and take her weight. Darnell was Lottie's friend. She knew him and talked to him and had a sympathy for him that was real and not for show. The scream frozen inside my throat is for all the things that can't be changed.

I hold Lottie up, and when the time comes for us to throw dirt on the coffin, I lead her to the graveside step by steady step. For her, I am the mountain. Mrs. Vincent and Nancy Breeland, the best voice at Keziah, sing "How Great Thou Art" and then "To God Be the Glory."

Darnell loved music.

I didn't know.

...

We return to the big-girls' dorm with swollen eyes. Our footsteps are slow and drag along the ground. If it was nighttime, we'd fall straight to sleep, but it's late Saturday afternoon and the hall is filled with curious girls waiting for us to get back from the funeral at the Parns farm. They keep their distance, and some girls take shallow sips of air, to avoid being contaminated by grave dust. Peaches crosses her arms and purses her lips.

"Crocodile tears." Delia's loud voice carries the length of the hallway. "Imagine crying for a dimwit just to get attention."

"Shame," Natalie intones. "What a thing to do."

Lottie lets out a ragged sigh and turns to Dead Lorraine's room. Her defense of our honor will have to keep. She's spent. I reach across and grab the door handle, exhausted from the service and the heat and the sadness.

"What would your mother think, Adele . . . the way you're

213

carrying on," Delia says. "You didn't speak one word to that boy when he was alive."

The pressure builds inside me. It floods my arms and my fingertips, and makes a hard drumming noise inside my ears. I walk over to Delia. I have no words. The pressure animates my hand and I slap her hard across the cheek with an open palm. Her face jerks to the right, and a red mark blooms across her skin. I lift my hand again, aiming to even out the blows.

"Don't." Lottie grabs my arm and pulls me back. "Only we understand, Adele. Only we know."

And that is the saddest and truest sentence I have ever heard.

25

Witches and Worse

Mrs. Thomas lets us eat dinner in our room on Saturday, Sunday, and Monday night, a privilege normally reserved for students who are too sick to get out of bed. Lottie and I are healthy in our bodies, but Darnell's death has wrapped us in a sadness we cannot shake. Breakfast and lunchtimes are hell. Whispers follow us wherever we go, and the seats on either side of us at the dining table clear as if by magic. Dinner in our room is better, though. We sit shoulder to shoulder, alone but together.

In the hour before Monday lights-out, I pull open my drawer and I take out a piece of paper and a pen. I write:

Dear Mother,

I have a bruise the size of a kaffir lime on my back from when I fell off the path and into the valley. The color of the bruise has changed from red to dark purple to yellow, which Lottie says is a sign that the bruise is about to fade.

Other things have changed but in the good to bad direction. After the fire we were heroes, Mr. Vincent sent you a letter about that, and little girls carried our books from one classroom to the other. Final-year girls congratulated us. Boys smiled and winked. We were queens.

Nobody talks to us now.

We stayed with Darnell's dead body in the valley and threw handfuls of dirt onto his coffin at the funeral. We live in Dead Lorraine's room. We survived the fire not because God loves us but because the devil looks after his own. It was him who stayed the flames. We are witches and worse. And if you brush against our skirts, even for one second, you might die.

It's cracked but that's what the others believe. Mr. Vincent gave a special sermon on superstition. "Trust in the Lord," he said, "only His word has the power to save you from false devils and spiritual corruption." Nobody listened. Americans! If the Vincents talked to Swazis, even the white ones, they'd know that bad spirits are real.

My hands are unclean. Lottie and I are unclean.

All we have is each other and if we really were witches we'd fly far, far away from here, but we are just ordinary girls who stayed with a dead boy and helped to bury him. I don't regret staying with Darnell. We did the right thing not to leave him there alone and to help lead his spirit away from the valley.

There is good news.

Lottie and I still get the Golden Sun Award for bravery. The ceremony and the celebration dinner have been pushed back eight weeks to the last Wednesday of term out of respect for Darnell's passing and because, I think, Mrs. Vincent wants everyone to leave for the school holidays with good feelings about us. There'll be roast beef and sponge cake with jam and cream at the dinner, so her plan might work.

It's time to go now. The generator is down and the hour of grace candle is low. Shadows crawl over the walls and I dread the coming darkness. My mind won't stop talking to me. Round and round it goes from the tall flames eating the trees, to Darnell lying so quiet in the valley, to the crack of the rifle shot over my head.

I've changed, Mummy. The daughter you know is different now. I slapped Delia on the face the other day and I was glad! She deserved it and I'd do it again. It turns out that behind my smiles and my good manners there's an angry and confused Adele Joubert who might, without Lottie's strength, have watched the school burn down.

Love,
Adele

I fold the paper, stuff it into an envelope, and write Mother's name and address on the front. I drop the letter on top of the chest of drawers and lie down with a sigh. I feel better for writing it. For telling the truth. John 8:32. *And you will know the truth, and the truth will set you free.* The Bible makes sense sometimes.

"Are you going to mail it?" Lottie asks with a sleepy yawn.

"No way. The letter is for me. To let off steam." Writing it also helps to remind me that there's more to the world than Keziah, and that Keziah is only one small part of the world. Mother will never read what I've written. The truth has set me free, but it would hurt her to know I've become an outcast.

Lottie pinches out the candle flame between her fingertips, and we lie in the newly fallen darkness. Murmured voices come from the other rooms: talk of boys and clothes, and theories on the bad luck that haunts Lottie and me. I'd rather the girls talked to us face-to-face so we could tell them what it was like to stay in the valley with Darnell, but they don't really want to know, so they whisper behind our backs and step aside when we pass. Cowards.

"He did it." Lottie's voice fills Dead Lorraine's room.

"Who?"

"Bosman," she says. "He killed Darnell."

I sit up, startled. "Seriously?"

"Think about it, Adele. Darnell was slow, and Bosman's daughter is slow. They knew each other. They might have been close."

"And Bosman killed Darnell why?" I ask.

"To keep Darnell away from his daughter, of course. You know how these things go," Lottie says, and brown boys have died for less: a careless look, a smile, a shoulder bumped against tender white skin. Even Father, who is gentle and turned gray, threatened to buy a gun to keep boys from climbing through my window at night. Not that he'd ever use it. Bosman, on the other hand, has a temper, and a rifle that he delights in using. Still, Lottie must be wrong.

"The doctor from the Norwegian hospital said that Darnell fell and broke his neck," I say. I quote the *Swazi Times*. " 'His injuries were consistent with an accidental death.' It was bad luck—an accident."

Lottie shakes her head in disagreement. "You saw Darnell climb the riverbank, Adele. No way did he fall over the edge like you did. He was a climber."

"Ja, but Bosman has guns," I say. "Four of them. He could have shot Darnell and buried him only God knows where. It's stupid to leave a body out in the open for the vultures to find."

"True . . ." Lottie punches her pillow into shape. "It's just . . . Bosman was involved, Adele. I feel it in my heart. And, if his daughter and Darnell were friends, he'd find Darnell and punish him for getting too close because he *hates* mixed-race people."

"Bosman hates everyone, Lottie. Even Mr. Vincent—and he's white," I say.

"One day, when I was visiting Mama Khumalo, Bosman came looking for a Swazi boy who, he said, was on his land.

She hid me inside her hut. 'Don't move,' she said. 'Don't make a sound. Bosman is sick in the head, and mixed-race people make his sickness worse.' She didn't know why. It just did. And, you saw how he was with us, Adele. You know he's capable of murder."

Bosman is dangerous, no question, but I'm not convinced by Lottie's argument.

Accusing a white man of murder is no small matter, and our hearts can't be relied on to tell us what really happened. Our hearts are broken, and we need evidence of Bosman's guilt or else the constable at the Howard's Halt station will just brush us off. Colored girls and their overactive imaginations! Brown girls and their malicious accusations against white men!

"We've got no proof of murder. We don't even know if Darnell and Bosman's daughter said one word to each other." I turn one way and then the other, putting off the moment that I close my eyes and meet the tall flames again, hot and blue around the edges, or else the deep valley and the soft halo of flies floating like rain clouds around Darnell's head. "Besides, my mind is full. I've got no space for Bosman. Or his daughter or his sons. All I want to do is get through to the end of term and go home."

"If you knew Darnell, you'd understand," Lottie says, and turns to face the wall. I grip the blankets to my chin and peer at the outline of her body.

"Understand what exactly?" I ask.

"That Darnell was kind. He spent hours out in the bush looking for gifts for the people he liked. If he was still alive, he would have brought you bird eggs and impala lilies and ripe figs and . . ." She turns to face me. "If anyone in the world needed Darnell's kindness, it was Bosman's daughter. You saw how she acted when we took his body away. She wanted to keep him."

Lottie also wanted to keep Darnell, and I feel guilty for brushing off her concerns about how he died. Maybe it's like she said after the fire, that your mind goes over and over a bad thing, till one day it stops. Sometimes the bad thing stays with you forever and, for now, Darnell's death won't let Lottie go. She already has the memory of her dead father and the reality of her sad mother to carry.

"How did you meet Darnell?" I ask because, to most Keziah students, he was just the slow-witted boy who ran from school every chance he got.

"I caught Richard B hitting Darnell for fun, and I hit Richard B till he wasn't having fun anymore. Darnell never forgot." Her smile flashes bright in the semidarkness. "Last year, Darnell left a honeycomb on the windowsill of the big dorm room where I lived. Wasps found the honey and we couldn't open the window for days. Poor Darnell. The idea was nice, but the details were all wrong. I hope he was friends with Bosman's daughter. It would have been a sweet thing for the both of them."

"I'm sorry he died," I say and I leave it there. No words will fill the hole that Darnell's death has left inside Lottie. I don't even try.

"Good night, Adele. Sleep well," she whispers, and the subject of Bosman closes for now. The two of us have more urgent business to attend to. Tonight we will fight our demons in our dreams, and tomorrow morning we will rise up from our cots, tired and wrung out, and get on with the day. And the next day. And the next fifty-six days till the end of term.

I stare at the ceiling and conjure up memories of our house in Manzini. My bed. Clean sheets and thick blankets. Milk tea and sugar biscuits. Ripe mangoes in a bowl on the kitchen table. Even the memory of walking to the telephone box at the end of Live Long Street takes on a sweetness. I will soak in the bathtub for hours and sleep late during the holidays. I will become Adele Joubert again.

Not Lottie. Lottie has to fight for what little she has, and how tired she must be. Each day is a struggle, yet still she has space in her head to think about finding justice for Darnell.

"Good night," I whisper back, and lie awake wondering how to make things different.

26

Fast Post

The late bus to Manzini, a dusty brown behemoth with the name *Lord Have Mercy* painted on the side, passes us on our way from afternoon study hall to the senior-girls' dorm. Dinner is in half an hour, and we have just enough time to wipe the dust from our shoes and wash our faces. Mrs. Vincent has decided that it's time for Lottie and me to "reintegrate" into the student population, so no more private dinners.

I comb the knots from my hair and drop the brush onto the chest of drawers. My hand stills, and my mind spins. I pull open the drawers and search them one by one, and then I drop to the floor and sweep my hands over the floor while my heart goes flip, flip, flip.

"What is it?" Lottie asks.

"The letter to my mother. It was right here on top. Right here. Did you take it?"

"No. I've been with you the whole time, remember?" Lottie runs a plastic comb through her short-cropped hair, and it's true that we are a society of two. We eat together and walk from blue classroom to blue classroom together, all the while pretending that being outcasts doesn't bother us one bit.

"Then it might . . ." Two terrible thoughts hit me at once. Either Delia has stolen the letter as payback for the slap and plans to read it out loud to anyone who'll listen, or something far, far worse has happened.

I hurry outside, sick with fear. Socks the cat sleeps in the last rays of sunlight to fall across the front stairs of Mrs. Thomas's cement-brick house. I knock, and, on the off chance that Jesus is in the vicinity, I pray. *Please let the letter be inside and propped against the endless row of wedding photos.*

Socks yawns and stretches out, a hundred miles from care.

"Ah, Adele." Mrs. Thomas smiles to see me at the door—still in her soft, dreamy mood. "You came about the letter?"

"Yes." I shift from right foot to left foot. "That's correct."

"It was a rush, but I got it into the *Lord Have Mercy* mailbag. It will be in Manzini this evening, and your mother will get it tomorrow or the next day." She reaches out and touches my shoulder.

I am speechless.

"It's good that you write to your mother, Adele. Keeping contact with the outside world is important. I'm sure she'll be delighted to hear from you."

I hold back the bad words burning on my tongue. *Stupid.*

*Idiot. You had no right. You know the rules. Hands off other peo-
ple's stuff.* Instead, I shape my mouth into a smile. It's almost
mid-February, and in eight weeks, I'll go home for the holidays.
From what I hear, Mrs. Thomas leaves the school only during
the Christmas break. She's stuck at Keziah from late January to
mid-December, and that fact melts my anger away. I'm sorry for
her. I take a big breath in.

"Thank you for posting the letter, Mrs. Thomas. Mother
will be pleased."

"No trouble, Adele. No trouble at all."

Each footfall on her stairs is like a hammer that echoes across
Swaziland, all the way to my mother, who will read the letter
and think I am insane.

Lottie stands on the other side of the dry lavender hedge
with a startled expression. She's guessed what happened.

"She was trying to help," she says of Mrs. Thomas's backward kindness. "What was in the letter?"

"The truth."

"Oh." Lottie says. Then, "Ohh . . ."

"Exactly," I say.

• • •

What to do? What to do? The question runs circles inside my
head until my brain is dizzy. I list the facts to try and calm my
mind: *Mrs. Thomas posted the letter. Fact. The letter is gone,
and there's no stopping it. Fact. There is nothing I can do to
change the situation. Fact.* My mind, however, refuses to listen.
My mind insists that there must be a way to fix the situation.

225

"Here. Take this." Lottie reaches over the side of her cot and offers me her dreidel. "Spin it and watch the symbols go around. Don't think. Just watch."

"All right." I grab the spinning top and crouch on the floor. Playing with a child's toy won't change anything, but lying in bed with the same stupid question looping through my head won't change anything either. I spin the top, and it falls over. I try again and get a good spin going. The painted symbols on the wood move in a blur of motion.

"What was in the letter?" Lottie asks.

"I already told you. The truth." I spin again, faster this time.

"Which part of the truth?"

"The fire, and Darnell dying, and us being outcasts at Keziah. Also, that I'm different from the girl that she put on the bus to school."

"Did you tell her that you met Mama Khumalo and that Mama asked after her?"

"No." The dreidel wobbles and tumbles over, and, right then, it's as if a hand has reached into my head and stopped my mind from spinning long enough for me to focus outside of myself. The visit with Mama Khumalo left me with questions that only my mother can answer.

If I don't ask, I'll never know why she abandoned her family and why she never again set foot in her village on the edge of Bosman's farm. My hands reach for the drawer with the pen and paper, and I pull my fingers back from the metal handle, uncertain. Children who ask personal questions of adults get a slap across the head and are told to *keep your nose out of my business unless you want to lose that nose, girl!* Do I have the courage to challenge "the way things are" by asking Mother to share with me her reasons for leaving?

I pull open the drawer. Mother is miles away in Manzini, I reason. If my curiosity offends her, she'll have eight weeks to cool down before I go home for the holidays. Writing another, more personal letter to Mother is a risk worth taking.

> *Mother,*
>
> *I met your cousin Mama Khumalo the other day and I have so many questions. First and most important, why haven't you come back to visit your cousin? I ask because the village is so full of life while our house in Manzini is neat and quiet. If I was you I'd miss the children and the stray dogs and the women singing in the fields. After all those people and closeness, I wonder if you're lonely with just me and Rian and the porcelain angels on the sideboard for company. Also, was Granny Agnes the one who taught you the African proverbs that you like to throw into conversations at the strangest times? Two of them have crossed my mind this term. When everyone stared at Lottie and me in chapel, I remembered that "the higher the monkey climbs up the tree, the more you can see of its bum," and when Darnell crossed the river at twilight, I knew he had to get to the shore fast because "the strength of the crocodile is in the*

water." I haven't yet had a chance to use your favorite saying, "When the ground is hard, the women dance." The truth is, I don't really understand why the women dance or how their dancing helps to fix the hard ground. Maybe you can explain it to me during the holidays.

Love,

Your Adele

PS: Mama Khumalo said that when you lived in the country, your eyes were always on the hills and what lay beyond. We have that in common. When Lottie and I were talking the other night I realized, for the first time, that I want to study overseas. A crazy idea, I know, but the world is big and full and I want to see it all.

Lottie spins the dreidel while I fold the letter into an envelope and write Mother's address on the front. "Are you going to send the letter on purpose this time?" she asks. "No accidents with Mrs. Thomas?"

"I'll post it," I say. "Who knows? Mother might actually answer my questions." Writing the second letter is the only way that I can think of to make things different.

The electricity cuts out, and the room goes from light to dark in a blink. I lie on my cot and turn to face Lottie.

"Why did you let me try your dreidel?" I ask. The Jewish spinning top is the last piece of Lottie's dead father, who is now, according to her, "just bones in the ground."

Cot springs squeak as Lottie turns to face me in the gloom.

I hear the slow inhale and exhale of her breath from across the room.

"When Delia stole my undies, you gave me a new pair and you never asked for it back. We fought the fire and sat with Darnell's body in the valley. We both hate Bosman and love to read." Lottie sighs in the darkness. "I gave you the dreidel because you're my friend, Adele. You're the best friend I've ever had. And when I get that farm, that's what I want. Friends."

The lump in my throat makes it hard for me to swallow, and tears sting my eyes. Lottie has put my feelings into words, but writing the second letter to Mother has eaten up all my courage, so I turn to the wall and mash my face into the pillow.

"Night, Lottie," I say through my tears.

"You big baby," she says, and her insult makes me laugh.

• • •

The next morning, the Go Lucky Boy bus to Manzini pulls out of the school grounds with the second letter to Mother in its mailbag. Two letters in one week—won't she be surprised? Maybe she'll reply to one or both of the letters. Maybe she won't reply at all.

That night, I reopen Jane Eyre and dive back into the story, desperate to take my mind off the letters and Mother's reaction to their content. Darnell's funeral and the whispers that followed us afterward threw us off course. Jane was pushed to the back of our minds but, once again, Jane is here to save us. Jane will take us far from Swaziland and from our troubles.

Lottie reads her fair share of the story, and I find that I actually enjoy being a listener, free to imagine the windswept moors and the poor schoolhouse where Jane found work after she ran away from Rochester and the mad wife he kept hidden in a secret room.

On the fourth night of feverish reading, we finish *Jane Eyre* and pick apart the ending in the flickering candlelight. Lottie is pleased that Jane married Rochester and had a child. I'm pleased, too, but less so. Mother, it seems, is right. Money is important. Money changes everything. Where would Jane be without that inheritance from her long-lost uncle? If she was in Swaziland, I'll tell you where she'd be: Living in a grass hut with nothing to eat but porridge. A blind and crippled husband. No running water. No money for school fees. No happy ending.

Without her uncle's money, Jane is a righteous pauper. And where's the harm in being Rochester's second wife so long as he takes care of her and her children the way that Father takes care of Rian and me? Mother would find Jane foolish to have run from linen sheets and shelter only to return to the ashes of Thornfield Hall.

I keep my thoughts to myself, because Lottie is "ecstatic" that Jane remained true to herself and got what she wanted in the end. Jane is "steadfast" and "tenacious." A "heroine."

"Lucky about that inheritance," I say, feeling disloyal to both Jane and Lottie.

"True." Lottie laughs and lifts her dreidel so the light catches the Hebrew symbols painted on the sides. "When my father died, he left me this and his work boots. What will you get?"

I shrug. "Rian and I are a secret, so Father's other children will probably get whatever he has. That's why my mother likes money. The coins and paper notes are right there in her hand. She doesn't have to wait, and she doesn't have to guess what's around the corner."

"Do you love him?" Lottie asks.

A strange feeling shoots through me. I have no answer for her question.

She persists. "Do you love your father?" she asks, and I puff out a breath, annoyed at her. Lottie waits for my reply.

"Of course I love him," I say, and then I add, "He pays the bills, so what choice do I have?"

"That's not how love works," Lottie says.

"Says who?"

"Says me and the books and the songs and the Bible. Do you love him? Yes or no, Adele."

She won't let go till she has her answer. I flex my hands to pump warmth to my fingertips, which are suddenly cold.

"I don't know him. Not really." I try to explain. "And I don't know if I love him or if I'm just grateful to him for giving us a house and paying my school fees. He visits us when he can, and Mother calls him every Thursday. When he comes to Manzini, we're glad to see him and he's glad to see us . . . I don't know."

"Well, all right . . ." Lottie spins the dreidel between her fingers and changes the subject. A kindness. "We can still be Jane. But without the inheritance."

"And live in a hut with a blind old man? Even if he's white . . . Even if *we* were white? I'll pass."

Lottie grins. "I already live in a hut, so we have to do what my mother says: we have to take care of ourselves and make money that we can leave to whoever we want."

I tuck *Jane Eyre* under my pillow and stretch out on the floor where we read books. Jane's uncle sailed to Madeira to make his fortune. Jane was stuck in England in the cold in the same way that we're stuck in Swaziland in our brown-girl bodies. Does Lottie really believe that we'll make enough money for her to buy a farm and for me to travel overseas? How? It's an unreal dream of an idea, and she's cracked in the head to say it. Even so . . .

"That would be nice," I say.

27

Echoes from Outside

"Sandi Cardoza. Mary Lewis. Claire Naidoo. Alison Carter."
I grit my teeth as the Elephant calls out the names of students
with parcels and letters in the afternoon postbag. I grind the
toe of my right shoe into the dirt, hoping to hear my name
boomed out and praying to God that it won't be. The bag empties, and my breath hitches in my chest. Six days have passed
since the *Go Lucky Boy* took my second letter to Manzini, and
I have to finally accept that Mother will not reply to either of
my letters.

Lottie makes excuses for her, but I feel in my heart that I've
let Mother down. She prefers the old Adele, who was part of
the top girls' circle. New Adele slaps former friends across the
face. New Adele reads till the grace candle burns down and
dreams of living in a faraway country—any country—where
things are different.

"Adele Joubert." The Elephant calls my name, and panic grips me. Mother *has* replied, and I'm not ready to read what she's written. The second letter was meant to change "how things are." Maybe it worked, but not like I wanted. Maybe things *have* changed—but for the worse.

"Quick sticks." The Elephant holds up a thin piece of cardboard. "I haven't got all day."

"Thank you, Matron." I take my mail. It's a postcard with a photograph of a traditional Swazi maiden, wearing a beaded skirt and not much else, on the front and Rian's scrawled handwriting on the back.

> *Adele,*
>
> *Father came to visit last Saturday and he and*
> *Mother talked about you in low voices. When they went*
> *to bed, I heard Mother crying. Did Mother lie when*
> *she said that the fire didn't burn you? If you are hurt,*
> *you can come back to Manzini and I'll show you how to*
> *make wood-block puzzles in the lean-to.*
>
> > *Your brother,*
> > *Rian*

"Bad news?" Lottie asks, and I give her Rian's postcard to read. Lottie doesn't send or receive mail, and, in our ten years at Keziah, not once has the Elephant called her up to the mailbag. She grins at the photo of the topless girl on the cover and flips over to Rian's words.

"Your brother is worried about you," she says. "It's nice."

"Still nothing from Mother," I point out. "Father came and Mother cried, and I'm not sure what it means."

"Let's walk." Lottie pulls me in the direction of the chapel and steers me away from my own thoughts. I let her. Since the mistake with the first letter, Lottie has taken care of me. When I might have sulked or bitten my nails, we walk to the cattle grids, the woodworking shed, and the curtain of burned trees that stand behind the school shop, black and stark against the sky. We avoid the river and the far hills, afraid to test our luck.

Sunlight falls across the graveyard and makes the granite in the headstones shine. I lean my arms on the smooth wood fence that separates the cemetery from the main road and rest my head on my arms, something I could never imagine doing at the beginning of term. The dead scare me less now.

"I'm glad Darnell isn't buried here," Lottie says. "He'd make mischief for sure."

"And who would blame him?" I say. "Being this close to the chapel for eternity would send anyone cuckoo."

"Darnell is better off lying next to his mother with a view of the mountains," she says. And, though she's careful to avoid mentioning his name, I know that Bosman looms large in her imagination, the evil white man who broke Darnell's neck.

I've pointed out the lack of evidence and thrown in terms from articles that I've read in Mother's racy gossip magazines: *eyewitness accounts, lack of probable cause,* and *false accusation* all have the power to sway a judge in the negative . . . especially in divorce cases, where shady motel rooms and dark alleyways are common, though I'm sure the same rules of evidence apply to murders.

"Darnell probably did die by accident," Lottie says with a hitch in her voice. We've gone over the dozen ways that Darnell might have fallen, by fair means and foul, and come by slow circles to the same conclusion every time: we will never know what happened or why. We stand before the great mystery that is everything in this world and fumble for answers.

"Why did God take Darnell and my father instead of Bosman or any of the other terrible people in the world? It's not fair," she says. "There are so many to choose from!"

"You're right," I agree. "It's not fair."

There's nothing else to say, so we remain quiet, and the quiet is soothing. When I was with Delia and the other popular girls, we never stopped talking. We discussed fashion and boys, and gossiped about other students including Lottie. We talked to pass the time. Life's heavy loads—trouble with our parents, confusion at our changing bodies, life and death, and the pain of being stuck in the narrow space between white and black— those subjects were left unspoken. It's different with Lottie. When we speak, the words have meaning, and when we are silent, the lack of words has meaning also. I don't understand how the sounds and the silences balance out between us, only that they do.

•••

"Adele! Adele!" Mrs. Thomas's frantic voice breaks the grave-yard peace. "Thank heavens I found you. Mr. Vincent's office. Now."

"Why?" I spin and face Mrs. Thomas, who appears to have been running. Mrs. Thomas runs only when being chased by lions. My heart thumps. "What's wrong? What is it?"

"Phone call," she pants. "Long-distance. For you. Go. Mr. Vincent is waiting."

Long-distance calls are for death and emergencies. Maybe Rian is in hospital. Mother is injured, and that's why she hasn't written. Father is dead.

"Adele . . ." Lottie grabs my arm and brings me back to reality. "Come on. Let's go."

She gets me to run to Mr. Vincent's office, and I wait outside the door till the stitch in my side stops hurting. I knock, and Mr. Vincent says to come in. Lottie tries to stay outside, but I pull her in with me, too afraid to face the bad news alone.

"For you." Mr. Vincent hands me the phone and walks out to give me privacy, something I can't imagine a Swazi headmaster doing in the same situation. I press the receiver to my ear and try to calm my breath.

"Adele?" His voice comes over the line.

"Father?" I say. "But it's only Tuesday."

His voice belongs to Thursday nights and to whenever he visits Swaziland. During the school year he is silent, a ghost. He laughs at my astonishment, and I know that Mother is fine and Rian is still breathing.

"Your mother told me about the award when I visited her last week." He takes a breath and explains. "This Golden Sun must be special."

"We—my friend Lottie and I—we saved the school shop

and the classrooms from burning down. There was a fire. We stopped it. There were monkeys running from the bush, and I got burned on my arm." I am rambling, but I don't know what to say or how to say it. This is the first time I've talked to him without Mother over my shoulder, urging me to be grateful.

"You did well," he says, and there is another pause. This phone call is awkward for him also. "I . . . I just wanted to say that I wish I could be there for the ceremony, but I can't."

"I understand," I say.

And I do understand. Father shares himself out in pieces: some to his family in South Africa and some to us in Swaziland. No wonder his hair has turned gray.

"You're a wonderful girl, Adele. Not just because of this award. And your mother . . ." He takes a long breath. "Your mother is the lov—" Three sharp knocks interrupt him, and he says, "Ja. Come in."

His voice is muffled. His hand is cupped over the telephone to hide my voice, the sound of his secret life. A door opens, and a female voice speaks a few words, some of which I can hear over the line. "Mr. Joubert," is said, as one speaks to a superior, then "waiting," and he replies, "Tell him I'll be right out."

I imagine him at work, seated behind a wide desk covered in contour maps and important papers. The door shuts, and he comes back on the line.

"Sorry about that. I . . . There is too much to say, and . . . I can't . . ." He stops to gather his thoughts. "I'm proud of you, Adele. Well done on being so brave."

Static crackles in the miles of telephone wire that connect us. I want to say something, but I don't know what.

"Well, I have to go," he says. "Work. It never ends."

"Oh." I finally get my mouth to work. "Yes. I understand. Thank you. Thank you for calling. I hope I see you soon."

"Till next time, Adele." He hangs up, and he's gone, absorbed back into a European world I will never live in but one that pays our bills and keeps me in school. I wonder if he's nervous about living a double life, or do we give him a feeling of closeness that is missing in his other family? I think back on his interrupted sentence. *Your mother is the . . .* I fill in the rest. *Your mother is the love of my life.*

"Are you all right?" Lottie asks, and I realize that the receiver is still in my hand. The sound of static fills Mr. Vincent's office, and I hang up.

My chest burns. He loves me. I love him. I feel the pain of it for the first time.

•••

Evening study hall. I write one obvious quote from Shakespeare's *Romeo and Juliet* into my English homework book, "*Parting is such sweet sorrow / That I shall say good night till it be morrow,*" and a second, more substantial quote, that secretly thrills my heart with its mad love and whispered prophecy, "*These violent delights have violent ends, / And in their triumph die; like fire and powder, / Which as they kiss consume.*" Just think. If Father loved Mother the same way, he'd do anything to be with her, but people behave differently in plays and books than they do in real life. When I'm done with my English home-work I move to history. I make a list of countries of the British Empire in alphabetical order for geography class. It doesn't take long. The list is shorter than it used to be.

Lottie sits next to me and finishes a math problem without counting her fingers to get the right answer. She's been quiet since the conversation with Father, knowing somehow that I need time to think about what he said. I chew my pencil and remember the hours I've spent imagining the details of Father's house in Johannesburg: the velvet curtains on the windows, the cool marble tiles in the kitchen, and the grand piano taking center stage in the lounge room. And, most vivid of all, my certain belief that Father's European house is a better version of ours in Manzini and that the lives being lived inside it are richer and more real than my own.

After Father's phone call, I'm not sure that's true. He loves my mother, and keeping her, Rian, and me hidden from the world must be painful. I wonder if all knowledge comes with a bitter trace of sadness. Mother has her sleep-in-till-afternoon days, but how does Father manage the burdens of his cut-in-two life and his secrets? I hurt for Father, who has chosen to ignore his own heart and lives a lie with his white wife and children. I especially hurt for Mother, who is always second in line for Father's time and attention. Mother who survives on small parcels of love but deserves a banquet of smiles and kisses to feast on. Mother who did not reply to my letter.

28

Parcel Delivery

A week after Father's call, Lottie and I sit in Health and Hygiene and pretend to be interested in this afternoon's topic: "How to Make Soap Your Friend." From outside the open classroom window comes the rumble of the *Ocean Current* as it pulls to a stop across the road from the dining hall. The engine idles. On board is a canvas bag stuffed with letters for Keziah students and seed catalogs for farmers who live on isolated farms at the end of barely used washboard roads. I shut my ears to the siren call of the brakes and the ticket seller calling "Durban, Durban, Durban" in a lilting voice. If Father can telephone, then surely Mother can write. But she won't. She hasn't. Not in almost two weeks.

The bell rings, and the boys rush out of the classroom to the dining hall for morning tea. Lottie and I let the others get ahead of us. It saves on awkward silences and skittish glances, both of which happen whenever we get too close to the other students. We can't shake the rumor that we're infected with germs from Darnell's dead body. Lottie and me are bad luck charms, to be avoided.

We walk the concrete path through the haze of blue buildings and step out onto the main road. A gang of boys, both tall and small, gathers under the branches of a jacaranda tree and gazes, slack-jawed, in the direction of the *Ocean Current*. The girls ahead of us stop to whisper behind cupped hands, their attention drawn to the idling bus. Everyone should be stampeding toward the dining hall, where thick slabs of white bread and apricot jam are waiting to be eaten.

Lottie and I push through the gawkers, and I see her. Mother stands in the swirling dust in a too-short daisy-print dress and white lace-up boots with stacked high heels. A dozen gold bracelets circle her wrists, and her lips are painted ruby red. Mother breaks every rule of our godly society with insulting ease. She could, with one swing of her hips, open the gates of hell and drag us all down into the fiery pit with her. She is irresistible, dangerous, fabulous.

I shut my eyes, squeeze tight, and then reopen them. No mistake. Mother is dazzling and real, and right in front of me.

"Mummy . . ."

"Adele . . ." She holds out her arms, and the gold bracelets chime on her wrists.

Mum . . . My heart beats out the word, and I run to her in front of a dozen witnesses who will call me crybaby for the rest of the term. Who cares what they say? Father called and Mother is here, and I burrow into her shoulder.

"My baby," she croons into my hair. "My baby girl."

"You came." I soak in the sound of her voice and the scent of tea-rose lotion on her skin. "You came all this way, and the Golden Sun Awards aren't for six weeks."

"Adele, I wanted to see you before then."

"And Rian?"

"With Mrs. Button. He'll be fat as a hippo by the time I get back. You know how she loves to cook." Mother turns to face our spellbound audience, which stares and gapes at the beautiful creature who's dropped into Keziah as if by magic. Lottie keeps her distance, self-conscious in her faded school uniform and worn shoes. Compared to Mother, we are all shabby.

"And this must be your friend, Lottie," Mother says.

"Yes." I motion Lottie closer. "This is Lottie Diamond. We share Dead Lorraine's room, and we just finished reading *Jane Eyre*, the book that Father brought me from Johannesburg."

Mother reaches out and touches Lottie's shoulder with an easy familiarity that makes the boys groan with envy. She claims Lottie as her own and anoints us both with an air of mystery and glamour. Delia and the others pretend they are indifferent to Mother's bombshell appearance, but they cannot look away. They are mesmerized.

The dust and isolation of Keziah disappear. Lottie and I belong to Mother, a worldly creature who lives in the city and wears white lace-up boots and fiery lipstick.

"All aboard." The ticket seller leans out of the bus and calls in a booming voice, "Next stop, Howard's Halt. Howard's Halt, next stop."

He's putting on a show for Mother. Nobody stops at Howard's Halt unless they were born there or have a sick relative to visit.

"I have a few things to buy. Is Old Man Lander's store in Howard's Halt still open?" Mother wonders aloud. "It had a strange name, I remember."

"Hebron," Lottie answers. "Old Man Lander died, but the store is still open. His daughter Ophelia runs it now."

The *Ocean Current*'s double doors swish shut, and the driver releases the hand brake. The engine throbs. Mother knocks on the metal—*tap, tap*—and smiles through the glass. The driver happily reopens the doors.

"Where to, my sister?" he asks.

"Three tickets to Howard's Halt." She motions Lottie and I on board, and I hesitate.

"We don't have permission to leave the school grounds," I say, fretting. "And we have Scripture class this—"

"You're holding up the bus, Adele," Mother says, and I realize that Lottie is halfway up the stairs, ready to run to Howard's Halt and all points beyond. Shamed by my fear, I climb aboard. The three of us find seats in the middle row, with Mother and I together and Lottie across the aisle. The bus rolls past the blue classrooms and the woodworking shed and the boys' dormitories. A gang of little boys and girls runs behind the *Ocean Current* chanting, "Runaway! Runaway! Runaway!"

I laugh for no reason, and Mother squeezes my hand. She

answered my letter in person, and the heat of her skin against mine warms every part of me.

"Ask me anything." Mother turns to look at me, and my heart hitches in my chest. If I'm ready to ask, she's ready to answer, and how could I have believed that she'd ignore my letters and never write back? Lottie is right. I am ignorant. My own mother is a stranger to me, and now is a good time to change that.

"Mama Khumalo says that you haven't visited the village in fourteen years. How come?"

"Many reasons, Adele." She motions to the long fields and deep valleys all around us. "The hunger and the hard hills, and the farmers who act like they're God because they own the land you live on and they have all the power. And things happened that . . ."

Mother turns her face away, and my breath catches in my throat. My mother, who Father says can talk underwater, is silent, and her silence scares me. I have an uneasy feeling that whatever happened to her out in those desolate hills is too terrible to speak of.

"Well." Mother forces a smile. "Let's say that some memories are best kept in the past. To do that, I had to leave the village behind. Can you understand?"

"I think so."

Mother peers through the dusty glass and back through the decades. "I left Keziah when I was your age, Adele. I found work at the land title office, and I met your father in the map room, just like he tells it. I made a good life for myself in Man-

245

zini, and after Mama Agnes died, there was no reason to come back."

"Until now," I say. "Until me."

"Only you could ever bring me back here, Adele," my mother says, and having her next to me is a dream and it is real at the same time.

"Were you alone at Keziah? No friends? No nothing?" I ask, and Mother tenses up.

"I got plenty of attention from the boys and mouthfuls of spite from the girls, but I had no one to stick up for me, Adele. That's why I'm here. To tell you that Daddy, Rian, and me . . . we're on your side. Always."

The postcard from Rian, the phone call from Father, and now Mother in the flesh are all proof that what she says is true. I am not alone. I have my family and . . .

"I have Lottie Diamond," I tell Mother. "And she has me."

Mother leans across my lap and says to Lottie, "You should come and visit us during the holidays. Stay as long as you like. We have room."

Lottie blushes, her famous Zulu pride dented by Mother's charm. "If Adele wants," she mumbles, leaving the decision up to me.

At the beginning of the term, my answer would have been no way, definitely not. Lottie is trouble. Her hair is too short. Her clothes are ugly. Her mother's a disgrace, and her manners are too close to native. Now, the idea of her in our house in Manzini makes me smile. The world is bright and sad and pressed close against my skin when she's around.

Then a shocking thought hits me like a fist. It takes my breath away. Lottie, with her Swazi medicine and Jewish spinning top and dog-eared *Oxford Dictionary*, is the first real friend I've ever had. Lottie Diamond is, in fact, my very best friend, and, this time, I have the courage to say the words out loud.

"You're my best friend, Lottie. I want you to come," I say, and that's the truth.

29

Face-to-Face

Howard's Halt is dust and flies, and a handful of buildings huddled together under an endless sky. A stray dog limps past the one-room police station, the deserted tearoom, and the Hebron General Store, painted pale orange with green trim around the windows. Four or five houses dot the area nearby, and a farm store supplies seeds and tractor parts to outlying farms.

"Now. Where are the sweets?" Mother says when we enter the cool darkness of the general store. Rows of hessian sacks filled with sugar, wheat, flour, and rice run along either side of us, and at the very back of the store is a small wooden counter with weights and scales, and behind the counter is a dark-skinned woman with bright-red hair. Ophelia, Lottie said.

"Over here." Lottie leads us deeper into the gloom, and I switch Mother's overnight bag from one hand to the other and then place it safely between my feet when we reach a row of glass containers filled with black licorice sticks, hard toffees, peppermint strips, and gold-wrapped chocolate éclairs. My mouth waters.

"One sweet each?" Ophelia asks with a sour twist to her lips. Everything in the store goes bit by bit to poor farmers and poor natives, and she'll be dead long before the candy jars run empty.

Lottie's cheeks flush at the poke, but Mother is calm. She tilts her head to consider and then says, "Three bags each of the peppermint twists, the chocolate éclairs, and the hard toffee, and five bags of the licorice, if you please."

More than enough to add an extra note of sweetness to the end of dinnertime. Mother has come to Keziah armed with charm and money. She's got what Father gives her and the "walking-around cash" that she earns working two days a week at Bella's Beauty Salon for All Types. Her goal: to lift the bad-luck curse that clings to Lottie and me. Her weapon: four kinds of sweets. An unheard-of luxury on our boarding school menu.

Ophelia hurries to the counter to collect the paper bags for the candy, and Mother whispers, "I remember this shop being huge and filled with treasure that I couldn't touch, let alone buy. Now see it."

Hebron is nothing compared to the hypermarket in Manzini, and Mother is delighted. She left this far end of Swaziland a poor girl with holes in her shoes, and she's returned with money in her pockets and white boots imported from London. This homecoming is a sweet victory, even though the memories of growing up here make Mother turn her face and hide.

Ophelia scoops and weighs the right amounts and drops the packets into a cotton sack that's roughly the same size as the one that Lottie brought her comb, her two pairs of underwear, her one sweater and one checked dress to school in.

Mother pays, and opens the sack to release a delicious cloud of sugar. "Take one each for the walk back, girls."

Old Adele reaches for a licorice, not wanting to appear greedy. New Adele stops and takes a chocolate éclair from the paper bag instead. Being good for the sake of appearances is the same as telling a lie. Lottie's straight talk and actions taught me that, and I really do prefer éclairs. Lottie scoops out a peppermint twist and throws me a half smile that says, *And you wanted to stay behind for Scripture class!*

I laugh at my foolishness. Scripture class, of all things! It's barely a subject, and I already have the most verses memorized of anyone. We walk to the shop exit, happy with our daring escape from school. Mother, who's used to talking to white men, will make excuses to Mr. Vincent, and we'll be forgiven.

Hebron's front door opens, and a man walks in with the light at his back. He's an outline, a silhouette with sloped shoulders and slack arms hanging loose by his sides, but I know who it is straightaway: Bosman. His sons stand to either side of him and block the exit, and I grip the handle of Mother's overnight case till the plastic bites into my fingers. Bosman said he'd remember Lottie and me. He promised.

"Mr. Bosman." Ophelia chirps false cheer from behind the counter. "How can I help you today?"

Bosman ignores her. He ignores me, and he ignores Lottie.

His catlike eyes narrow on Mother, who keeps her gaze pinned to a spot on the floor, a vague smile on her ruby-red mouth. She makes herself invisible. She makes herself small. She follows the rules to survive, but Bosman sees her.

"I know you," he says in gruff English. "I know you."

"I live in Manzini." Mother's voice is thin and scared. "Maybe you saw me there."

"No." He snaps his fingers. He's placed her. "You're that girl Mbali, the little flower who lived in the kaffir village. You used to wander around singing, like one of those birds I shoot from the trees."

Birds killed for singing: Bosman's world summed up.

Mother holds still and holds her tongue. She endures. But I can't, for one minute longer, endure the sight of her made mute by a cruel man. I go to her side, and, of course, Lottie follows.

"Mother has a beautiful voice even now," I say.

"Beautiful voice." Bosman snorts. "That's what everyone used to say. 'Oh, what a lovely voice. Beautiful.' She certainly thought so."

Bosman's sons sift through bags of rice and flour with nervous fingers. Their father's interest in a mixed-race woman embarrasses them and horrifies me. The youngest son, in particular, is tense: his shoulders are tight and his jaw twitches, and I wonder where the daughter is hiding.

Bosman ignores his sons and leans in to Mother, voice low. "The sound of your tweeting grated on my nerves, but you never paid me any mind. Too good for the valley, you. Too proud to stay in your place till I taught you otherwise."

I gulp for breath, and Lottie makes a *shh, shh* sound to calm me. The hair on my scalp prickles, and every fiber of my being tells me that the bad things that happened to Mother out in those hills were Bosman's doing. That day on his farm, Bosman said I was born to sell myself to a man with money. The poisoned words rolled off his tongue, smooth as butter. He'd said them before. I think he said them to Mother, and he did worse to break her pride and teach her rightful place in the valley.

I imagine Mother in the crosshairs of Bosman's rifle. A girl alone, singing to blunt the sense of danger that lurks in the forests and the tall grass. A girl alone, singing to let the world know she is alive and well, and to come and look for her if her song ever stops.

A hot, spiky rage floods through me. Lottie was right to wonder why God took Darnell and her father instead of this man. Bosman lords his power over his family, and now over Mother, who remains absolutely still, patiently waiting for the storm to pass. If I could call down lightning from the sky, I would. I want Bosman gone from the world. I take a half a step forward, ready to swing a fist. He notices me, and he smiles. *Go on*, his amused expression seems to say. *Do it, girl. The police station is just next door.*

"Ground coffee was it, Mr. Bosman?" Ophelia tries to break up the dangerous mood. "I have salt pork and dried apricots half-price, and a loaf of sugar bread, baked fresh this morning. I have samples."

The fear in Ophelia's voice brings me back to reason. I want to strike Bosman's face for shrinking Mother's voice and body to the size of a child, but he is taller, stronger, and whiter than I'll ever be. And even if by some miracle I could beat him to the ground, I'd lose Mother and Lottie and my freedom. The law favors Bosman. The law is forever on his side.

"I see you got your girl from a white man," Bosman says to Mother, and his ugly expression makes me flinch. "A man with deep pockets from the look of those fancy boots."

I understand why Mother left this place and never came back. She left to save herself. She left so that when Rian and I were born in far-off Manzini to a white engineer, we'd have what she didn't: enough food to eat, an education, the freedom to dream of a better future, and the power to reach out and grab it. I suddenly know it's my turn to be brave.

"Come." I take Mother's hand and squeeze warmth into her cold fingers. "We have a long walk back."

With my heart in my mouth, I push past Bosman, who probes Mother's blank expression, hoping to catch a glimpse of the frightened girl he stalked across the hills all those years ago. He wants to feel her fear. He feeds on it.

Mother gives him nothing and raises her head. She shuts him out as if he isn't there. Lottie shoves past Bosman's other shoulder and opens the door to the sunshine.

30

Joyful

I stagger onto the pavement and give Mother a sideways glance. Beautiful Mother, who ran from this place and came back to save me from humiliation. Clever Mother, who found a gentle man to love her, even if his love is part-time and given to her in secret. Her hand trembles in mine, and I stop to catch my breath. A few seconds at most, but it's enough to regain control of my emotions and find the high ground from which to view Bosman in the right perspective: Small, mean, left behind. And a liar. To hate my mother's singing is to hate life and all the joyful moments in it.

"This country," Mother says in a shaky voice. "Oh, this country."

Bosman has resurrected the scared girl dressed in second-hand clothing and eaten up by the shame of being poor and unprotected. I need to swallow my rage and get her back to our thick carpet on the living room floor and our moonlit walks along the length of Live Long Street, and the sound of Father's voice on the end of the line.

"Adele," Lottie says. "We should leave."

Bosman's red truck is parked by the curb, with his daughter huddled in the back. She's dressed in a thin cotton shift with bare feet and a black eye the size of a bird's egg. I take one step and then another on the road to Keziah. We draw level with the truck and the girl throws her arms over the side, fingers flexed.

"Dee-Dee," she says. "Dee-Dee is gone."

"You mean Darnell?" Lottie asks.

The girl nods.

"Yes," Lottie says in a quiet voice. "Dee-Dee is gone."

"For me." The girl stands and reaches for the sky, her hands grabbing at the air. "Butterflies for me."

Lottie and I exchange blank stares. The girl has lost us. She reads our clueless expressions and sighs as if we are the ones who are simpleminded and need help understanding.

"Purple. Butterflies. For me." She dances from one end of the tray to the other with a strange grace as she chases and grabs at phantoms. Then with a final lunge, she jerks and falls down onto the tray of the dirty truck. She lies with her arms and legs sprawled, a wisp of brown hair caught in the corner of her mouth.

"I ran," she says with a knot in her voice. "I ran away."

Lottie understands, and then I do too:

A cloud of purple butterflies hangs suspended in the air, their shimmering wings reflecting the sunlight. Darnell grabs for one butterfly and then another, always a second too late. The perfect present just out of reach. The purple wings are so close. The lip of the ledge is closer. Then the air takes him and the ground catches him, and the world goes dark.

Lottie has her answer to the why and the how of Darnell's death, and I wonder if the truth hurts more than the fantasy she spun with Bosman at the center.

Mother comes out of her fog and pulls a strand of hair from the corner of the girl's mouth. Her fingers trace an eyebrow, cheekbone, smooth jawline, and dimpled chin—every touch a sorry.

The door to the general store opens, and Bosman's voice growls at his daughter. "Get up, you useless girl. Get up before I make you."

Mother's hand jerks back as if stung, and the familiar pressure that built in my throat at Darnell's funeral builds again; a burning. Men like Bosman will always win if we let them. Are we forever helpless? Weak girls and women born to suffer in silence and do nothing to fight back? It breaks my heart to think so. Then, like rain falling, Mother's favorite proverb comes into my mind: "When the ground is hard, the women dance." I understand what it means now. Darnell's death, Bosman's cruelty, and Mother's pain are the hard ground that we stand on. The ground itself can't be replaced, but it can be changed. It can be made new. That's why the women dance. They dance to bring joy. They dance to soften the ground beneath their feet. They dance for change.

Lottie takes Mother's other arm, and the pressure fills my

mouth and finds a voice. I lick my lips and start out slowly and self-consciously. Mother normally leads the singing and leaves me breathless in her wake. Now it's my turn to lead the dance . . .

"This little light of mine"—the simple words are a whisper on the wind—"I'm going to let it shine. This little light of mine . . ."

"I'm going to let it shine." Lottie Diamond, who mouths the words to hymns in chapel and refuses to answer the preacher's call-and-response, joins the song in a high, sweet voice. "This little light of mine. I'm going to let it shine."

Bosman's daughter smiles to hear the music, and her happiness brings Mother back to me. She squeezes my hand and lends her voice to the chorus, "Let it shine. Let it shine. Let it shine. Everywhere I go, I'm going to let it shine. Everywhere I go, I'm going to let it shine . . ."

We link arms, the three of us, and walk the length of the main street with easygoing steps. I sense Bosman watching us from the front porch of the Hebron General Store, and I glance over my shoulder. He stands with his hands on his hips, a powerful man powerless to drown out our song or stop the music from rising over the mountain and into the valleys and the hidden, lonely places of the heart. A man left behind.

The road leads us away, and our voices rise, clear and certain. We sing to heal Lottie's mother's fractured heart. We sing for Darnell, gone so soon, and his father left behind. Our song flies over the fields and into the sky.

We sing the light into being.

Turn the page for a sneak peek of
Malla Nunn's latest book

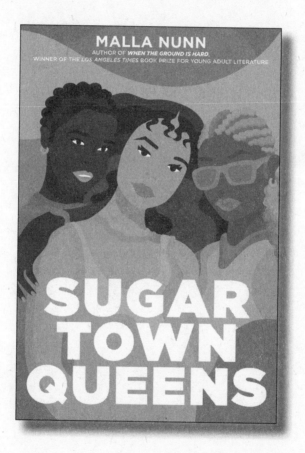

White stars dance across my field of vision. The blindfold is tied too tight and I want to rip it off. Instead, I sit and try to rub the goose bumps off my arms. It's cold inside our one-room house, the cracks in the corrugated-iron walls wide enough to let the air in from outside. It's winter, so we have stuffed rags into the spaces we can reach. I shiver and wait patiently for the two surprises that my mother has planned.

The thing is: not all surprises are good.

"Happy fifteenth birthday, Amandla." My mother, Annalisa, who refuses to be called Mother in any of South Africa's eleven official languages, unties the blindfold and hands me a bowl of lumpy porridge decorated with multicolored sprinkles, icing sugar, and whatever canned fruit was in the cupboard. This year's fruit is pears in syrup, a step up from last year's ancient mandarins. Loaded porridge is the closest I will ever get to a birthday cake: a blessing. Annalisa is a terrible cook and a worse baker.

"Thank you." I take the bowl (surprise number one) and our fingers touch, hers pale, mine brown, both with long fingers, elegant, waiting for jewelry, or a piano. In another life, maybe. Our room is too small for a piano, and there is no money for jewels.

"Today is extra-special for two reasons. It's your birthday, plus . . ." She takes a deep breath and cups my cheek with a shaky hand. "Last night, I had a vision. It was wonderful, but we have to do our part to make it come true."

The lumpy porridge sticks in my throat and stops me from cursing. Annalisa's visions have taken us into the cane fields to sing to the stars at midnight. They have told us to eat eggs, and only eggs, for four days in a row. They have led us into the heart of a storm to wait for the lightning to send us instructions. The instructions never came.

My mother is out of her mind.

The lightning was eight months ago. Every night since, I have prayed for the spirits to leave Annalisa alone and go whisper directions to someone else.

"Tell me what we have to do." I use a fake calm voice to mask the anxious feeling gathering inside my chest. I have to stay cool and make my next move carefully. "But hurry. I have to get to school."

"Hands over your eyes," she says. "Here comes the second surprise."

I cover my eyes and peek through the space between my fingers as Annalisa walks across the cracked linoleum floor in black tailored trousers, a white silk shirt, and a cropped leather jacket with silver buckles. This is her best outfit. This morning, she will disappear into the city of Durban and come home with bags of the basics: socks, underwear, soap, and a special something for my birthday.

"Open your eyes now." She pulls a piece of blue material from her wardrobe and holds it up with a flourish. "Look. Isn't it beautiful?"

"It" is a folded bedsheet with two holes cut in the fabric for the arms and another larger hole, for the head. The material is stained and held together by stitches that zigzag in different directions. She drapes the sheet dress across the foot of my cot as if it is made of raw silk and sewn together by cartoon birds with golden needles.

"If you wear this . . ." Her pale skin glows like there's a fire burning out of control inside her. "All our dreams will come true."

No. All my nightmares will come true.

"Which dreams are you talking about, exactly?" Annalisa's dreams can be anything. A brick house with ocean views. A holiday under swaying palms. Cold lobster rolls chilling in a fridge for when the temperature rises . . . if only we had a fridge instead of a cooler.

"Wear this dress," she says. "And your father will come back to us. Blue was his favorite color. You see?"

No, I do not see.

My father is not an actual person. He is a collage of blurred images thrown together by Annalisa in the half hour before we

3

go to bed. Less now than when I was little. She would whisper that father was tall as a lala palm and black as a moonless night. He wore a sharp gray suit with a blue tie, iridescent like peacock feathers. He loved to dance, and he stole her breath away when he kissed her.

No matter how pretty a picture she paints of him, there is only one thing that I know for sure about my father.

He is doing fine without me.

"Is he here in Sugar Town?" He isn't, but I ask just in case. I have to be sure, even though I hate that there is still a tiny shred of hope left in me that he is out there somewhere.

Annalisa smiles wide, and her lips stretch tight across her teeth. "He's not here yet, but he'll come when he sees your blue dress." She grabs my hands and squeezes tight. "The wind will carry the message to him quicker than a text. Get dressed now. It's time to leave."

Today is Friday, a school day. On school days, I wear a uniform. Blue skirt or pants, white shirt, black shoes, and white socks. A black sweater or a black blazer for now in winter. Nothing fancy, but Miss Gabela, the principal, is clear about the rules: No uniform, no school. Annalisa's magic sheet will get me suspended, *and* it will frighten away the few friends I have. This is the last day of second term, but the scandal of the blue sheet will survive the holidays and live on to haunt me for the rest of the year.

No thanks. I'll pass.

"Hurry." Annalisa tugs at my nightgown. "Lift up your arms and put on your new dress. There's a good girl."

"It is not a dress." I pull away. "It is a sheet with holes in it, and I won't wear it. Ever."

"You have to wear the dress." Annalisa's smile disappears, and her expression turns dark. "It's the only way to get him back."

We stand face-to-face, breathing hard. Mother is a few inches taller than me, with fine blond hair and pale blue eyes that remind me of the sunlit ocean. She is delicate, with slender limbs and narrow hips, while I am all bumps and curves. What did the nurses think when I slipped into the world with different skin, different hair, different everything from Annalisa? They must have wondered how the two of us fit together. Sometimes, I look in the mirror and I wonder the same thing. Who am I, and where do I fit in?

"Put the dress on," Annalisa says. "Do it for me. For us."

Annalisa angry is scary. Annalisa with a bottomless darkness welling up inside her is terrifying. I see that darkness well up now. More resistance from me and she'll tumble into it. She will curl up and sleep for days. She won't talk or eat. I have been to the bottom of the well with her once. I will never go there again—if I can help it.

"Here. Give it." I take the sheet from her with jerky movements and point to the mirror hanging to the right of the sink. "Don't forget your lipstick."

"Of course." Annalisa digs through her faux-leather hobo bag that acts as a portal to another dimension. At different times, she has pulled out an orchid bulb with dangling roots, an owl feather, five mother-of-pearl buttons, a vintage Coca-Cola yo-yo, and a porcupine quill. I'm surprised my father isn't in there, too.

She takes out a tube of Moroccan Sunset, her favorite color, and leans close to the mirror to put it on. The moment her back is turned, I grab my school uniform out of the bed-side drawer and push it deep into my backpack. I slip the sheet dress over my head and bend low to tie the laces of my school shoes, working up a plan to switch the dress for my uniform somewhere. Somehow.

Got it.

"Lil Bit and me are meeting early to finish up an assignment in the school computer lab." The "lab" is a room the size of a cleaning closet. One door, one window, and the faint smell of bleach coming up from the concrete floor. Come to think of it, the room might, in fact, have been an actual cleaning closet before the donated computers arrived from a Christian school in Denmark. "Got to run."

"Lil Bit and I," Annalisa automatically corrects. "And we're not finished yet. Sit, and I'll do your hair. It has to look the same as in my vision."

Shit.

"Fine." I take a seat and work through the next steps. I have a plan. For the plan to work, I'll have to leave home five minutes before Annalisa, and then I'll have to run. Not my preferred activity. But run I will. Today, I will be the great sprinter Caster Semenya—strong, fast, and focused.

Annalisa wraps a curl around her finger, remembering. "You got your father's hair, that's for sure. Don't ever straighten it."

"I won't." No lie. I will keep my kinked-up curls, not because they tie me to an invisible man who haunts our lives, but because straightened hair is an imitation of white hair, and I am not white. I am brown with a snub nose sprinkled with freckles. I have hazel eyes flecked with green. I'm a genetic mutt. And I am happy to let my hair be.

"Today, your hair will be a halo," Annalisa says. "That way, your father will see the angel that we made together."

On a normal day, she plaits my hair into a single French braid that dangles between my shoulder blades, but today is not normal. Today she pulls the metal teeth of an Afro pick through my springy curls to make a bumping 'fro that casts a shadow onto the kitchen table. It is huge. An alien spacecraft could crash-land on the surface of it and sustain no damage. Beyoncé rocking a Foxxy Cleopatra wig has nothing on me. The style is loud and proud, and damn, I gotta admit that it is impressive.

"Last and best of all." Annalisa dips her hand into her bag and pulls out a tiara. An honest-to-goodness rhinestone tiara with BIRTHDAY PRINCESS spelled out in fake pink diamonds. Hideous.

"You bought this?"

"Of course not." She anchors the tiara to my head. "I found it lying on the side of the road. It's ugly, but it's perfect for today. The stones will catch the light, and the light will fly over the hills to wherever your father is."

I can barely breathe I am so angry. The 'fro I can deal with, but the sheet dress and the tiara are too much! Instead of screaming, *It's my birthday! Be normal. Just this once,* I make a list in my head. Lists soothe me. Lists are anchors to rational thought. Lists are how I survive.

This morning, I will:

1. Keep calm.
2. Run fast.
3. Get help.

"Catch you this afternoon . . ." I grab my backpack and rush to the door that leads to the lane. Annalisa blows me a goodbye kiss and tucks a strand of blond hair behind her ear. I am stunned to see her so cool and elegant. She belongs in a magazine, and I wonder, for the millionth time, how she ended up in this tiny house on a dirt strip that runs between Tugela Way and Sisulu Street. The lane doesn't have a real name. "The lane between Tugela and Sisulu" is description enough for the bill collectors to find us. When I used to ask Annalisa where she came from, she'd say, *Next door and a million miles away.*

I don't ask anymore.

2

I step outside our one-room house and into a small patch of dirt that murders every plant that's planted in it. Our front yard is a graveyard for living things. Behind me, the corrugated-iron walls of our home glow like a sunrise and rocks and old tires hold down the flat tin roof.

Annalisa calls our room "snug," as if the word alone has the power to change the fact that we have a single light bulb dangling over the kitchen table and a rusty tap with an off-and-on-again water supply. It's the twenty-first century, but we live like the people in black-and-white photographs from the 1950s.

"Ah, shit," I whisper under my breath. The lane is busy with people on their way to work—or on their way to look for work—in the city. Children skip to school, and stray dogs trot between houses, sniffing for scraps. I stand paralyzed in the yard. If I cross the lane, I will be seen in my blue sheet. If I stay frozen, I will be seen in my blue sheet. Either way, the word about me will spread like a grass fire.

You heard about that white woman's daughter? Dressed in a sheet. Big hair like an exploded watermelon. Wearing a crown. A crown! Madness runs in the family, my sisters.

The sound of keys rattling inside our shack gets me moving. I sprint out the gate and across the lane. The world around me blurs into shapes and sounds. Mrs. Mashanini's blue front door is all I see. Behind the blue door is sanctuary. I run for it although I've never been inside before.

"Mrs. M!" I pound my fist against the wood. "It's Amandla. Please open up. I need your help."

A long moment passes. Footsteps shuffle across a grass mat, and the door opens a crack. Mrs. M's blind aunt peeks through the gap, and her blindness spares her the sight of me sweaty and wild-haired.

"Yebo?" she says in Zulu. "Ubani?"

"It's Amandla, from across the lane," I answer in Zulu, and check over my shoulder. Our front door is still closed, but any second now, it will open. Annalisa has a bus to catch, and she is never late. "Auntie, *please* can I come in?"

Blind Auntie steps back and makes space for me to squeeze through. Three children and a woman sleep tangled together on a pullout bed squashed against the wall. Mrs. M's daughter and grandchildren: refugees from a bad husband and bad father who was never home anyway. Six people in one bedroom. Somehow, they all fit.

"In the back." Blind Auntie leads me through the room to a narrow kitchen with a woodburning stove and old wooden crates nailed to the walls for storage. Mrs. M, a tall Zulu woman with a tight-knit Afro, scoops seeds from a small green eggplant the size of a brussels sprout. She's busy, and my being here is awkward. In the six years that Annalisa and I have lived on the lane, we have never entered her house. Annalisa prefers to keep our neighbors at a distance.

"Sorry to disturb you, Mrs. Mashanini, it's just that . . . uh . . ."

"Your mother had another one of her notions." Mrs. M takes in the whole of me without a flicker of amusement. She is also a retired nurse who keeps an eye on the neighborhood. When Annalisa and I returned from that night in the cane fields, Mrs. M smiled at me through her window, but I looked away.

"Yes. One of her notions." A blush burns my cheeks, and the roots of my hair tingle. It shames me to remember Mrs. M watching the two of us dragging ourselves home in the rain, barefoot and soaked to the skin.

"Are you here for the day or just for the time being?" Mrs. M asks, and I get the feeling that, if I decided to stay for five hours, she'd somehow find a space for me to sit and wait.

"Just for the time being. I brought my uniform to change into. When my mother leaves, I'll head off to school."

"Auntie, go see if Miss Harden is gone," Mrs. M says, and I wonder how a blind woman will know. Yes, she knits scarves for the children at the Sugar Town Orphanage without dropping a stitch, but that's different from spying on our house across the lane.

She shuffles out of the kitchen, and I have to ask: "Mrs. Mashanini, how will she know?"

"That one can hear a pin drop in Zimbabwe," Mrs. M says. "If your mother is home, Auntie will know. If your mother is gone, Auntie will know. Put on your uniform and get ready to run. You don't want to miss the first bell."

I shrug off the blue sheet dress and pull on my school uniform. Standing half-naked in a strange room for even a short while should embarrass me. Strangely, it does not. Mrs. M sips tea and spreads the eggplant seeds on a piece of paper to dry. She worked in the emergency ward of the Inkosi Albert Luthuli Hospital for twelve years. A round-hipped brown girl in plain cotton undies is nothing compared to what she must have seen on the wards. Babies being born. The tragic aftermath of traffic accidents. Bones shattered by gunshot wounds. Death delivered by the hour.

"Unyoko akasekho," Blind Auntie says. *Your mother is gone.* She sits at the kitchen table and takes up knitting the last panel of a scarf made with leftover red, pink, and brown yarn. "But your tap is dripping. Mr. Khoza, there by the red roof? He can fix it."

Mr. Khoza. Short legs. Wide chest. Bald head. Twin daughters. He lives four doors down from us, but we don't talk. We nod hello in passing. That is all. *Why make friends, Annalisa says, when we'll be leaving Sugar Town soon?* That is my mother's dream. We're no closer to leaving now than the first time she said it. I can't even remember the first time she said it.

And now it is my dream, too. At night, I lie awake and imagine the wide road that will lead me away from the dirt streets and back alleys of Sugar Town. At the end of that wide road is a brick house with picture windows and separate rooms. On the kitchen table is an invitation to a cousin's birthday party, and on my mobile phone is a long list of family names and contacts. The house is a safe place for friends and the network of aunts and uncles who exist only in my imagination. Best of all, the house is built in the middle of a far-off town where the color of my skin doesn't mean anything, a town where I am at home in my roundness and my brownness.

I think that escaping from where we are is going to take longer than my mother imagines. Right now, though, being here inside Mrs. M's house, Sugar Town isn't so bad.

"Sit, Amandla. Auntie will do your hair."

I wrestle the tiara from the whirlwind of Afro curls and sit on a low stool next to Blind Auntie, who stops knitting and runs her fingertips over the contours of my skull. She parts my hair down the middle, a first. Then I feel her fingers working in rhythm. It's firm but gentle—no hair pulling, but nice and tight. My breath matches the rhythm of her fingers, until suddenly, she's done. She has plaited the sections into two chunky braids that dangle over my shoulders. Another first. When she's done, she pats my shoulder and goes back to knitting. I'd love to see what I look like, but asking for a mirror is rude, so I don't.

"Go, now," Mrs. M says. "Or you'll be late."

"Thank you. For everything." The words come out stiff and embarrassed at having to ask for refuge inside an already crowded house. *Nothing comes for free*, Annalisa says. *Favors have to be paid back one way or the other.* How will I repay Mrs. Mashanini's kindness? My pockets are empty. Mrs. M sees my awkwardness.

"Neighbors help each other, Amandla." She pours her aunt a mug of red bush tea, adds six teaspoons of sugar, stirs, and adds another scoop to make seven. "That's ubuntu."

Ubuntu. We learned about it in primary school: the Zulu idea that a person is a person through other people. We are all interconnected in a living, breathing ocean of compassion and humanity. If that is true, then Annalisa and I are the anti-ubuntu: two individuals who live in the community but are not part of it. Maybe it's better that way for everyone.

Social interactions are awkward. Annalisa's voice might drift off when her memory hits a blank spot. Or visitors might be held prisoner by a ten-minute lecture on how to brew the perfect pot of tea. Or she might suddenly stare at the ground. Or at the sky. Or just walk away.

"Come by anytime, my girl. Bring your mother," Mrs. M says. "My door is always open."

I nod, speechless, and creep through the narrow front room, afraid of waking the sleeping children, all under five and too young for school. A strange feeling burns in the pit of my stomach. Not from the lumpy birthday porridge, which was all kinds of wrong, but from Mrs. M's simple *Come by anytime, my girl. Bring your mother.* Mrs. M knows Annalisa is strange—and she doesn't care. And now her daughter has crashed into her house looking for help. Despite all that, her invitation stands. *Anytime, my girl.*

Outside, the lane is quiet, and the sun's rays slant over the rusted rooftops. On either side of me, Mrs. M's winter garden glows green with broad beans, thyme, and winter gem lettuce. Today will be long and hungry with just that spoonful of porridge to keep me fueled.

"Amandla!" Mrs. M is right behind me. I turn, and she puts a piece of steamed corn bread with butter in my hand. "Go!" she says. I run without even saying thank you.

The bread is still warm.

* * *

Brown, white, and mostly black teenagers pack the schoolyard outside a low classroom building painted with sunflowers on the outside and rolling ocean waves on the inside. Lil Bit, my best and only real friend, waits for me in the shade of the parsley tree where the poor but ambitious students gather.

"What happened?" Lil Bit's gaze narrows on my face, all-seeing. "Your hair looks amazing, but you're sweating a river."

Lil Bit's real name is Esther, but she hates that name, and Lil Bit suits her better anyway. She is a "little bit" of a girl: dark-skinned and slender as a dancer. Inside her delicate skull, her planet-size brain is always thinking and making connections. I don't need to pretend with her. I lay it all out:

"Annalisa had another vision. She cut up an old blue sheet and tried to get me to wear it to school. The sheet was meant to bring my father back. Blue was his favorite color, apparently."

15

Lil Bit is the only one I tell about Annalisa's highs and lows. We are both only children. We both have parent problems. I have my mother and her visions. Lil Bit has her father, the Reverend Altone Bhengu, who was caught behind the church altar with a teenage girl named Sunshine. Both of them were naked. That was a year ago, but the scandal is still fresh. Together, Lil Bit and me spend hours plotting a path out of Sugar Town to the University of KwaZulu Natal in Durban, fifteen kilometers away on the map but an epic journey for two girls with no money.

"I think it's nice," Lil Bit says, and I raise an eyebrow.

"Which part is nice exactly?"

"My mother wants my father dead. First, she'd cut off his legs and make him crawl through the streets to beg for forgiveness. Then, she'd dump his body in the bush for the wild dogs to eat. Your mother loves your father and wants him back," Lil Bit says. "That was the nice part of your story."

"I guess . . ." I can't imagine what it would be like to have Annalisa tell me a bedtime story about wild dogs feasting on my mythical father's corpse. I get a love story instead. Pale girl meets dark boy under a sky full of stars.

We move to the far side of the parsley tree and into the shadow of a concrete water tower with Nelson Mandela's face painted on the side. This is our place, set apart from the others and right under Nelson's beaming smile. Nelson Mandela, aka "Madiba," is our patron saint. He gives us hope that one day the South Africa he dreamed of will come to pass. His dream is slow in coming. Money and race divide us. The rich are still rich and the poor are still poor and none of us is truly colorblind. Not yet. The black kids give Lil Bit a hard time for hanging out with "that colored girl" instead of "one of her own." The white and mixed kids do the same to me. Old habits die hard, I guess.

"Happy birthday, Amandla." Lil Bit hands me a brown paper parcel tied with twine. "If you don't like it, I'll get you something different."

I have my first genuine smile of the day. "Thanks." I untie the string and carefully peel open the brown paper wrapping. Lil Bit is poor like me. A gift from her is worth more than the money that she spent to get it. My breath catches at the sight of a square sketch pad and a set of high-quality graphite drawing pencils. Nothing this fine is for sale in Sugar Town.

"You shouldn't have." I hug her, and then I hug the parcel to my chest, torn between delight and guilt. "You could have been caught."

"Please!" She snorts with amusement. "This girl never gets caught, Amandla. The lady in the store followed me around for ages, but she had no idea who she was dealing with. The Lightning Thief."

Lil Bit has a quick brain and even quicker fingers. Her talent for theft borders on the supernatural, but much as I'd like to scold her for taking stupid risks, I aim to keep the sketch pad and pencils. They are perfect, and now they are mine. Besides, Lil Bit only "shops" in the city on special occasions and never

17

here in Sugar Town, where the store owners scrape by on the thin trade that comes through the doors. She's a thief with a conscience, which helps to ease mine.

"Thanks again." I pull her into another quick hug as the morning bell rings. "I love my present. You're the first person I'll sketch."

She shakes her head, *Not me*, and her lack of confidence is painful. I want to tell her that the Bible is wrong, that the sins of the father are not visited on the daughter. Reverend Bhengu's sins are his alone. She is Esther Junia "Lil Bit" Bhengu, a separate and sovereign being with a heart and a mind that are all her own.

"I want to try to capture your inner criminal," I tell her as we walk side by side to class.

"Sorry, my sister. I have to stay invisible. It's the only way to be free."

Acknowledgments

When the Ground Is Hard has deep roots in my family history. Adele and Lottie's story is my mother's story and my aunties' story. It is also my story. I gave the book its title to honor and show respect to all the women worldwide who give life to my mother's favorite African proverb, "When the ground is hard, the women dance."

Thank you and lots of love to my children, Elijah and Sisana, for understanding that Mummy sometimes has to talk to the people in her head at dinner instead of them. Thank you also to my husband, Mark, my first reader extraordinaire, and the only man brave enough to tell me when I'm wrong. I love you. (Yes, I know, babe . . . I still owe you a trip to Fiji.)

Thank you also to my agent, Catherine Drayton from Inkwell Management, who stuck with me through difficult times and provided me with great insight. I'm so grateful you have my back.

Lastly, thank you to my editor, Stacey Barney of Putnam Books, who believed in the book at every stage and asked me all the right questions to help me make it better.

After her family migrated to Australia to escape apartheid, MALLA NUNN graduated with a double degree in English and history and then earned a master of arts in theater studies from Villanova University. Faced with a life of chronic underemployment, she dabbled in acting and screenwriting. She wrote and directed three award-winning films, including *Servant of the Ancestors*, which won best documentary awards at film festivals in Chicago, Los Angeles, and Zanzibar and was shown on national television in Australia. She married in a traditional Swazi ceremony. Her bride price was eighteen cows. She now lives and works in Sydney, Australia.

You can visit Malla Nunn at mallanunn.com